Murder
at Piper's Gut

Also by Eugene McEldowney

A Kind of Homecoming
A Stone of the Heart
The Sad Case of Harpo Higgins

Eugene McEldowney

Murder
at Piper's Gut

HEINEMANN : LONDON

First published in Great Britain 1997
by William Heinemann

3 5 7 9 10 8 6 4 2

Random House UK Limited
20 Vauxhall Bridge Road, London, SW1V 2SA

Random House Australia (Pty) Limited
20 Alfred Street, Milsons Point, Sydney,
New South Wales 2061, Australia

Random House New Zealand Limited
18 Poland Road, Glenfield
Auckland 10, New Zealand

Random House South Africa (Pty) Limited
Endulini, 5a Jubilee Road, Parktown 2193, South Africa

Random House UK Limited Reg. No. 954009

A CIP catalogue record for this book
is available from the British Library

Papers used by Random House UK Limited
are natural, recyclable products made from wood grown in
sustainable forests. The manufacturing processes conform to
the environmental regulations of the country of origin.

ISBN 0 434 004340

Typeset by Deltatype Ltd, Birkenhead, Merseyside
Printed and bound in Great Britain by
Mackays of Chatham plc, Chatham, Kent

For my friends,
Fanny de Burgh Whyte and *Stephen Heron,*
who love a good mystery,
in grateful thanks for all their help and encouragement.

Lizzie Borden took an axe,
gave her mother forty whacks.
When she saw what she had done,
gave her father forty-one.

American nursery rhyme

Gut: narrow water-passage,
sound, straits.

Concise Oxford Dictionary

Book One

1

Joe Boylan always swore that if he had known what was going to happen that day, he would never have gone out in the boat, no matter how many fish they caught.

As it was, things started badly and that should have been a sign. The forecast had been for good weather, but instead they got a mist. It rolled in from the sea, thick as cotton, so that they could barely see the island where it lay, just beyond the harbour, like a great green-backed whale.

Then the engine wouldn't start. Joe's son, Sean, pulled on the cord, stopped, pulled again. He was a tall, broad-shouldered man, red eyes of a whiskey drinker. The engine whimpered and died. Sean kicked the side of the boat and cursed.

'Damned thing's cold as hell,' he said. He appealed to his father. 'Why don't we just pack it in? We can go out again later when the mist has cleared.'

'Are you kidding?' the older man said. He was small, hunched, white bristles on a leathery chin. 'You want the God-damned seals to get anything we've caught?'

He went into the little cabin at the prow of the boat and came back with a spanner and a new sparking plug. He worked for a few minutes at the engine, stood back and rubbed his hands on a rag.

'Try it again,' he commanded.

The younger man tugged at the cord. At first there was nothing. He tried again. This time there was a revving sound. It hovered for a moment, then accelerated. The engine coughed into life.

'You know your trouble, Sean?' the small man said with disdain. 'You've no staying-power. No perseverance. You give up too easy.'

The younger man said nothing. He took the wheel and slowly steered the boat past the harbour wall, into the open sea. The mist closed around them like a glove. They could just make out the outline of the cliffs, rising sheer from the sea. There was a stillness in the air. No wind. There had been no wind for days.

The little boat stopped now and then and the men pulled up lobster pots. They were nearly all empty. At last, the small man walked to the side of the boat and trailed his hand in the dark water. They had reached the shelter of the Bailey Lighthouse. The man gave directions to his son in a thin, clipped voice.

'Closer, Sean. Easy now. That'll do. Slow it. Slow it.'

The younger man cut the engine and the chug-chug sound died away across the waves. All that remained was the screeching of the gulls and the murmur of the sea against the rocks.

'That'll do,' the small man said and waited while the boat came to rest in the lee of the cliff. Above them, they could see the lighthouse shimmering in the mist. Every now and then it sent a beam of light sweeping like a finger across the sea.

The small man dragged his hand in the water till he caught a rope tied to a marking buoy. He paused before speaking again.

'Want to bet?'

Sean Boylan shrugged.

'You want to bet, for God's sake? A pint says we've made a catch. Are you on?'

'I'm on.'

The younger man left the engine and together they pulled on the rope. A net rose out of the sea and shook water in a silver spray. There were fish caught in its web. They could see the shine of their white bellies.

The small man gave a shout.

4

'Jesus, Sean! What did I tell you? Look at the bastards. Look at the size of them.'

They began pulling frantically now, dragging the net over the edge of the boat. The fish tumbled from its folds, spilling on to the floor. The small man tried to count.

'Twenty,' he said. 'At least. Big fat sea trout.'

Beside him, the younger man threw back his head and howled and the sound came echoing from the cliffs.

The two men tugged at the rope and the last of the net came shivering into the boat. There were pieces of seaweed caught in its folds, black and brown beside the silver fish.

Something caught the younger man's attention. It looked like a plastic ball, round and white, tucked away in the corner of the net. He bent to examine it and, all at once, he gave a gasp.

'What is it?' Joe Boylan said. He was busy now, picking up the plump fish, laying them carefully in the fish box.

There was no reply. Out of the corner of his eye he saw his son move quickly to the side of the boat. There was a splashing sound as he vomited into the sea.

'What the hell . . .?' Joe Boylan began.

He turned to look and felt his blood run cold.

'Christ!' he muttered. His hand moved quickly to make the sign of the cross.

A human head was lying on the floor. The mouth was open. He could see the teeth, the bloated face, the pocked skin, the empty eye sockets staring into the cold mist.

At that very moment the foghorn started from the lighthouse and its loud wail shattered the silence of the morning.

2

Megarry heard it too. He'd been listening to it all morning. It was one of the things he was gradually getting used to since he'd packed up the house in Belfast and come to live here in Howth. Things like street signs in Irish, the angelus bell at noon, the gulls that gathered on the roof outside the kitchen, squabbling over the crusts of bread that Kathleen threw out to them each morning after breakfast.

There was one there now, yellow beak and flinty eye, watching as he bent with the secateurs to trim the dead heads off the roses. He pretended to ignore it, lopped off a fat orange bud. It would never blossom, its folds enveloped in a sickly mould. The roses should have been sprayed months ago. Now it was too late. He sighed and looked around the neglected garden.

It had lain idle all autumn and winter, just like the house which still felt damp and cold, despite his wife's insistence on keeping the central heating running night and day. There was weeks of work to be done, hedges to be trimmed, grass to be cut, weeds to be pulled. Strangely, he found himself enjoying it.

He sat down on a wooden seat and took out his cigarettes. The early morning mist was beginning to clear and the sun was streaming into the garden through the knotted branches of the grisilenia, making patterns on the lawn. There was a fresh, salty smell and the scent of gorse drifting over from the East Mountain. He heard the phone ringing somewhere inside the house. Most of the calls now were for Kathleen. She was up to her neck in women's groups, charities for this and that. Half the time he never saw her.

He hesitated with the cigarette packet, allowing his fingers to caress the smooth surface, feeling the indentations where the brand name was stamped into the cardboard. He wasn't supposed to smoke at all now, but it was very hard to stop.

He had gone to see Dr Henry, who told him to take off his shirt, probed him with a stethoscope, took his blood-pressure, pressed his head against his chest and listened to his heartbeat while he held an old-fashioned pocket-watch in his hand.

At last Dr Henry sat down, his plump little stomach straining against his waistcoat, while Megarry self-consciously buttoned up his shirt. Dr Henry pushed his glasses hard against his nose and tried to look serious.

'You know what this means, Cecil, don't you? It means a change of life-style. That's what it damned well means. You've got to slow down.'

Megarry waited.

'It's a warning. You're a lucky man you're not dead. You're not young any more. All this stress, all this gadding about. It's not doing you any good.'

'Yeah, yeah,' Megarry said. 'That's not what the doctor in Spain told me. He said I'd be okay.'

'Those guys don't know horseshit,' Dr Henry said, looking displeased. 'I'm your doctor. I tell you what to do. Now listen to me. You get some exercise. You cut down butter, meat, cheese, alcohol. You give up those God-damned cigarettes.'

'You smoke yourself,' Megarry said.

'Don't take me for an example. If I want to kill myself, that's my business.'

Dr Henry took a pen from his breast pocket and fiddled with it while he studied Megarry from the side of his eye.

'There's something else.' He coughed, as if embarrassed. 'You ever thought of taking early retirement?'

In the end it had been so easy it left him with a feeling that it hadn't happened. He made an appointment to see his boss, Chief Superintendent Drysdale, who sat and listened patiently to what Megarry had to say, only his fingers betraying his irritation as they strayed from time to time to smooth down an imagined crease in his tunic.

'You can't do this, Cecil,' Drysdale said at last. 'They're going to reorganise the force, for Christ's sake. You could be in line for promotion.'

He poured more Bushmills into Megarry's glass and started in trying to persuade him.

'You're at that stage in your life when you want to settle back. A nice management job, sitting behind a desk giving the orders, letting other people do the running around. What's wrong with that?'

Behind him were all the little trophies of his career, medals, citations, certificates, framed pictures of his wife and children, smiling for the camera. The rewards of loyalty and faithful service.

'Don't do this, Cecil. Think of your wife, think of Kathleen.'

Megarry laughed and some whiskey ran down his chin. He took out a handkerchief and wiped it dry.

'What's so funny?' Drysdale asked.

'Kathleen. It's her idea. Hers and Dr Henry's. She's been at me for years to pack it in. She says the job is killing me. She says other things as well.'

'Like what?'

'Like I'm not appreciated here. Like nobody gives a continental whether I roll over and die as long as I don't stain the carpet.'

Drysdale looked shocked.

'That's not true, Cecil. You bloody well know it's not true. We all care about you.'

'Oh yeah? She's also got this idea in her head that I should have got further up the greasy pole after thirty-five years.'

'You made superintendent. That's quite good.'

'But not as good as Chief Superintendent.'

Megarry found himself laughing again. After the months of agonising, he felt an amazing sense of freedom.

'You can't be persuaded?'

8

'No. It's too late.'

'We'll miss you.'

Drysdale raised his glass and drained the whiskey.

'I just hope you're not in here in six months' time looking for your job back, you sonofabitch.'

It had been that easy. After thirty-five years.

They sold the house in Belfast and moved to Howth, where Kathleen's sister lived. Megarry wanted a clean break, somewhere far away from his old haunts with a lifetime's memories. But not so far that he couldn't go back from time to time when the mood took him.

He had fond memories of Howth. He had spent a couple of weeks here recuperating after Spain. And he had helped to solve a murder case.

He put the cigarettes back in his pocket and started in once more on the roses. You were supposed to make the incision just above the stem, according to the manual. He heard footsteps and saw his wife hurrying along the path from the kitchen.

'Peter Kelly phoned. He's down in the Capstan Bar. Something has happened. He says he'd appreciate your advice.'

'Did he say what it was?'

'No. Just that it was urgent.'

Megarry started to take off his gloves.

The Capstan Bar was down beside the harbour. There was a white police car outside with its lights flashing and a young constable in shirt sleeves sitting nervously at the wheel. Megarry walked quickly past and into the pub. There was a smell of sweat, beer, stale tobacco smoke.

The snooker-room was empty, but as he approached the lounge he could hear raised voices. There was a crowd around the bar, talking and drinking excitedly. They stopped when he came in and turned to examine him.

'Morning,' Megarry said and looked around the room.

There were two men in oilskins, seated on a faded leather banquette, clearly the centre of attention. They had glasses of brandy in their hands. Sitting alongside was Peter Kelly.

9

Megarry squeezed in beside him.

'I got your call,' he said. 'What's this all about?'

'We've got a problem. I need to talk to you.'

Kelly started to explain but immediately was interrupted by a plump man in braces who stood behind the counter. Megarry recognised Tom Reddin, the proprietor.

'I can tell you everything,' Reddin began. 'I saw it all with my own eyes. About ten o'clock this morning. I was just getting the place ready, when I heard this awful banging on the front door. When I got it open the two lads there came tumbling in. They looked like they'd seen a ghost. Hardly able to talk. How they got that damned boat back I'll never know. Sure, that sort of thing would put the heart across you.'

Reddin gripped his braces.

'What sort of thing?' Megarry asked.

'They found a head in the fishing net.'

The bar fell silent.

'A human head. In the net. Can you beat that? It was me rang Inspector Kelly there to tell him.'

The excitement around the bar started up again. This was a story that would be retold for years to come.

Megarry turned to the two men beside him. They were typical fishermen, rough, calloused hands, faces tanned by the sea. The older man was small, about forty-eight, with greying hair. The other man was taller, broader. He had a wild look in his eye.

Megarry lowered his voice. 'Just tell us exactly what happened. Start at the beginning.'

The older man lifted his glass and drained it, then wiped his mouth with the back of his hand. Megarry noticed the six empty glasses already piled up around the table.

'We were dragging up our net at the back of the lighthouse, and there's this head in among the fish.' The man hesitated. 'An awful-lookin' thing. All worn away. Like as if the crabs had been eating it. I tell you, it nearly turned my stomach.'

'Caught in the net?'

'Yeah. Just like the fish. There were bits of seaweed round it.'

'You keep the net there all the time?'

10

'Just sometimes. We have different places. There's a channel at the back of the lighthouse. Good deep water and you often get a run of fish in the evening.'

The man lit a cigarette. The other man sat nervously biting his nails.

'How does it work?' Megarry asked.

He heard the low murmur of laughter from the bar at his ignorant question. Everyone in the room knew exactly how it worked.

'It's simple,' Tom Reddin said, and started to explain, but Megarry waved him to be quiet.

'Let him tell me himself.'

He leaned forward and looked into the fisherman's face.

'What's your name?' he said.

'Joe Boylan. This is my son, Sean.'

'I know you, Joe. Haven't I seen you round the town?'

'Sure you have. I live in St Patrick's Lane.'

Megarry remembered the place, a jumble of small fishermen's cottages beside a field that blazed with yellow gorse all summer long. The houses and streets ran on top of each other, higgledy-piggledy, so that a man could easily get lost.

'Tell me how this netting business works, Joe.'

Megarry smiled and this time no one laughed. The man started again.

'Like I said, there's a channel at the back of the lighthouse. We stretch the net across the channel and tie it to the marker buoys.'

'And then what?'

'We leave it. Sometimes at this time of year there's a run of fry. The bigger fish, like the sea trout, they go after them. The fry can get through the net because they're small, you see, but the bigger fish that's chasing them, they get caught.'

'So when's the last time you put down the net?'

'Yesterday morning. We have a few lobster pots as well and we go out every morning at seven o'clock, weather permitting.'

'So the head could only have got there in the last twenty-four hours?'

'Yes,' the small man said and someone put a pint of Guinness in front of him and another for his son.

Megarry glanced at Kelly. Maybe it would be better to bring the men down to the station and finish the interview there. He tried to ignore the noise around him.

It wasn't there yesterday morning, if that's what you're getting at,' Sean Boylan said.

Megarry turned his attention to him. 'And no sign of . . .'

'The rest of him? You must be joking. Seeing that thing is enough to last me for the rest of my life. If there's any more bits of him floating around, somebody else can find them.'

Sean Boylan sat forward and gripped his glass.

'How do you think it got there?'

Boylan shrugged.

'The tide,' somebody said, and other voices took up the suggestion.

'What time was high tide?'

'Ten past six.'

'Have you ever found other things in your net?'

'From time to time.' The older man took a sip from his pint.' Dead seabirds, things like that. But we never found nothing like this before.'

Megarry paused. There was one important question left to ask.

'Where is it now?'

The clinking of glasses ceased and the chatter died away. It seemed that every ear was straining for the reply.

'It's in the boat,' Sean Boylan said. 'In the lobster bucket. I was going to throw it back in the sea, but me da told me to keep it. I just dropped it in the bucket and put the lid on and started back to the harbour as fast as I could.'

'You did the right thing. We'll have to identify him.'

'You'll have a job,' the man said. 'You want to see it. It's an awful bloody sight. Jaysis.'

The chatter in the bar started up again. Kelly leaned forward.

'One of you will have to give us a statement. But not now. Tomorrow will do. I'll send someone to your house. In the meantime, we have to collect that head. And one of you will have to take us to the place where it was found. Who'll do that?'

Sean Boylan finished his drink and stood up.

12

'I will,' he said. He looked around the room at the faces, staring at him in awe.

He shrugged. 'C'mon,' he said. 'Let's get this bleedin' thing over.'

Kelly was excited as they came out from the pub.

'Well, Cecil. What do you think?'

Megarry paused. 'How do you mean?'

'Head in a fishing net? It sure as hell beats the stuffing out of some guy getting stabbed in Limerick. Looks like we've got a real job on our hands here.'

Megarry's fingers went to his pocket, felt the hard edge of the cigarette packet.

'Let's get this straight. You've got a job, Peter. Singular. You.'

Kelly put a friendly arm on his shoulder, pretended to look disappointed. 'But why do you think I called you, for God's sake?'

'Kathleen said you wanted my advice. I'll give it to you in three words. 'Identify the head.'

'And what if we can't identify it?'

'Then you've got a problem.' Megarry started to walk away. Kelly went after him.

'A big case like this, Cecil? Here in Howth. Right on your doorstep. I thought you'd be offended if I didn't invite you in.'

'Don't give me that bullshit.'

'It's not bullshit. You're the best cop I know. They're still talking about the Harpo Higgins case back at the station.'

Megarry stopped. 'You know what happened on that one. Your superintendent ordered me off the God-damned inquiry. That's the thanks I got.'

'It won't happen again,' Kelly said quickly. 'You've got my word. You're retired for one thing. They can't pull that stunt about working in a different jurisdiction.'

'That's right. I'm retired. I'm supposed to be taking it easy.'

'But you'll enjoy it, Cecil. I'll do the spade work. You can take the cerebral stuff.'

'Jeeesus,' Megarry said. 'You're so full of shit. Where do you guys learn it? Do they teach you this at training college?'

Kelly began to laugh.

Megarry looked at him, smirking like an idiot in the morning sun. Do I need this? he thought. I could be playing golf, sitting in the Lighthouse Bar drinking pints and listening to some good traditional music. Do I need the aggravation of another investigation? All that God-damned footslogging, the endless interviews, the lies and evasions, the disappointments, the blind alleys?

'I don't know,' he said at last. 'I'm not sure Kathleen would like it. I'm supposed to be clearing out the garden for her.'

'But you told me yourself she's hardly ever at home now, Cecil. I'm relying on you.'

Megarry studied the young man beside him. Underneath the banter, he was uneasy. This could turn out to be the biggest thing he'd had to face since becoming Inspector. And then another thought came to him. I'm partly responsible. I encouraged him. I told him to go for the job.

He sighed. Pulled out the cigarette packet. The first one of the day. Jesus, he thought. Here we go again.

'On one condition,' he said. 'No interference. The first sign of your super poking his nose in, and I'm off the case. Is that understood?'

'Of course,' Kelly said.

'I mean it,' Megarry said. 'And wipe that stupid grin off your face.'

At the harbour wall, Sean Boylan was waiting for them.

'What do you want me to do?' Megarry asked.

Kelly thought for a moment.

'Why don't you go with Boylan in the boat? I'll take the head into Forensic and see what Finnegan can make of it.'

'But I don't like boats,' Megarry protested. 'In fact, I hate the God-damned things.'

'It's not far,' Kelly said soothingly. 'It won't take long.'

They began walking along the cobbled stones of the pier. Boylan's boat was moored against the wall. It was a tiny craft, capable of holding three or four people at most. *Star of the Morning*, it said in painted letters on the prow.

Sean Boylan jumped down and Megarry clambered after him, puffing from the exertion. He noticed the lobster pots and the boxes filled with trout, their little eyes gleaming like buttons in the hard morning light.

Boylan moved along the boat towards the engine and stopped when he came to a bucket with a plastic lid. Megarry could see his hand tremble as he lifted it.

'It's in here,' he said.

He slowly withdrew the lid to reveal the contents. Megarry felt his gorge rise. The head looked like a large ball of soap. It had been badly mutilated, empty eye-sockets, a large hole where the nose should have been, part of an ear missing. The hair was practically all gone and a strand of seaweed clung across the forehead like some ghastly wreath.

'Seen enough?'

Megarry nodded.

Boylan replaced the lid and handed the bucket out of the boat to Kelly. He seemed relieved to be rid of it. Boylan pulled on the cord and there was a phut-phut sound as the engine fired.

For a while they travelled in silence. Then Megarry said, 'You had a good catch.' He gestured towards the boxes filled with fish.

Boylan seemed reluctant to talk. He averted his eyes and pretended to concentrate on steering the boat.

'I said, you had a good catch. How much will that lot fetch?'

'God knows. It depends.'

'Where will you sell them?'

'The local restaurants. Maybe the fish shops.'

Megarry watched him as he handled the wheel, the strong arms, the broad shoulders like a footballer's, the eyes that had a crazy look. He's nervous, Megarry thought. Maybe he's still in shock. And then it occurred to him that Boylan distrusted him. Maybe he was collecting social welfare on the side.

'Would you get a catch like that every day?'

Boylan grunted. 'Are you kidding? Some days you get nothing at all. Some days the bleedin' seals eat the fish if you don't get there soon enough. Some days you can't get out because of the weather.'

The weather. Megarry thought of the trawlers tied up in the harbour for weeks during the winter, unable to put to sea because of the storms. But today the weather was kind. He looked at the sea. The earlier mist had burned off and the water stretched blue and green across to the island.

'How far is this place?'

'About fifteen minutes. Just below the lighthouse.'

Megarry watched Boylan steer the boat into the waves. There was a strong smell of the sea but scarcely a breath of wind. A couple of gulls followed, screeching and diving into the water.

He looked around the boat. Apart from the lobster pots and the fish-boxes, there was a can of diesel, several lengths of rope, a grappling hook, a couple of oars and a box with 'Flares' written along the side. He was surprised to see no evidence of buoyancy jackets or even a lifebelt. He gripped the side nervously as the boat began to shift in the swell.

'Do you enjoy your work?' he asked.

'It's a job.'

'But all this good fresh air? And the scenery.' He waved his hand towards the expanse of ocean, the cliffs climbing sheer out of the sea, the heather and gorse burning bright along the hillside.

Boylan spat. He turned a sullen face to the policeman. 'You didn't mention the danger.'

'Danger?'

'Of drowning. Fishermen drown all the time. The sea is treacherous. You have to respect it.'

'You can swim, can't you?'

Boylan shook his head. Megarry stared, incredulous.

'No?'

'Fishermen never learn to swim. It's an old tradition. If you're going to go down it's best that it happens quick. Swimming only prolongs the agony. I never learnt to swim. I don't want to learn.'

They were passing close in along the cliffs. Megarry saw that they were covered with sea-birds, gannets, gulls, guillemots, hundreds of them clustering in the crevices and ledges. He watched as a cormorant swooped low over the water and dived below the waves, surfacing far out beyond the boat with a fish in its mouth.

They were approaching the white battlements of the Bailey lighthouse, its fog-horn fallen silent. He could see the spires of Dun Laoghaire and, beyond, the dark humps of the Dublin mountains. At last they came to two large rocks rising sheer out of the ocean. Boylan turned off the engine and the boat drifted to a halt so that Megarry could almost reach out and touch the dark stone. He saw a channel running between the rocks, the water clear and blue and deep. Two red marker buoys bobbed in the water.

'This is the place?' he asked.

'Yes. This is it. This is where we found it.'

'What's it called?'

'Piper's Gut. It's an old name. A man called Piper owned this place hundreds of years ago.'

There was a swell in the channel, but scarcely a wave, just the gentle lapping of water on stone. There was a stillness, a sense of peace. Megarry let his eye travel across the scene, the marker buoys tied with rope, the rocks, the cliffs rising above them towards the sky. He took in the details, filing them away.

He saw a look of concern cross Sean Boylan's face. The boat was drifting now that the engine had been knocked off, and they were being drawn further into the channel.

'Have you got what you wanted?'

'I think so.' Megarry gave one last look along the cliffs. He could smell the rich scent of the gorse. It mingled with the smell of the sea. Smack in the shelter of the lighthouse, his eye caught the dark blue slate of a roof.

'Is there a house up there?'

'Yes.'

'It's very exposed, isn't it?'

'Some people like it that way.'

Megarry nodded.

They pulled away from the rocks and started back. Boylan hesitated, then spoke again.

'What is it?' he said. 'Is it murder?'

Megarry gazed out across the sea, the sun sparkling off the

water in spangles of light, the sky blue and empty of cloud. The very thought of murder in a place like this seemed like an outrage.

'It could be,' he said. 'It could be many things. Murder is certainly one of them.'

3

Megarry left Boylan to tie up the boat and made his way towards the town, thankful to be back on dry land. His stomach felt queasy, even though it had been a smooth enough trip. When he came to the Pier House Inn, he decided to go in and ring Kathleen.

The place was crowded and it was obvious there was only one topic of conversation passing back and forth along the bar. It was also clear that the story had been embroidered in the telling. He heard one grizzled mariner claim that an arm and a leg had been found. Another man said it was a hand with the fingers missing.

The barman gave the counter a wipe and waited for Megarry to order. He felt like something strong after the boat trip, but he was mindful of Dr Henry's advice.

'Sparkling water,' he said and went out to the hall to ring home.

'It's me. Cecil.'

'Peter Kelly rang again. He said to tell you he'd meet you at the Bailey lighthouse. What's going on, Cecil?'

'He's got a case,' Megarry said.

'I heard. Bits of a human body washed up in Doldrum Bay.'

'*What?*'

'It was on the radio.'

Megarry felt his heart sink.

'Well, the bloody radio's got it wrong. It was a human head and it wasn't washed up anywhere. It was caught in a fishing net. Jesus Christ.'

'A head?' Kathleen said. 'How did it get there?'

'I don't know. That's what Kelly has to find out. He wants me to help.'

'Are you sure that's a good idea?'

'It's not much. It's really just the . . . eh . . . cerebral stuff.'

'The what, Cecil?'

'It's Kelly's phrase. What it really means is he wants me to solve the God-damned case for him.'

He put the phone down and went back into the bar. It was only after he'd finished his drink that the thought came to him that Kathleen hadn't even mentioned the garden.

He found Kelly and another man on a narrow road that ran towards the lighthouse. They were standing on the edge of the cliff and gazing down into the sea. Below them, a blue police dinghy bobbed in the water while a team of divers in wetsuits and breathing apparatus searched the gulleys that surrounded the channel where the head had been found.

Both men looked up when they saw him approach. Kelly made the introductions.

'This is Inspector Walshe of the sub-aqua unit. Cecil Megarry. Cecil used to be with the RUC, but he's retired now.'

Out of the corner of his eye, Megarry thought he saw Kelly smile.

'Have they found anything?' Megarry asked.

'Not so far,' Walshe said. 'But I'm confident. If there's anything down there, they'll get it. They're professionals. But, you know, it depends.'

'On what?'

'Tides, currents. How the head got into the sea to begin with.'

'I'm assuming it was dumped,' Kelly said.

Walshe turned his pale blue eyes on him. 'You think it's murder?'

'It crossed my mind.'

20

'Have you considered an accident?'

Kelly kept a straight face. *'Accident?'*

'Yes. The propeller of a boat, the hawser of a ship. It could have happened out in the middle of the ocean somewhere. Maybe a seaman fell overboard and got caught up in the machinery. The body could be washed up anywhere.'

Walshe made a sucking noise with his teeth. 'Like I said. My men will trawl every inch of this shoreline. If there's anything down there, they'll find it. Now,' he said, 'I have to go.'

He nodded politely to Megarry. 'Nice to have met you, Mr Megarry. You picked a beautiful place to live. You know, there are some fine walks around here.'

'Yes,' Megarry said. 'I've tried them.'

Walshe turned away and strode purposefully up the road. The two men watched him go.

Megarry spoke to Kelly. 'Someone has tipped off the press. It was all over the radio. *And* they've got it assways, as usual. In my experience, this is never a good development. There'll be reporters crawling all over the place, asking questions.' Megarry paused. 'And if this *is* murder, it will have alerted the murderer. Now he knows we'll be coming after him. It gives him time to prepare.'

The house at the top of the cliff was called Paradise Regained. It was perched on an outcrop that seemed to have been hewn from the rock. It was a bungalow, painted white. There was honeysuckle in the little front garden and daffodils in bloom. As they approached, Megarry could hear the sighing of the sea, a gentle sucking of water against the shore.

The door was opened by a young woman in jeans and halter-necked top. She had her blonde hair tied with a kerchief and there was a dusting cloth in her hand. Immediately she stood back and put her fingers to her mouth.

'I don't believe this. Cecil Megarry.'

Megarry stared at her, struggling for recognition.

'We met before,' the woman said quickly. 'At your house. I know your wife. Kathleen. We're in the women's group together. Trish Blake.'

'This is Inspector Peter Kelly.'

She stared for a moment and then a smile curled the corners of her mouth. 'Let me guess why you're here,' she said. 'It's about this body they found. Isn't it?'

'I beg your pardon?'

'The body that was washed up in the bay. I heard it on the radio. I suppose that's what all this racket is about.' She pointed with a thumb behind her. 'That boat down there. Those divers. Is it to do with the body?'

Megarry and Kelly exchanged a glance.

'Yes and no,' Kelly said.

'You'd better come in,' Trish said.

She held open the door and they entered the house. There was a smell of polish. She led them through the hall and into a kitchen where a large window gave out over the sea. The room felt warm from the sun. There was a telescope fixed on a tripod and a painting of a seascape on one wall. Megarry bent to examine it.

'Is it a local scene?'

'Yes,' the woman said. 'A place called Gaskin's Leap. Not far from here, along the cliffs.'

She put down the dusting cloth. 'I was just doing some cleaning. I have a routine, you see. Every day I do something different. One day it's cleaning. Then washing, baking, gardening. I find if you organise your time you get more done. Today is my cleaning day.'

'Are you at home all the time?' Kelly asked.

'Good Lord, no. I'm up to my neck in all sorts of things. I used to work in PR before I got married. I still do a little bit from time to time. On a freelance basis. And then there's the women's group.' She glanced quickly at Megarry. 'I'm very involved with them.'

'You're a very busy woman.'

She smiled again. 'I like to be busy. I like to be organised. I like everything in its proper place. I find there's a comfort in routine. Security. Do you know what I mean?'

'How long have you been married?'

'Five years.'

'Have you any family?'

She shook her head. 'It's too early for that. We want to settle down a little bit. Get established. Get things on a sound financial footing. Then we'll plan our family.'

'And what about your husband?'

'He's a factory manager. He works in town.'

She suddenly clapped her hands. 'Look, why don't I make you a nice cup of tea?'

'Brillo,' Megarry said and watched as she went to the sink to fill the kettle. Everything was spotless. Even the taps on the sink had been polished till they shone.

'This is a beautiful house,' he said. 'You keep it so tidy.'

Mrs Blake looked pleased. 'Like I said. It's all down to routine. Running a house is just like any other business. You make a plan and you stick to it. You don't let things pile up. That's the secret.'

'How long have you lived here?'

'Three years. Before that we lived in the town.'

'The house is new, isn't it?'

'Yes. We built it ourselves. Well, not physically, although Jim was able to help with some of the construction work. We bought the site and designed the house to our own specifications. We always wanted a house with a view. No point living in Howth if you don't have a view. Don't you agree, Mr Megarry?'

'Of course.'

Mrs Blake put down cups and saucers. 'Would you like some cake? I baked it myself.'

'You're very kind,' Megarry said.

She went off to a cupboard and came back with a coffee cake. She poured the tea and then sat down across from the policemen and rested her chin in her hands.

'Now, maybe you'd tell me what this is all about?'

Kelly hesitated. 'It's not very pleasant.'

Mrs Blake moved closer.

'Shock me,' she said.

'Something was found in the water down there this morning. In a fishing net. It wasn't a body like the radio said. It was . . . part of a body.'

'Part?'

'It was a human head.'

Mrs Blake gave a little cry. A look of horror filled her face.

'Oh, my God! I don't believe it. Howth is so quiet. Nothing happens here!'

'Look,' Kelly said quickly. 'We don't know how it got there or where it entered the water. The sub-aqua people think it could have happened miles away and got washed up here. But we have to make inquiries.'

'The radio said Doldrum Bay.'

'The radio got it wrong.'

'And how long was it there?'

'We think less than twenty-four hours.'

'So where's the rest of it?'

There was a pause and Megarry became aware of a clock ticking on the kitchen wall.

'We don't know. That's what the divers are searching for now.'

Mrs Blake looked at the two men and took a deep breath. 'I'm sorry,' she said. 'Forget about me. It's just the shock.'

Megarry spoke: 'Were you at home yesterday?'

'Yes.'

'All day?'

'Most of it. Yesterday was my baking day.'

'Did you see anything unusual down there?'

'Unusual?'

'Any activity? Boats? Anything like that?'

'No.'

A frown suddenly crossed her face. 'You're not suggesting . . .?'

'I'm simply asking.'

'No,' she said. 'I saw nothing.'

Megarry finished his tea and stood up.

'I'm sorry to have bothered you. You understand we have to make inquiries. Thanks for the tea and cake.'

'You're welcome.'

She walked the men back through the house. At the front door, Megarry paused.

24

'One final thing,' he said. 'What time did you go to bed last night?'

'Eleven thirty. It's the same every night. Jim has an early start.'

'Did you hear any noise? Cars stopping on the road? Anything like that?'

Mrs Blake considered.

'There was something,' she said. 'About one o'clock. The dog was barking. Jim went out to investigate.'

'And what did he find?'

'Nothing.'

The forensic laboratory was closer into the city, at Clontarf. It was an ugly building of red-brick and smoked glass like something a child might construct from a Lego set. They drove down from the Summit, past the big houses standing defiantly back from the road, with their security gates, warning signs, Volvos parked in the driveways, cherry trees coming into blossom.

They went in by the coast, the smoking stacks of the Pigeon House, the waves rolling relentlessly on the grey shore at Dollymount strand. The spires and domes of the city shimmered before them in the heat.

It was almost three o'clock when they arrived. There was a man on a tractor cutting the lawn. The air was filled with the sweet scent of new-mown grass. At the entrance, they came upon a surly-looking cop lounging at the security desk.

'Can I help you?' he said.

Kelly produced his ID.

'You can get your God-damned feet off that desk for a start.'

The man sat up straight.

'I didn't recognise you.'

'Where's Dr Finnegan?'

'He's in the lab.'

'We're here to see him.'

'Right away,' the policeman said and spoke quickly into a phone. Megarry looked around the empty foyer. It had been painted a depressing shade of grey. Close to the door, a solitary spider plant was wilting in a tub.

The policeman put down the phone. 'He says you can go down. Do you want me to take you?'

'It's all right,' Kelly said. 'I know where it is.'

He started along a corridor. There was a smell of disinfectant. It got stronger as they went, till at last they saw an open door and light spilling out. Kelly entered without knocking.

They were in a large room with benches and dissecting tables and glass jars filled with odd-coloured liquids. In the corner, beside a sink, a small man in a white medical coat was bent over a desk. He heard them approach and turned to greet them.

'Inspector Kelly,' he said and held out a chubby little hand. He had a bright red face like he'd been out in the sun. Megarry smelt the whiskey on his breath. So did Kelly.

'You've been drinking, Herbie,' Kelly said.

The man looked indignant. 'Hell roast it. It's my day off. I was at the golf club. I came in here to do you a favour. Maybe I shouldn't have bothered?'

He looked expectantly towards Megarry. 'I don't believe we've met.'

'Cecil Megarry.'

Finnegan wiped his hand on his coat before presenting it. 'Where're you from? That accent. Somewhere north. Donegal?'

'Belfast.'

'Belfast? Knew a girl there once. Protestant. Decent type. No hang-ups. None of this Catholic horseshit about leg-over situations. Know what I mean?' He winked at Megarry.

'What part of Belfast?'

'Ardoyne, I think.'

'I know it. It's ninety-five per cent Catholic,' Megarry said.

'Is it? Oh, well. She was a decent sort. Enjoyed her bit of slap and tickle. Wasn't running off either to tell it all to the priest in the confession box.'

He turned back to Kelly. 'Where'd you get this?'

'In the sea.'

'I know that, for Christ's sake. It had seaweed on it.'

'Howth.'

'Well, it's very interesting. I don't think I've seen anything like it before.'

He indicated the desk where he had been working. The head was resting on a plastic stand. It had been washed and cleaned but it was still an awful sight. The eye sockets were empty, two pale holes staring blankly from the yellow face. The skin had been scraped from the right side. It hung in shreds down below the neck and spilled into a little tray.

Kelly wrinkled his face in disgust.

'Do we know how it got separated?'

'I think so.'

'Was it an accident? A propeller or something like that?'

'A what?'

'We thought maybe it might have been an accident at sea. Guy mangled by a propeller or something.'

'No,' Finnegan said. 'It was done with a saw.'

He drew the men's attention to the flesh at the bottom of the neck.

'See how neat the cut is? And here.' He pointed to the spinal cord, clearly visible at the base of the skull. 'You can almost see where the saw went through. Like a knife through butter, to coin a phrase. If this had been an accident there would have been much more damage. The head was cut from the body and *then* put in the sea. And there's something else.'

Finnegan turned the head sideways so that the left part was facing up. He pointed again. At the bottom of the neck there was a little round wound.

'A bullet?'

'Exactly. Entrance wound. Here.' He rotated the head once more so that the right side was now visible where the skin had been scraped away.' Exit wound. Notice the damage. You can still see where the flesh is torn and bruised. This person was shot first and then the head was removed.'

Megarry felt the temperature in the room suddenly increase. It was as if the air had been withdrawn. He turned to the window and pushed it open. Finnegan was still talking.

'There is one piece of good news. The teeth are still intact. That should help your identification.'

'How long was the head in the sea?' Megarry asked.

Finnegan coughed, took out a handkerchief and wiped his

eyes. 'It's difficult to say. There's been a lot of damage. Crabs and fish and things like that. The nose and the eyes, for instance. I'd need more time to work on it.'

'Give us an estimate.'

Finnegan sniffed. 'This *is* only a guess. I'd say about ten days.'

He spoke again to Kelly. 'Is this all you've got? Just the head?'

'Yes. The sub-aqua unit is searching for the remainder of the body.'

'I hope they find it.' He began to take off his gloves. 'Looks like you've got a murder.'

Finnegan walked with them along the corridor towards the hall. 'I'll have a preliminary report for you by tomorrow and a fuller one in a few days.'

At the door they stopped.

'Is there anyone could do a reconstruction of the face for us?' Kelly asked.

'Sure,' Finnegan said. 'I can do that.'

'That would help. Once we know what he looked like, we can begin to match him with the Missing Persons file. The sooner we can identify this guy, the sooner we can make progress.'

Finnegan's bright eyes were twinkling. 'You're jumping to conclusions.'

'What do you mean?'

'This wasn't a man,' Finnegan said and pushed the door wide so that they could see out over the lawn. 'This was a woman.'

4

The next day, Megarry rose soon after 7 a.m. It was a dull morning; heavy sky, low cloud. There was a tension in the air as if a storm was coming. He left Kathleen sleeping, an arm thrown upwards across her chest, went down to the kitchen and made tea. By 7.30 a.m., he was striding across the golf course, a film of perspiration dampening his brow.

This early morning walk was now part of his daily routine. Regular exercise, Dr Henry had said. He found it difficult at first, a man like him who had never taken exercise in his life and who took the car everywhere, even to the corner shop to buy his cigarettes. But he had got used to it, even discovered after a while that he'd come to enjoy it. There were advantages. For one thing, it gave him a chance to think.

The golf course was deserted, the grass wet with dew, the air heavy with the scent of hawthorn in bloom. As he climbed, he could see the town falling away behind him, the chimneys and roof-tops, the spires of the churches, the boats packed together in the harbour.

He entered a wood and a rabbit scurried for cover. He heard a bird call and then an answering reply from a nearby oak. He pressed on till at last, through the darkness of the wood, he caught the glint of light on water. Soon he came to a small lake. He stopped and sat down.

This was one of his favourite places, particularly at this hour, when everything was still. Later in the day there'd be little boys with fishing poles, angling for perch. His thoughts turned to the case.

Kelly had driven him back to Howth after they left the forensic lab the previous evening. He kept talking over his shoulder as he wrestled with the rush-hour traffic on the Clontarf Road.

'What do you think we're dealing with here?'

Megarry shrugged. 'It's too early to say.'

'Some sort of madman? Some sort of animal?'

'Why do you say that?'

'He cut her up, for God's sake. Bad enough shooting her. But then to take a saw. Why'd he want to do that for? Jesus Christ.'

'He probably cut her up to make it easier to dispose of the body,' Megarry said. 'That's the obvious reason.'

'Why didn't he just bury her?'

Megarry shifted in his seat.' You ever hear of Dennis Nilsen?'

'Sure I did.'

'Remember the case?'

'Some of it.'

'Dennis Nilsen murdered at least a dozen young men. Dismembered them, boiled their limbs in a pot in his kitchen. He took some of the corpses to bed with him, slept with them for weeks.'

'What are you trying to say?'

'That Nilsen appeared normal. Nobody suspected him. The police only discovered the murders by accident after someone complained about the smell and workmen found rotting human flesh in a blocked drain. Our murderer may be just some ordinary Joe Soap. Someone who helps old ladies across the road, goes to church on Sunday. Someone who leads a perfectly respectable life, not a raving madman.'

Kelly drove for a while in silence.

'There's one thing that bothers me,' he said at last. 'Something that Walshe hinted at. What if we don't find the rest of the body?'

It was 8.30 a.m. when he returned to the house. He could smell breakfast cooking. Kippers. Low cholesterol. Kathleen was sitting at the kitchen table. He kissed her softly on the nape of the neck, ran his hands slowly along her face.

She turned her head and smiled. 'How was your walk?'

'Good.'

'Take a look at this.'

She had a morning newspaper spread out on the table. There was a banner in bold type. 'Horror Find in Howth.' Beneath it was a report of the discovery of the head. It was written in tabloid prose and accompanied a picture of the Boylans sitting at the counter of the Capstan Bar. A plump figure sat between them.

'Of course,' Megarry said and thumped the table with his fist. 'I should have known.'

'Known what?'

'It was Reddin who tipped off the press. The owner of the bar. Look at him. He's grinning from ear to bloody ear as if he's just won the lottery. He's publicity-mad. He probably thinks this will be good for business.'

'He could be right,' Kathleen said and put a plate before him. 'People love this sort of thing. Look at the way they make pilgrimages to that pub in London where the Kray twins used to drink.'

Megarry grunted and began to pick at his kipper.

'It was also on the news at eight o'clock. The reporter said the police were looking at the possibility that there could be other killings. Some maniac going about cutting people up.'

Megarry put down his fork. 'Jesus Christ! Where do they get this stuff? That's the most irresponsible thing I've ever heard. It's just going to put the fear of God into people.'

Kathleen poured tea into his cup.

'So, is there a maniac on the loose or is there not?'

'Of course there's not. All we have is a head. We haven't even identified her yet.'

'It was a woman?'

'Yes.'

'So now they've got a sex angle.'

'I know,' Megarry said mournfully.

He decided to walk to the station. As he passed through the narrow streets of the town, he thought again how much he relied on Kathleen, how much he needed her. She was like a good right arm to him.

Memories of those awful times in Belfast came flooding back. The vendetta against his father's killers that drove him night and day like a madman consumed with passion for revenge. The crazy drinking bouts in the backroom of the Montrose Hotel, the only place it was safe to drink. Watching a child slowly starve herself to death because he had been a bad father.

Kathleen had rescued him from that, saved him from a breakdown, incarceration in a drying-out clinic, maybe even something worse. There were times in that terrible period when he had been tempted to end it all. But she had never wavered in her love for him. How did you repay someone for something like that?

As he walked along Main Street, he noticed the little knots of people chatting outside the gates of the church. They glanced about them as they spoke. There were more outside the library and the newsagent's. He knew they were talking about the murder. It would be the only topic of conversation in the town for days to come. And if the media kept up its campaign, the agitation that was palpable in these people's faces would grow to panic and then to hysteria. Silently, he cursed Tom Reddin.

The station was dark and cool. An exasperated sergeant sat behind a desk, face flushed with irritation. He was a big, heavy-built man in shirt sleeves and belt, thick farmer's wrists, tie loosened, hairs crawling out from under his collar. Megarry introduced himself and the man pumped his hand.

'See that damned phone?' he said and pointed. 'Bloody thing hasn't stopped ringing all morning. I'm tempted to take it off the hook and let them all go and shag themselves.'

'The media?'

'Yes, the bloody meedya. Reporters wanting to know if there's more bodies out there, if we know who the killer is, if we've identified the victim yet, if there's a Jack the Ripper on the loose, if I can tell them any damned thing at all that'll help them make up a story. There was a television crew here only half an hour ago. I had to chase them. I sent them down to Tom Reddin in the Capstan. He started it after all.'

'Damned right,' Megarry said. 'Reddin's problem is he doesn't know when to keep his bloody big mouth shut. Tell them the Press Office are the only people who can give out information. Eventually, they'll get the message and leave you alone.'

'But it's not just the meedya,' the sergeant continued, reluctant to let go of a sympathetic ear. 'It's Joe Public as well. You know we have practically no crime in Howth. The occasional burglary or drunk-driving or fellas parking on double yella lines. That's about the extent of it. Now we've got this. That radio bulletin this morning didn't do any good. People are ringing in to ask if it's safe to go out. Old folk, particularly. This sort of thing just scares the shit out of them.'

Megarry sighed. 'Just try to reassure them, sergeant. Tell them we've no reason to believe this is anything other than a one-off murder. It may not even have been committed here.'

The phone started to ring.

'Talk to you later,' Megarry said and walked quickly past and into the station.

Kelly's office was a small place at the back. It had 'Interview Room' written on the door. Kelly was sitting at a desk with a young woman officer. They were deep in conversation. Kelly saw him and stood up.

'Cecillll! How are you, this fine morning?'

He indicated the young woman. 'Annie Lawlor. Cecil Megarry. He's an old friend. You're going to be working together.'

Megarry raised an eyebrow. 'Working together?'

'Sure. Since the murder victim was a woman, I decided to draft Annie in.'

Lawlor smiled. 'I've heard of you,' she said.

'You have?'

'You solved the Harpo Higgins murder. *After* the superintendent had ordered you off the case. There were some noses out of joint over that one. And a lot of glee among the foot soldiers. If you want my opinion, nothing energises the troops better than watching management making eejits of themselves.'

Megarry glanced quickly at Kelly who was lying back in his chair and staring at the ceiling.

'I'm afraid you've got this wrong. I was only assisting. Inspector Kelly made the arrests. And prepared the case. And got the convictions. Any credit is entirely due to him.'

Kelly blushed. What the hell is this? Megarry thought. Put one good-looking woman on the case and Kelly's behaving like a schoolboy on a first date.

'Enough bullshit,' he said. 'You heard the news bulletin?'

'Of course. You know, I could joyously strangle that fat bastard Reddin.'

'Get in the queue. The sergeant's way ahead of you. And I'm a mile in front of him.'

Kelly stuck a matchstick between his teeth and sucked on it.

'What can I do? Newspaper editors decide to get the head-staggers, it's beyond my control.'

'Don't talk to them,' Megarry said. 'Refer all inquiries to the Press Office. It's the best way, believe me. I've just given the sergeant the same advice. And while we're at it, why don't you get someone to check the murder files? Just in case?'

Kelly stared.

'You don't believe that stuff, Cecil? A mass murderer loose in Howth. What tablets are you taking?'

'I didn't say I believed it. But let me put it this way. What are you going to say when the superintendent starts asking questions?'

Kelly sat up straight.

'Get someone to go through the files. And get them to check with the RUC and Scotland Yard. Cover your back, Peter. Don't give them any opportunity to do a number on you when the shit starts to fly.'

'All right,' Kelly said quickly. 'I'll do it.'

He shifted some papers on his desk and glanced at Lawlor.

'Anyway, I've asked Annie to join us. She's been around a bit. Worked with the Women's Refuge and the Sexual Assault Unit. She's used to this sort of thing.'

34

'What sort of thing?'

'Sex crimes.'

Megarry took a deep breath.

'Aren't you jumping the gun? Where's the evidence?'

'Cecil. We have to look at all the possibilities.'

Lawlor spoke. 'There's been a spate of attacks on women in the past eighteen months. They've largely gone unreported in the media. But now, with this case, more women are coming forward.'

'What sort of attacks?' Megarry asked.

'Rapes, sexual assaults. Mainly in the Kilbarrack area. It's only a few miles away. Maybe they're connected. Why don't I check if anyone's been arrested? At the very least, the Kilbarrack cops must have a list of suspects.'

Megarry took out his cigarettes and saw Lawlor frown. There was a 'No Smoking' sign on the wall. In police stations, nobody usually gave a damn. He put the packet away.

'Slow down,' he said. 'Let's not get carried away. Maybe this is a sex crime. We can't tell. The first thing we've got to do is identify this woman.'

'On that very point,' Kelly said and opened a drawer. He took out a folder.

'Missing Persons file. I got it this morning. There's something of interest.'

He took out a sheet of paper and began to read.

'Mary Elizabeth Grogan. Single. Thirty-two years of age. Five feet, seven inches. Auburn hair, blue eyes. Financial consultant. Place of employment: Custom House Docks complex, Dublin. Last seen leaving work on the evening of Friday, 20 April.'

'Get to the point,' Megarry said.

'Her address, Cecil. Crow's Nest Cottage. West Heath. Howth.'

5

West Heath was a dark, foreboding place, a bleak expanse of moorland covered in heather and gorse that stretched from Howth summit to the foot of Shielmartin Hill. When they arrived, it was shrouded in shadow.

Lawlor parked her car at a disused quarry and they got out. The clouds were low in the sky. A light breeze shook the elms along the rim of the moor. There was no sign of a living thing.

Lawlor shivered. 'This place gives me the creeps,' she said.

Megarry said nothing, let his eye travel down the wide stretch of moorland to where it sank into the green margin of the sea. Not a thing moved. Not a bird. Not an animal. He buttoned his coat tight against his chest.

'Let's go,' he said and took her hand. They started to pick their way carefully along a bridle path that ran deep into the heath.

For a while they walked in silence, listening to the sounds their feet made as they crunched through the heather.

'What were you doing before this?' Megarry began.

'Hitting the bricks out in Ballymun.'

'Foot patrol?'

'That's right. General dogsbody. Car thefts, drugs, juvenile crime. There's a whole bag of social problems out there.'

'Who are you telling?' Megarry said.

'Before that, I worked with the Sexual Assault Unit. And before that, I was at UCD.'

'What did you study?'

'Sociology.'

Megarry nodded. 'Makes sense.'

They pressed on, their trouser legs slowly getting damp from the wet gorse. Megarry cursed once or twice as his foot stumbled on a stone.

'I have a daughter your age,' he said.

'What's she do?'

'She's a teacher. In the North. Seaside town. Bit like Howth in a way.'

He thought briefly of Jenny. The time she lay in the grey hospital bed in the psychiatric ward outside Belfast, slowly starving herself to death. Because he had been an absent father. A father out drinking every night with the good ol' boys in the Montrose Hotel. He had a memory of her as a child. She'd been playing out the back of the house with a little friend. He'd overheard their conversation. 'My daddy's a policeman,' Jennifer had said. 'He's brave and he's strong and he puts bad men in jail.' She'd been proud of him then, and he'd let her down. Never there when she needed him. That's where the damned anorexia had come from. He knew it in his bones.

'She's fine now,' he said without thinking.

The cottage caught them by surprise, rearing out at them from behind a clump of ancient sycamores, half hidden by the gloom. It stood in a sheltered position with its back to a rocky outcrop of the mountain. On a fine day it would have given a view across the broad sweep of the heath, down across the fields to the sea. But today the cloud curtailed their vision to a few hundred yards and the cottage had an eerie, isolated look.

They stood for a moment to inspect it. It had once been a shepherd's hut, before someone restored it. It had Howth stone walls, wooden windows, a blue slate roof. There was a picket fence and a gate and a little lawn running up to the front door. Megarry could smell the heavy scent of wet earth. It mingled with the strong smell of gorse from the heath. He opened the gate and started along the path.

'Let's see if anyone's at home.'

He grasped the knocker on the front door and rattled hard. The sound seemed to reverberate across the moor, shattering the silence. From inside the house there was nothing. He knocked again, louder this time, and heard the sound echoing back from the bleak hillside. There was no response.

They went round the back. There was another lawn that seemed to have been hewn out of the rocky ground. Here, the grass was tangled and overgrown. There was a bicycle leaning sadly against a wall and a clothes line with washing drooping in the dim light.

'I think we can safely assume the place is empty,' Megarry said. He turned to go and at that moment, Lawlor saw that a window was partly open.

They stopped and considered. They had no warrant. Technically, if they went into the house it would be breaking and entering.

He spoke to her. 'What do you think?'

She shrugged.

'I think we go in,' Megarry said. We've got a responsibility to secure the place. In case of vandals. What do you say?'

Lawlor smiled. 'I say you're right.'

He climbed awkwardly into the room and Lawlor followed. Megarry locked the window and stood for a while to recover his breath. There was a pervading silence, not a sound, except for their own breathing.

The room they were in was a kitchen. It was furnished in pine with a large table and benches in the middle of the room. There were shelves and cupboards along the walls and an antique sideboard with plates and dishes. The floor was tiled and covered with straw mats. A wine glass had been left to dry on the draining board and on the table a bottle stood, three-quarters full, with the cork pressed firmly into the neck. Beside it, a small glass vase held decaying bluebells, their petals wilting and turning brown.

No one spoke. There was a clock on the wall but it had stopped. The hands showed 11.10. Megarry moved out to the hall and Lawlor followed.

There was an overpowering smell of must and trapped air. Megarry bent to pick up the mail that lay scattered on the floor, half a dozen letters and bills, made out to M. Grogan or Ms Mary Grogan. The postmarks showed they had been delivered over the past few weeks. The most recent one, a demand from the telephone company, had arrived just the day before. Megarry pushed open another door.

The curtains were drawn. He pulled them wide and a thin light filtered in. A large double bed dominated the room, neatly made, the duvet pink to match the pillows and the painted walls. There were pictures around the room and he stopped to examine them. They were local scenes, the Bailey lighthouse, Howth Castle, Ireland's Eye. The initials in the corner said M.G. On a bedside table, a couple of books rested.

He opened a wardrobe and caught a scent of perfume. Rows of expensive-looking suits and dresses hung in a neat line. He pulled out a drawer. It was stuffed with underwear, stockings, black-lace bras. Another drawer held scarves and handker-chiefs.

Suddenly he felt like an intruder, a voyeur violating this woman's privacy, poking about among her intimate things. He closed the drawer quickly and crossed the room. As he did so, his eye caught sight of a framed photograph on the dresser near the door.

It showed a young woman smiling for the camera. The photograph had been taken on a sunny day and he could see the shadows on the moor and the purple heather stretching away towards the sea. He thought of the description in the Missing Persons file. He put the photograph in his pocket and left the room.

The next door led into a bathroom. There was a shower and a shelf above the sink stacked with bottles and jars. Megarry saw a faint covering of dust on the mirror on the wall, a spider scuttling along the enamel surface of the bath. There was a lounge with comfortable settees and a rocking-chair beside the stone fireplace. Again, the curtains were drawn. Lawlor walked to the window and pulled them wide.

'All these damned curtains. Every room we've been in, the curtains have been drawn. Except the kitchen.'

39

Megarry stopped. 'Of course. Why didn't I notice it before?'

'What?'

'It could mean that she left the house at night. If she'd left in the morning you'd expect her to open the curtains. Unless . . .'

He paused.

'She might have wanted to create the impression that the cottage was occupied. For security reasons. It could be that she's gone off somewhere without telling anyone.'

'But what about the kitchen window?'

'Maybe she just forgot to lock it.'

They tried the remaining rooms. One had been fitted as an artist's studio. The floorboards had been sanded and varnished. In the corner was an easel with a canvas stretched tight. Someone had started work on a painting. Megarry recognised the towering outline of Shielmartin Hill with the sea in the background. Jars and brushes and pots of paint were scattered in disarray on a table. A smock hung from a peg on the door.

'Ms Grogan is an artist,' Megarry said. 'The paintings in the bedroom, the initials M.G. And she's not a bad one at that.'

The last room was an office with filing cabinets and shelves piled with Economics textbooks, statistical analyses, company reports. There was a heavy desk with a computer and printer.

Megarry's eye caught sight of a little calendar. The page said Friday, 20 April in bright red letters. It was the last day that Mary Grogan had reported for work.

Suddenly, he heard Lawlor give a shout. He turned to see her holding something up for his inspection. She had a look of horror on her face.

It was a doll's head. He saw the rolling eyes, the curling hair, the pale, pink, innocent face. There were jagged edges in the plastic below the neck where the knife had done its work. He felt his blood chill.

'Where was it?'

'There, on the desk.' Lawlor's hand shook.

'Concealed?'

'No. It was just sitting there. Like an ornament.'

Megarry took out a plastic bag and put the doll's head inside. Lawlor took his arm.

'I don't like this place, Cecil. It's spooky. Let's get the hell out.'

They returned to the hall. There was a key on a table beside the door. He tried it in the lock, then pocketed it. He closed the front door and pulled it tight.

As they left the cottage and turned onto the path, Megarry's eye was drawn to a curl of smoke drifting up from behind a clump of gorse, several hundred yards away across the heath. He looked at Lawlor and, without saying a word, they started off towards it through the heather.

As they got closer, they could see it was a dilapidated farmhouse. It had a desolate, abandoned look. There were a couple of slates missing from the roof and one of the window-panes had a crack like an ugly scar. Tufts of grass sprouted in the gutters.

Surrounding the house, there was a chicken-wire fence and a field of stony land which someone had tried to cultivate. Megarry could see a cabbage patch and several potato drills. Two bedraggled horses grazed behind the house, picking desultorily at the thin grass.

He found himself beginning to perspire. The breeze had died and the air across the heath suddenly seemed trapped, electric, as if waiting for the storm to break.

When they came to the fence, they stopped. Lawlor put her hand on the gate. At once, a ferocious shepherd dog came bounding to confront them.

Lawlor stepped back. 'Nice boy,' she said. The dog growled and bared its teeth.

'Nice boy,' she said again and moved once more to open the gate. The dog sprang forward, its great paws splayed, saliva dripping in a sticky mess from its open mouth.

'Bastard,' Lawlor said and quickly closed the gate.

They looked towards the house. The door had opened and a stocky figure in vest and trousers was now watching them from the shadows.

'We're police,' Megarry announced.

The man seemed unimpressed. 'What do you want?'

'To talk to you.'

'What about?'

Their voices seemed to boom and echo across the empty land.

'Can you call the dog off?' Megarry said.

'Can you identify yourselves?'

Lawlor held up her ID card in its plastic folder, but the man was not convinced.

'That could be anything,' he said. 'How do I know you're police?'

'Read it for yourself,' Lawlor said and tossed the card towards the door. The man examined it, turning it over as if expecting to find more information on the back.

'What do you want to talk about?' the man asked again. Megarry sighed. He felt his temper begin to fray. He turned and pointed back the way they had come.

'We want to talk about your neighbour.'

'Her,' the man said and there was scorn in his voice. 'What about her?'

Jesus, Megarry thought, we can't stand here like this, shouting at each other across the fence like fishwives in a market.

'Are you going to let us in, or do we have to take you away and talk to you in the station? It's your choice. And if you don't call that damned dog off, I swear to God we'll shoot it.'

The man seemed to hesitate. Then he gave a low whistle and the dog trooped obediently to the door and lay down. Lawlor pushed open the gate and they started tentatively along the path to the house. The man pulled the door open and stepped aside.

They entered a drab room. The wallpaper was peeling. There was a rash of damp-spots like ugly blisters along the ceiling and a pervasive smell of mould and rotting vegetables. Megarry glanced at the ancient furniture. It was scuffed and bruised. Some of it had been clumsily mended. A gash in a settee had been patched with sealing tape and the stuffing was poking out.

They followed the man into another room. There was

42

someone else here, a grey-haired figure hunched in a chair by the window. It was an old woman, her gnarled fingers twisting a string of blood-red beads. She didn't look up or speak.

'Ma, these people are police.'

The old woman made no response.

'They want to talk to me.'

The old woman grunted and stared out over the moor, oblivious to their presence.

'What's your name?' Lawlor began.

'Mick Dudgeon.'

Megarry studied the man. He was squat, sturdy, about forty years of age. He had strong, sunburnt arms, calloused hands, black unruly hair that hung down into his narrow eyes. There was a day's growth of stubble on his leathery chin.

'You own this place?' Lawlor continued.

'No,' Dudgeon said. 'She does.'

'Your mother?'

'No. Grogan. The one who lives in the Crow's Nest. I pay her rent.' There was a harsh edge in Dudgeon's voice.

'How long have you been living here?'

'All my life. I was born here.'

He pointed to the old woman. 'She's lived here these fifty years. This house and land has been in our family for generations.'

Dudgeon had taken out a packet of cigarettes and began to smoke. Megarry caught the sweet smell of burning tobacco. Hell, he thought, and fumbled in his pocket till he found his own. The man automatically stretched out his cigarette and Megarry took a light.

'How long has Mary Grogan lived in Crow's Nest?' Megarry asked.

'Three year.'

'How did she come by it?'

'Bought it.'

'Was it she who restored it?'

'Yeah. It was a wreck. Just the four walls. She got it for half-nothing and brought in these builders from Dublin to do it up for her.'

'So how come she owns your place as well?'

'She owns the whole parcel of land and the two houses. It was sold as one lot.'

'Why didn't you buy it?'

A pained look came into Dudgeon's face. 'I couldn't afford it. It's a long story. My father had a chance to buy the lease years ago, but he passed it up. The lease went to a property company and they sold it on to her.'

By the window, the old woman stirred.

'Who else lives here?' Lawlor asked.

'Just me and ma.'

'No other family?'

'No. There was six of us at one time, but they're all gone now.'

'You never married?'

'No.' Dudgeon shifted in his seat and his eyes darted uneasily about the room.

'How well do you know Mary Grogan?' Megarry asked.

Dudgeon tapped ash from the end of his cigarette. 'Not well. I hardly see her. Except when she comes looking for the rent.' His eyes flashed. 'She comes for that on the button, but she's not so quick with other things.'

'Like what?'

'She's meant to carry out repairs. It's supposed to be covered by the rent. Look at this place. It's falling apart, while she lives in her fancy cottage. Did you see that roof out there? It's leaking rain in the winter. I asked her to fix it but she refused. Just laughed and said I'd have to do it myself.'

'When was the last time you saw her?'

'About three weeks ago. She called looking for her money.'

'Do you mind if I ask you what you pay?'

Dudgeon stubbed out his cigarette on the flagstones of the floor. 'Forty pounds a month.'

Megarry nodded. It was hardly exorbitant. It was little wonder that Mary Grogan was refusing to carry out repairs.

'She's not at home. Do you know where she might be?'

'Not at home?' Dudgeon said. 'You're sure?'

'We just checked. Has she gone away somewhere?'

44

'How would I know? I don't mind her business.'

Megarry paused. It was the sort of interview he hated, where the information had to be dragged out piece by tiny piece and in the end amounted to very little.

'We'd like to know more about her,' Lawlor put in.

'Can't help you.'

'But you must know something. She is your neighbour, after all.'

'We don't mix with her. We keep to ourselves. That's how we like it.' He looked into Lawlor's face and his eyes were cold and hard.

There was a silence and then they heard the chair by the window creak.

'She's a bad woman,' the old woman said.

Megarry turned quickly to the hunched figure.

'A bad woman? What do you mean?'

The old, worn fingers twisted frantically at the red beads. 'She does bad things. Keeps bad company.'

He moved closer and stared into her face. It was lined and wrinkled, the skin like yellow paper.

'How do you know that?'

A wicked smile creased the old lips. 'I know. There's very little that passes me by.'

'What do you mean by bad company?'

'Men,' the old woman hissed. 'Men she has no right to be with.'

'Do you know who they are?'

She sniffed but said nothing.

'Can you give us the names of some of these people?'

'No,' she said. 'I don't know their damned names. But I know that God will punish her. You mark my words. God will not be mocked.' She kept her head fixed, the face turned resolutely towards the moor.

There's something wrong, Megarry thought. He turned to Dudgeon. 'Why doesn't she look at me?'

'She's blind,' Dudgeon said. 'Been blind this ten year.'

Megarry's cigarette had burned down to a stump. There was a fireplace, an open hearth and a small fire burning. He tossed the cigarette into the flames.

He turned and left the room. As he reached the front door, his eye caught something. It was a hunting rifle. It rested in the corner of the wall, just inside the door. He wondered that he hadn't noticed it before.

He stopped and ran his hand along the polished wood of the stock, up along the cold blue metal of the barrel. Behind him, he could hear Dudgeon's heavy breath. He turned to face him.

'You own this?'

'Yes.'

Megarry paused. 'What do you use it for?'

There was a scared look in Dudgeon's eyes.

'For shooting rats. And foxes. They come after my chickens.'

'You have a licence for it?'

Dudgeon hesitated. 'Somewhere,' he said. 'I'd have to go looking for it.' He turned back down the hall but Megarry reached out a hand to restrain him.

'Bring it to the station,' he said.

The dog growled as they stepped out into the yard.

'What about *him*?' Lawlor pointed. 'You got a licence for *him*?'

Dudgeon didn't reply.

'Get one,' Lawlor said.

6

The storm broke just as they got back to the quarry. There was a crash of thunder and the sky opened, a great black downpour of rain that covered the heath and rattled the roof of the car as if they were sitting inside a tin can.

Megarry watched the water running in streams along the windows, saw a flash of lightning somewhere out in the darkness over the bay.

'We should wait till it's over,' he said. 'It won't last.'

They sat for a while, staring out over the heath, watching the rain hammering from a leaden sky.

'You know,' Megarry said at last. 'There's something not adding up right.'

Lawlor turned her face to him and he realised how handsome she was, the pale skin, the dark, intelligent eyes, the wide, sensual mouth. He thought of a line from Yeats. *That is no country for old men. The young in one another's arms.*

He shook the thought from his mind, turned back to the conversation.

'If this woman really is Mary Grogan, where's she been for the past three weeks?'

'Dead,' Lawlor said.

'But Finnegan told us the head had only been in the sea for ten days.'

'Maybe she was held prisoner somewhere. You know. Before she was killed. That's happened.'

Megarry considered. 'This idea you had about the sex assaults in Kilbarrack. Maybe you should go ahead with it after all. Check when the attacks began. See if there's any recognisable pattern. Find out if anyone has been able to get a description of the attacker.'

'Sure.'

'And Annie. Be discreet. There's enough confusion on the streets already.'

The rain stopped as suddenly as it began, and out over the bay they saw the first rays of sunlight break through the clouds and slant silver and gold across the sea. Lawlor started the car and they drove back to the town.

As they were passing the top of Main Street, he tapped her arm. 'The Boylans live here somewhere. We've still got to take a formal statement from them. Why don't I do it?'

Lawlor stopped the car outside the church and Megarry began the slow plod back up the hill towards Saint Patrick's Lane. All this climbing, he thought. Everywhere you go in Howth, there's a hill.

He found the street he was looking for easily enough. The Boylans' house was at the end of a row of neat fisherman's cottages with hanging baskets and window-boxes. There was a blue van outside with a television aerial poking from the roof. A crowd of gaping onlookers surrounded a camera crew. Joe Boylan was standing on the footpath in his oilskins and cap even though he hadn't been fishing today. He was speaking confidently into the camera.

Megarry waited on the edge of the crowd and listened as Boylan recounted the events of the previous morning. He had obviously recovered from the shock, for he spoke with surprising calm, as if he'd been giving television interviews all his life. He retold the horror that had gripped him as they hauled in the net and found the ghastly skull among the glittering trout.

'And what was your immediate reaction?' the interviewer asked.

'That the cops would have to nail the guy who did this.'

'You suspected that it was murder?'

'Of course I did. From the word go.'

'And did you think there might be other bodies?'

'Well, it stands to sense, doesn't it? Once these guys kill, they get a taste for it. That's well known.'

'It must have been a terrible shock for you?'

'You've no idea,' Boylan said. 'I'm not the better of it yet. I've already lost two days' work over it. God knows when I'll be able to go back.' He turned a pained face for the camera.

'And what advice would you give to the women of the area?'

'Be on the watch for strangers. Don't go anywhere alone. There's a madman on the loose out there.'

A murmur went up from the crowd.

'Have you anything else to say?'

'Yes, I have. No stone should be left unturned till they catch this guy. If the cops can't do it, they should bring in the army. There's too much crime in this country. The politicians don't care. They don't have to put up with it. It's time the ordinary people showed them who's boss.'

'Perfecto,' the interviewer said as the lights dimmed. He gave Boylan the thumbs-up sign. 'You're a natural,' he said.

Yes, Megarry thought and pushed his way forward. He should have been an actor.

Boylan saw him and immediately began to apologise.

'I didn't mean you lot. You lot are doing your best. I know that. But you haven't got the resources. It's the bleedin' politicians I was gettin' at.'

'How much are they paying you?' Megarry asked.

Boylan sniffed. 'A hundred lids.'

'A hundred? That's easy money.'

'But think of the shock we've suffered, Sean and me. Plus we've lost two days' fishing. I'm entitled to get something back for that.'

'You seem all right to me.'

'Wellll,' Boylan said and added quickly, 'poor Sean's not all right. He's laid up with it. He's inside in bed. Poor divil's in bits.'

'I have to talk to you,' Megarry said. The crowd was melting away now that the excitement was over. 'I have to get a formal statement. Can I come in?'

Boylan hesitated, scratching his tanned face. 'I've just told you. Sean's not well.'

'It won't take long.'

Boylan turned reluctantly and went back inside the house. Megarry followed. It was a tiny place but warm and cosy. There was a video set in the corner of the room and two comfortable armchairs on either side of the fireplace. On a wall was a framed photograph of a mariner with a peaked cap. He was being presented with a scroll.

'My father, God rest him,' Boylan said. 'He was coxswain of the lifeboat for thirty years. They gave him a medal.'

'Where is Sean?' Megarry asked. 'I need to talk to him as well.'

Boylan slowly pushed open a door. The curtains were drawn, but in the dim light Megarry could see a figure propped up in bed with pillows round his head. There was an overflowing ashtray and a half-full bottle of whiskey. There was a stink of tobacco smoke and sweat. He felt a wave of disgust as he recognised Sean Boylan.

He was staring at the policeman with bloodshot eyes, like some ghastly gargoyle, his face pale, his lips trembling, a dribble of spittle on his unshaved chin. He looked like a man in the advanced stages of d.t.'s.

Megarry sat down softly on one side of the bed and Joe Boylan on the other. Megarry took out a notebook.

'Remember me?' he said. 'The Capstan Bar. Superintendent Megarry.'

Sean Boylan nodded and reached for the bottle.

'This won't take long. Just tell me again what happened. It doesn't have to be detailed. We'll start from when you left the harbour.'

Joe Boylan began. He outlined the course they took till they came to the lighthouse, the various stops to pull up lobster pots.

'It was a poxy morning's work. Three lobsters and two crabs. Until we got the trout, that is. The trout's what made it.

Otherwise we'd have been bollixed. What we'd caught wouldn't even have paid for the diesel.'

Sean Boylan watched from the bed, his face the colour of cold porridge. He poured a glass of whiskey and Megarry noticed how his hand shook as he raised it to his mouth. If he goes on like this, Megarry thought, he's going to end up in hospital.

'Who was the first to see the head?'

'Sean. Gave him an awful turn. Puked up his guts, he did. It was lying in the corner of the net covered in seaweed. Looked like a football or something. Maybe a buoy that had come loose. Jaysus. I couldn't believe my eyes, when I saw what it was.'

'What happened next?'

Sean Boylan grunted from the bed. 'I was going to hump it back in the sea. It was me da that told me to keep it. He realised there was something wrong. So I put it in the lobster bucket and started the engine and we high-tailed it back to the harbour.'

'Can you remember what the time was?'

Joe Boylan did a quick count on his fingers. 'Well, we'd been out since seven o'clock.'

'And you were back at the Capstan by ten.'

'It must have been about half-nine, then.'

'And the net had been put down at what time exactly?'

Again Joe Boylan counted on his fingers. 'About the same time the previous morning.'

'You don't put it down there regularly?'

'No.'

'When was the last time?'

'I can't remember,' Boylan said. 'A couple of weeks.'

'Did you notice anything unusual?'

The two men looked at each other and Joe Boylan shook his head.

'And there was only the head? Nothing else?'

'Jaysus. No. Isn't that bad enough. Seeing that thing. Christ!' Joe Boylan shuddered.

Megarry snapped the notebook shut.

'Will we have to go to court?' Joe Boylan asked.

'That depends. There may have to be an inquest when we find the rest of the body. You may be asked to give evidence.'

Sean Boylan finished off the whiskey and poured another one. This is suicidal drinking, Megarry thought. What's wrong with him? Shock couldn't have caused this.

'You told me there are long periods when you can't get to sea because of the weather. How do you spend your time?'

Sean Boylan shrugged. 'We mend the nets. We fix up the ould boat. We pay Tom Reddin a visit from time to time.' He tried to laugh but it turned into a cough.

'Do you have a girlfriend?' Megarry asked. 'A young woman?'

He saw the father's face turn into a sneer.

'Are you kidding,' he said. 'Sure who would have him?'

Megarry got up and Joe Boylan walked with him to the front door.

'You're enjoying this, aren't you?' Megarry said. 'This media attention. You're enjoying it.'

Boylan smiled. 'It's a few bob. Like I said. I see it as compensation for loss of earnings.'

Megarry looked into his pale blue eyes. 'You're an intelligent man, Joe. You're not a fool. Do you really believe there's a madman out there?'

'What do you think?'

'I'm asking you,' Megarry said.

Boylan smiled once more. 'To tell you the truth,' he said, 'I made that up. They like that. That's what the television people want. Plenty of excitement.'

Back at the station, Megarry found the sergeant looking more relaxed.

'Calls still coming in?' he asked.

The sergeant put down his pen, slowly scratched his ear with a fleshy finger. 'Not as many as before.'

Megarry thought of the interview Joe Boylan had just given for television. It would probably go out at 6 p.m. and was sure to inflame the situation further.

'Of course,' he said and walked quickly into the station, aware of the sergeant's eyes on his back as he went.

The main office was all activity. In a corner, close to the door, a radio tuned to the patrol car frequency was stuttering out messages. It was slightly off-kilter with the waveband and every now and then a taxi firm broke in and sent cabs to Coolock, Raheny and Bayside.

He saw Lawlor working at a desk near the window and waved, then passed through into Kelly's office.

'We found the place,' he said.

'Annie told me.'

'There was no one there. We gave it a quick check. Looks like there hasn't been anyone there for a while. Her neighbour said he hadn't seen her for weeks. We found this.'

He took out the photograph. Kelly held it at arm's length and studied it.

'You think it's her?'

'It fits the description.'

'Anything else?'

'Front-door key. Just in case we have to go back there and do a proper search.'

Kelly nodded.

'And this.' Megarry produced the plastic bag and slowly drew out the doll's head. He put it down on the desk.

Kelly gave a start. 'Jesus,' he said. 'You found that?' His face had gone pale.

'Annie found it. In Mary Grogan's study.'

Kelly looked up. 'You think it's a warning?'

'Well,' Megarry said. 'It's no coincidence.'

Kelly poked at the head gingerly with a pencil. It was a cheap, plastic doll that you could buy in any store. There was an ugly scar along the neck where it had been severed from the trunk. It rolled over and the eyes fluttered momentarily.

'Christ,' Kelly said. 'Take it away. Give it to Forensic or something. Get them to check for fingerprints.' He took out a handkerchief and wiped his face.

'Is there anything on file?' Megarry asked. 'If someone was threatening her, maybe she made an official complaint.'

'I'll get someone to check.'

Kelly sat back and made a steeple with his fingers. 'What do you think?'

'I think it could be her. Why don't you do a trawl of the local dentists? Somebody must have her records.'

'That's in hand.'

'What about Walshe?'

'Not good, Cecil. The sub-aqua team have searched the area twice and found nothing. He's thinking of calling it off.'

'And Finnegan?'

'He's completed the preliminary report. Says death was probably due to brain haemorrhage, consistent with gunshot wound. He wants to carry out more tests.'

'Probably?'

'That's the word he used, Cecil. He says the head was too long in the water to tell for certain. The tissue has decayed.'

'What about the weapon?'

'Says it could have been anything from a shotgun to a revolver.'

'A shotgun?' Megarry said. 'A shotgun would have blown her head clean off. Even I know that.'

'That's what he said, Cecil.'

'Jesus,' Megarry said. 'What a bloody clown.'

He went out to the main office and typed up the interview with the Boylans, then walked across and stood at Lawlor's desk. She was working at a computer terminal, the desk littered with files and notebooks and scraps of paper.

'How's it going?'

She looked up, pushed back a stray wisp of hair, reached for a pen, tapped some keys on her terminal. He noticed the way she moved, fast and graceful, like a cat.

'Let me show you something.' She gave him a sheet of paper. It was a mess of scribbled notes, arrows, telephone numbers, dates. 'There's a pattern. These attacks started eighteen months ago. November '95, December, through January. They stopped in February and March. Then there was one in April. None in May. Right through the summer, nothing. Started again in October. The last one was two weeks ago.'

'Why were there no attacks during the summer?'

'This guy operates at night. Maybe the summer nights were too bright for him.'

Megarry considered. 'What about suspects? Anyone brought in for questioning?'

She found another sheet of paper. There were six names on it.

'None of these guys was ever charged. The investigating cops couldn't build a case.'

'What about a description?'

'This guy has his face covered with a mask. None of the victims was able to give an accurate picture. But they all agree that he is young, five feet eight or nine. Speaks with a Dublin accent.'

The radio started up again. 'Capricorn to Cancer. Capricorn to Cancer.' Someone shouted to turn the damned thing down. A detective tore a fax sheet from a machine and went rushing across the room.

Megarry watched him go. He thought of his own office in Belfast that he had left forever, the excitement, the fraying tempers, the insults hurled without thought. The comradeship. It was what he remembered from a hundred cases, coffee in polystyrene cups and, later on, whiskey from cracked mugs. And cigarettes. One damned cigarette after another till the room was blue with smoke and someone invariably opened a window to let in the night air.

He turned to Lawlor. 'Have you eaten yet?'

She mumbled something and he knew at once she was lying. She'd been working flat-out all morning.

'C'mon,' he said. 'Let me introduce you to the low life.'

There was a lively crowd in the front room of the Anchor Bar, fishermen gossiping at the counter, a posse of bikers playing pool, a sprinkling of tourists with cameras, soaking up the atmosphere. The pub had the beaten-up look that some people find attractive, low tables scarred with cigarette burns, high stools at the bar, smoke-stained ceilings.

He led Lawlor through to the lounge and up to the food counter. At least it was clean. There was a range of salads, filled rolls, pies, soups and barbecued chicken pieces in a spicy sauce. He bent to examine them.

'Buffalo Wings?'

'It's just a name.'

'But where does the buffalo come from?'

'How am I supposed to know?'

'Forget it,' Megarry said. 'What would you like?'

Lawlor studied the plates piled with food. The smell was making him hungry. 'C'mon,' he said. 'You have to eat, for Christ's sake. Pick something.'

He took a salad roll and called out to the barman for a pint of Guinness. He saw Lawlor choose a sandwich.

'You're sure that's enough?'

'It'll do.'

'Why don't you have a pastry? Here. Spoil yourself.'

He took a slice of cake and put it on her plate.

'What about a drink?'

'Diet cola.'

'Jesus,' Megarry said. 'Diet bloody cola. It'll rot your stomach.'

'You should try to eat regularly,' he said as he lowered himself into a chair. 'Cops never eat regularly. That's why they all have ulcers.'

'I don't always have time.'

'Make time. If you're tired and hungry, you can't think straight. It affects your judgement. Plus your productivity level falls. And you get cranky.'

He saw a smile in the corner of her mouth. 'Does that apply to booze?' She pointed to his pint.

'This is nourishment too,' he said and lifted the glass. 'Anyway, I've cut down.'

'You're just a fraud,' she said and laughed out loud.

'Cheers,' Megarry said and took a bite from his roll.

She looked around the room. 'Is this your local? The barman seemed to know you.'

'I play darts here some nights. With my brother-in-law. He's a fanatic. Thinks of nothing else. Drinks two glasses of beer a night and believes he's having a riotous time.'

She wiped some crumbs from her chin. 'Where are you from?' she said.

'Belfast.'

'You used to be in the RUC? Right?'

'I was a Special Branch officer.'

'Dealing with the paramilitaries?'

'All the time.'

'You must have seen a lot of murders.'

'Too many.'

Lawlor nodded. 'But you're retired now.'

'It's a long story,' Megarry said. 'I'm not sure you've time to hear it.' He finished the roll and searched in his pockets for his cigarettes.

'Tell me about this women's stuff you're into. The Sexual Assault Unit and that stuff. How did you get involved in that?'

'It started as a project at university. I was going to get into social work when I graduated and then I decided to join the cops instead. I figured it's social work of a kind.'

'I suppose it is,' Megarry said. 'You should meet my wife. She's into women's groups too. When we moved down here I was afraid she might be lonely. Now she's hardly ever at home.'

He saw her look at him.

'Do you mind?' she said. 'Her not being at home, I mean?'

He thought for a moment. 'Not if she's happy.'

He glanced across the room. A big bow window looked over the harbour. He could see the fishing boats tossing in the swell.

'These sex assaults. You're convinced it's the same guy?'

Lawlor smoothed down her skirt. 'Not just me. The Kilbarrack cops are too. I told you there was a pattern. They all occurred within a radius of a few miles. They all occurred close to the DART railway line. In fact some of the attacks actually took place in the immediate vicinity of Kilbarrack station.'

'You think the DART line is significant?'

'Could be. Maybe the attacker lives somewhere along the railway line. Uses it to travel into the area. Maybe also uses it to escape.'

She stopped, made a circle with her finger on the table top. 'I think the dates are significant too. I told you there were no attacks during the summer.'

Megarry nodded.

'Maybe the attacker isn't here in the summer. Maybe he visits

57

at certain times of the year. Or maybe . . .' She paused. 'Maybe it's someone whose work takes him away during the summer months.'

Megarry finished his drink, put the glass down on the table.

'I'll tell you what,' he said. 'Why don't you get back to the Kilbarrack cops? Get a list of known sex offenders in the area. We'll bring them in for questioning.'

'And the guys who've already been interviewed?'

'Put them on the list. We'll talk to them as well.'

'As they were preparing to leave, Megarry said: 'You ever done this kind of thing before? Detective work, I mean.'

'Not much.'

'Some people like to make a big deal about it. They try to make it out to be a mystery. But it's just common sense really. Understanding what makes people tick. You can do it.'

She smiled. 'You think so?'

'Yes. I think you'll make a very good detective.'

As they walked back to the station along the narrow streets, Megarry had an inspiration. He turned to Lawlor.

'What are you doing tonight?'

'Working.'

'Not all night, for God's sake. Why don't you come to my house this evening and have something to eat?'

She began to protest, but he brushed it aside.

'A break will do you good. And you can meet Kathleen.'

'I'm not sure.'

'8.30 p.m.,' Megarry said. 'We'll be expecting you.'

Kelly was waiting for him in his office. Megarry knew at once that something was wrong.

'Sit down,' Kelly said. 'I've got bad news. I was wrong about the murders. There *was* another case. I just got confirmation half an hour ago.'

'A mutilation case?'

'Yes. November 1995. Bray. County Wicklow. It's a different division to Dublin. That's why, when you asked me earlier, it didn't register.'

58

'A woman?'

'Imelda Lacy. Eighteen years of age. Murdered and the body dismembered.'

'Dumped in the sea?'

'Worse. There was an attempt to burn her. The charred remains were found in a field outside the town.'

'Jesus,' Megarry said.

'She was strangled.'

'Sexual assault?'

'She'd been raped.'

'Was anyone charged?'

'No.'

'What was the extent of the mutilation?'

Kelly swallowed hard. 'Both arms were cut off and an attempt was made to sever the left leg.'

'Instrument?'

'It doesn't say.'

For a moment the two men looked at each other.

'It's bad, Cecil, isn't it? When word of this gets out, it's going to make us look awful stupid.'

'Word doesn't have to get out,' Megarry said sharply.

'But it's only a matter of time. The newspapers keep files just like we do. Sooner or later, some bright crime correspondent is going to remember the Lacy case and link it to the Howth murder.'

'Just keep it under wraps for the time being. Tell no one who doesn't need to know.'

He thought for a moment. 'How far is Bray from Howth?'

'About twenty miles.'

'So it would be easy to get between the two places?'

'Sure. The roads are good. And there's also the DART. The train runs right around the coast. You can make the journey in an hour.'

'The DART?' Megarry said.

'Yes.'

'These attacks that Annie has been looking at. They all happened along the DART line.'

'Maybe it *is* the same guy.'

Megarry placed a hand on Kelly's shoulder. 'Let me give you some advice, Peter. Things will probably get worse before they get better. The main thing is that you hold your nerve. You're the boss now. People look to you for direction.'

He paused and took a deep breath.

'We've got a long way to go. But I promise you one thing. We'll see it through to the end.'

He left the station and walked slowly up the hill. The sun was going down behind the West Mountain. After the storm, the air felt fresh and clear. He could smell the sweet scent of gorse in the fields above St Patrick's Lane.

Kathleen was in the back garden, trying to get the barbecue to light. She was dressed in jeans and shirt. He took her in his arms and kissed her.

'I've invited someone for dinner.'

'Who?'

'Annie Lawlor. She's a young cop working with us on the case.'

He went into the kitchen and poured a cold beer. After a while Kathleen came and curled up on the settee beside him.

'I had Nancy on this afternoon. She's all worked up about this murder. That Boylan man was on the television at six o'clock. He was warning women about going out alone. He said there was a madman on the loose.'

Megarry put his arm around her shoulder and pulled her closer. 'I don't want you to mention this, but we've uncovered another murder. Over in Bray. November 1995. A young woman raped and mutilated.'

'My God,' Kathleen said. 'Do you think they're linked?'

'Kelly only got confirmation this evening. But it's looking bad.'

He sat for a while staring out at the smoke rising in grey wisps from the barbecue.

'I've been thinking,' he said. 'Maybe we should invite Jennie and Rob to stay with us for a while.'

'But she's working, Cecil. She hasn't time.'

'They could come for a weekend. I worry about her.'

60

She stroked his forehead. 'There's nothing to worry about. I spoke to her on the phone only yesterday. She's fine, Cecil. She's happy. She's busy. She's enjoying her life.'

'I'd like to see her.'

'Cecil. She's a healthy young woman. She had anorexia. That was long ago and she's better now. There's no proof that you had anything to do with it. You have to forgive yourself, Cecil. You have to let go.'

Megarry finished his beer and went up to the bathroom and showered. He kept thinking of Kelly, the way his mood had changed with the news of Imelda Lacy's death, as if the case was being dragged into deeper and more treacherous waters.

The information would eventually leak out to the media and then there would be an even greater outcry than there was at present. That would bring pressure from the superintendent for arrests and charges. He thought of the young policeman sitting in his lonely office, poring over files, examining fax messages, waiting for phone calls that might never come. Would he be able to withstand it, when the pressure became intense?

After a while the smell of barbecued chicken began to drift up from the garden. He was on his way to the kitchen when Lawlor arrived. She had brought a bottle of wine wrapped in white paper, and thrust it into Megarry's hands.

He brought her through to the garden. It was growing dark, but the night was warm. 'Why don't you two go and get yourselves a drink? I'll look after this,' Megarry said.

There was a handful of stars, hanging in the sky, but no breeze. Kathleen had prepared a marinade, and he basted the chicken with it. He watched as the steam rose from the grill, chicken fat dripping down onto the coals. When the meat was cooked, he brought it into the kitchen where the two women were drinking wine, deep in conversation.

'You heard the news?' Lawlor said as he came in.

'Yes. Kelly told me.'

She lowered her eyes. 'This thing is getting out of hand. Women are afraid to leave their homes. We have to get this bastard.'

'Yes,' Megarry said and began to unload the chicken onto their plates.

They sat around the table and talked about life in Belfast. Megarry felt himself begin to relax, the wine warm in his stomach. If I could hold this moment, he thought, capture it. If life could always be like this, good food, good wine, good company.

When they had finished eating, he stood up. 'I'll wash the dishes. You stay and talk.'

The phone rang out in the hall. He left the kitchen and closed the door behind him. When he returned his face looked grim.

'They've identified the head. It *was* Mary Grogan. Kelly's just got a positive match on her dental records.'

7

He slept well, a seamless night, unbroken by dreams. When he woke, weak sunlight was already streaming in through the curtains on the bedroom window flooding the room with light.

The murder was the main item on the eight o'clock news and again at nine as he drove along the Howth Road to Kelly's house. 'Fear grips North Dublin suburb,' an excitable young reporter said and interspersed a sound clip from Joe Boylan's interview. But Megarry noted with relief that they hadn't yet made the connection with the Bray killing.

It was a dull morning, overcast, threatening rain. He could see the clouds like great bags of smoke, drifting in from the sea as he turned off at Bull Island. Kelly's door was opened by a young woman with a baby in her arms. There was the sound of activity from inside the house, a radio rattling and a voice reciting poetry.

'Hello, Sinead,' Megarry said.

'Cecil. You're looking well. You've lost a bit of weight.'

'Clean living,' Megarry said and followed her along the hall to the kitchen.

Kelly was seated at a table, the remains of breakfast scattered about. A boy of eight or nine sat beside him, a schoolbook spread out.

'Again,' Kelly was saying. 'I wandered lonely as a . . .'

'Cloud that floats on high, o'er vales and hills,' Megarry interrupted.

They looked up and the boy laughed.

'They're still teaching that stuff?' Megarry said and ruffled his hair. 'That's ancient, that is. Bleedin' daffodils? Why don't they teach you something exciting?'

'Like what?'

'*The Ballad of William Bloat*, for one. Ever hear that?'

'No.'

'In a mean abode, on the Shankill Road . . .'

'What happens?'

'Man gets hanged.'

'That's brill,' the boy said and thumped the table.

'How's the football, Jamie? Still supporting Celtic?'

'Sure.'

'You must be sick. The 'Gers stuffed them last week.'

'They were lucky. We'll get them back.'

'How much?'

'Fifty pee.'

'You're on.'

They slapped hands noisily.

'I've got witnesses,' Megarry warned. 'You'll be owing me.'

'No,' the boy replied. '*You'll* be owing me.'

'Get out of it,' Megarry said as Jamie ran out of the room.

Kelly poured him a cup of tea. Megarry stirred the spoon, looked Kelly in the eye.

'How're you feeling this morning?'

'Fine.'

'What time did you get away last night?'

'Shortly after midnight.'

Megarry nodded.

'You told your boss the news?'

'Sure.'

'How'd he react?'

'Like a scalded cat. You don't know this guy, Cecil. He's nervous as hell. He was shoved into the job by some political cronies. Spends all his time watching his back and spreading the blame as widely as he can, so it doesn't attach to him. He's going to hate this whole business like a stomachful of ulcers. And he wants to see you.'

Megarry put his cup down firmly on the table. 'You know what I said, Peter. No interference.'

'It's not like that. He just wants to talk to you, for God's sake.'

'We'll see,' Megarry said. 'Did you talk to the Bray cops?'

'Yeah. The case was never closed. They're pulling in the guys they interviewed before to grill them again.'

'Good. Annie has arranged with the Kilbarrack cops to interview their suspects this afternoon.'

'And we have to talk to Mary Grogan's employer. James Clarke. He reported her missing.'

'I'll tell you what,' Megarry said. 'Why don't I do that? I'll bring Annie. We can see you later at Bray. And then we can all go back to Kilbarrack.'

Megarry finished his tea. Jamie was coming down the stairs. He was reciting his poetry lines.

'I wandered only as a cloud . . .'

'*Lonely*,' Sinead said. 'Lonely. Get that into your thick skull, for God's sake.'

Megarry caught Kelly's eye. He patted him gently on the arm. 'It's starting to move,' he said. 'Things are going to work out just fine.'

James Clarke was middle-aged, thin, balding. He wore a pin-striped suit and button-down collar. He looked like a successful insurance salesman. He brought Megarry and Lawlor into his office and sat down behind a massive desk.

'I'm in shock,' he said. 'I can't believe this has happened.'

Megarry said nothing.

'You're sure there's no mistake? It's definitely her?'

'Yes,' Megarry said. 'It's definitely her.'

'Clarke produced a large white handkerchief and blew his nose. Then he took off his glasses and wiped his eyes.

'Have you any idea why . . .?'

'Not yet. That's what we're hoping to establish.'

'I'm devastated.' Clarke shook his head as if he had run out of speech. 'Such a lovely woman. It's just such a waste.'

Megarry took out the photograph they had found in Crow's Nest Cottage and handed it over.

'Is that her?'

'Yes. That's Mary.'

'Tell us what you know about her.'

Clarke fidgeted, turned his pale face on the two. 'I don't know where to begin, really. When she went missing, naturally we hoped there'd be some simple explanation. You know, like maybe she'd gone off some place without telling anyone. We didn't expect anything like this.'

'But you must have had some doubts? She's been gone now for three weeks. It must have crossed your mind?'

'Murder? That was the last thing I thought of.'

'What did you think had happened?'

'I thought it might have been some personal matter. Maybe a romantic involvement that had gone wrong. Something like that. I thought perhaps she just wanted some time to herself.'

'But to go without telling you?'

'Yes. That was unlike her.'

'And you were sufficiently concerned to report her missing.'

'I thought it was the proper thing to do.'

Megarry nodded. 'When did she join the company?'

'About four years ago. Maybe four and a half. I'd need to check our files.'

'And where did she come from?'

'National City Bank. She was an economist with them for several years. Before that she was with Hardcastle Stockbrokers. She had a very good track record. Very highly recommended. Excellent references.' Clarke took out the handkerchief once more. 'This is a terrible waste of talent. She was so bright. So full of vitality. She had a brilliant future. This is just so . . . unnecessary.'

'What about her educational background?' Lawlor asked.

'Degree in Economics from Trinity College. Postgraduate course in Statistics from Dublin City University. She was an achiever. A real high-flyer.'

'Any family?'

'Just parents. Somewhere down the country. She was an only child.'

66

'You mentioned romantic involvement. Did she have any men friends that you know about?'

'She had several. But no one permanent. She was going out with a young guy for a while. Brian Casey. There was talk of an engagement. But it all came apart in the end.'

'When was this?'

'Months ago. I'm not sure exactly.'

Lawlor had a notebook out and was beginning to write. 'Do you know where we could find him?'

'He's a producer with RTE.'

'What sort of work did she do?' Megarry asked.

'She was a financial analyst.'

Megarry looked puzzled. 'What is that exactly?'

'Her job was to draw up reports for people who were thinking of making investments. She'd ferret out information about companies. Things like market share, creditworthiness, financial performance, projected profit or loss. Then make recommendations.'

'She was a sort of financial detective?'

'Yes,' Clarke said. 'That sums it up neatly.'

Megarry glanced out of the window. They were on the seventh floor. All around was shining steel and glass. He could see the river, snaking out into the bay, the traffic moving slowly across O'Connell Bridge in the rain. He put a matchstick in his mouth and rolled it on his tongue.

'I don't really understand this business,' he said. 'Is it possible that she might have made enemies through her work?'

'Oh no,' Clarke said quickly. 'I don't think this has anything to do with her job.'

'But just say she found out information that someone didn't want her to know. Or perhaps she presented a report and the recommendations proved inaccurate and somebody lost a bundle as a result. Don't you think they might feel sore?'

'Sore enough to murder her? Good God, no. This business isn't like that, Mr Megarry. This is a respectable profession. We're not the Mafia.'

'What sort of money was she earning?'

Clarke paused. 'The whole package, salary, company car, insurance, pension entitlements. About eighty K.'

Megarry exchanged a glance with Lawlor.

'That's an awful lot of money.'

'But she earned every penny of it. She worked extremely hard. When she was preparing a report, she would go flat out. Weekends, evenings. Her salary was related to performance and believe me, she performed very well.'

'Can you tell us something about her private life?' Lawlor asked.

Clarke turned to face her. 'I'll tell you what I know. It's not something we discussed very often. She came to dinner several times at my house. Always brought a male companion.'

'Do you have their names?'

'I'll have to ask my wife. They were just companions. Just to make up the numbers. There was no romantic involvement.'

'Anything else?'

'Not really. Mary was interested in what any normal young woman would be interested in. She liked to dress well, take good holidays. She did some sailing out of Howth. And of course there was the painting.'

'Ah,' Megarry said. 'She was an artist.'

'Yes. It was something of a passion with her. Most of her spare time, I think. She had this cottage up near Howth Head.'

'We've been there.'

'I believe she was quite good. I'm no critic, mind you. But if you look at this . . .' He pointed to the wall above Megarry's head. 'That's one of Mary's.'

It was a small watercolour. Megarry recognised the location. Boats moored in Howth harbour. He saw the initials in the corner. M.G.

'When was the last time you saw her alive?'

'Just after seven. Friday evening, April 20th. She had stayed behind to clear up some work.'

'Did she have any plans?'

'I've no doubt she did, but she didn't discuss them.'

'And when she didn't show up for work on Monday, what did you do?'

'Rang her home. Must have called half a dozen times. Always got the phone ringing out.'

'But you waited till Wednesday before reporting her missing.'

'Like I said. I was hoping it was something minor. Some personal problem.'

'I have to ask you this. I realise it might be difficult for you. Did Mary have any enemies?'

Clarke pressed his glasses hard against his face. 'Good God, no. She was ambitious. She was successful. Some people might have been envious of her. She had little time for failure or weakness. But people respected her. Even people who might not have liked her.'

'But someone killed her, Mr Clarke. They must have had a reason.'

Clarke sighed and lowered his eyes.

'You can think of nothing? No reason?'

'No.'

Megarry sat for a moment in silence. It seemed that the interview had come to a natural conclusion. He stood up.

'Will there be some kind of funeral?' Clarke asked. 'Or service, or something? I just thought . . .' He suddenly stopped.

'I understand,' Megarry said. 'The fact that we've just got a head and no body. It makes things very awkward. To tell you the truth, I don't know what the drill is.'

They went in Megarry's car to Bray, across the toll bridge, then out past Ringsend and Sandymount. It was raining steadily now, grey clouds shrouding the ocean, fat raindrops slapping against the glass.

Megarry turned to Lawlor. 'You'll have to check out her men friends. And this Brian Casey guy. And you'll have to locate her parents.'

'I'll organise it,' Lawlor said.

'Make sure they break it gently.' He turned to look at her. 'It's going to be hard for them, Annie. They're probably old and she was their only child.'

He felt her hand warm on his cold cheek.

'You really do care, don't you?' she said.

Kelly was waiting for them at Bray railway station. He was

wearing a thick lumber jacket and peaked tweed cap. Megarry thought he looked anxious, though he tried to hide it.

'Took you long enough,' he said and checked his watch. 'How'd the interview with Clarke go?'

'So-so. I'll fill you in later.'

'Okay,' Kelly said. 'The man here is Inspector O'Connor. He led the Lacy inquiry.'

'And he doesn't mind me poking in?' Megarry asked.

'Not at all. And I read the case notes. Turns out there were three main suspects. A neighbour and two guys with records for sex offences as long as your arm. The cops tried every trick in the book to get a confession but they wouldn't break. And since they'd no forensic evidence to link them, they had to let them go. The neighbour is particularly interesting.'

'Why's that?'

'He's a butcher.'

'Well,' Megarry said and pursed his lips.' That *is* interesting.'

They drove through the damp streets and out along the Bray Road. The rain had turned to a fine mist, a grey blanket covering the town. Two men in suits met them at the station. Kelly made the introductions. Inspector O'Connor was a tall man in his mid-forties with bad teeth and an honest face.

'This is a very difficult case,' he said. 'Caused a lot of local outrage. Imelda Lacy was only eighteen. Fresh out of school. She was very popular.'

He paused, looked at Megarry and Lawlor. 'She died a horrible death. Ill-feeling was running very high. Still is. I'd be anxious not to stoke it up.'

Megarry nodded.

'There may be no connection at all,' O'Connor went on. 'So I'd appreciate it if you can make sure this visit is kept quiet. You know the way the media can twist things.'

'Tell me about it,' Megarry said.

O'Connor opened a drawer and took out a file. 'I suppose you want to see the case notes?'

Megarry and Lawlor studied the file together. Imelda Lacy had been abducted on her way to meet some friends in a pub in Dalkey. She was last seen alive with a man variously described

70

as young, well-built, unkempt and of middle height. She had been raped and strangled and then her arms had been cut off. The forensic notes said that it had been done with a hunting knife. An attempt had been made to burn her body.

'We conducted a very thorough investigation,' O'Connor continued. 'Interviewed over a hundred people. In the end, we narrowed it down to the three men we have now.'

'But you had no case against them?'

'No. We tried everything that was legally permissible to get a confession. But we drew a blank. And we had practically no forensic evidence. The attempt to burn the body caused us serious problems in that regard.'

'What about the murder weapon?'

'It was never found.'

'So why did you suspect them?'

'Previous form. Two of them had records for rape. In the case of one man, Gerard Quinn, there was also evidence that he had tried to strangle his victim.'

'Both local?'

'Yes.'

'And the third man?'

'John Delaney was a neighbour of the dead girl. Her family claimed he'd been pestering her for months to go out with him but she kept turning him down. They say he was a bit strange. Kind of distant, intellectual type. That sort of thing.'

'And he's the butcher?'

'Yes,' O'Connor said gravely.

'You said he *was* a neighbour?'

'That's right. He had to move away as a result of the murder. As I told you, feeling was running high. He was assaulted on a number of occasions. We advised him to move for his own safety.'

'Where does he live now?'

'Right across the bay. On the north side. Kilbarrack.'

Lawlor looked up sharply. 'Kilbarrack?'

'That's right. He's got a flat there.'

'Where is he now?' Megarry said.

'We have him in a holding cell.'

'Well, let's go and talk to him.'

John Delaney sat at a table with his head erect and his arms folded neatly across his chest. He was young, about five foot eight or nine. He had long greasy hair and a squirrel face. There was a day's growth of beard on his pock-marked cheeks. He wore a faded blue anorak and jeans. Megarry thought he could detect an odour, like the smell of unwashed clothes, stale alcohol sweat, dried blood.

Megarry sat across the table from him, with Lawlor and Kelly on either side. O'Connor and another detective who had worked on the Lacy case stood at the door.

Kelly began. 'John Delaney?'

The man looked up. There was an arrogance in his eyes, a taunting smile in the corner of his mouth.

'Of course,' he said. 'Who the hell else? You didn't think you'd pulled in Charlie Manson, did you?'

Kelly ignored the remark. 'We have to ask you some questions.'

'Questions. Questions. I answered all the questions the last time. I even signed a statement, for God's sake. It was witnessed by my solicitor.'

'This is about a different matter.'

Delaney raised an eyebrow. 'Is that a fact? Maybe you'd like to tell me?'

'We'll come to that in a moment.'

'Come to it now. What is this crap? What am I here for?'

'Just answer the questions,' Lawlor said.

Delaney stared across the table at her. 'Who the fuck are you? What are you doing here?'

'That's none of your business.'

'None of my business?' Delaney began to laugh. 'You bring me in here and you start putting me through the wringer. And you haven't even got the decency to tell me what I'm being questioned about. I think I've had enough of this.' He started to get out of his seat, but O'Connor moved quickly to restrain him.

'Now,' Kelly said. 'Let's begin again. Are you married?'

'No.'

'Do you have a girlfriend?'

'Girlfriend?'

'Yes. You know what I mean.'

'Jesus,' Delaney said. 'This is the exact same crap as the last time.' He looked around the room, the solid phalanx of policemen staring with fixed faces.

'Do you have a girlfriend?' Kelly persisted.

'Not regular. I have different women friends.'

'So you live alone?'

'Yes.'

'Do you know Howth?'

'Of course I know Howth. It's only up the road.'

'How well do you know it?'

'I go out there sometimes at weekends. For the music. There's some good sessions in the pubs.'

'You know West Heath?'

'Where?'

'West Heath. It's up near the Summit.'

'Never heard of it.'

Kelly paused, glanced at the others.

'You're a butcher?'

The muscles on Delaney's neck seemed to tense. 'Sure I am. It's all in my statement.'

'How long have you been a butcher?'

'All my working life. Since I left school.'

'So you'd be pretty skilled at your trade?'

'Sure.'

'And you'd be used to cutting up carcasses?'

'Of course. That's my job.'

'And cutting up an animal wouldn't be much different to cutting up a human being?'

They watched for Delaney's response. There was silence for a moment and then his face broke into a grin.

'You guys never learn, do you? The same old bag of tricks. I thought you were into psychology now.' He shook his head in mock despair. 'Is it any wonder the crims are creaming you out of it?'

'Answer the question.'

'I answered it before. I happen to be a butcher. That doesn't make me a murderer. I'd nothing to do with Imelda Lacy. I never laid a finger on her.'

'Who mentioned Imelda Lacy?'

'You did.'

'No. I didn't.'

'Don't try to fool me. This is what this is all about, isn't it?' He pointed at O'Connor. 'He interrogated me about Imelda Lacy for nearly twelve hours. And in the end he had to let me go because I was clean.'

'You asked her several times to go out with you?'

'Sure I did. She was a good-looking kid. That doesn't mean I killed her.'

'And she refused?'

'She fancied some other bloke. Look, why don't you read my statement. I wasn't even in Bray that night. I was miles away. In Dublin.'

'You don't seem to have much success with women, do you?'

'Get out of it,' Delaney said. 'What would you know about that?'

'Do you know a woman called Mary Grogan?'

'Who is she?'

'Just a woman we're interested in. Do you know her?'

'Never heard of her.'

'She was murdered,' Kelly said. 'Cut up, just like Imelda Lacy. Her head was dumped in the sea.'

'So that's why I'm here, is it?'

'We're questioning various people. You're only one.'

'Well, you're barking up the wrong tree, mister. I don't even know the woman. And I'll tell you something else for nothing. If I'm being questioned for murder, I want my solicitor here.' He sat back and folded his arms again. There was a hard, resentful look in his eyes.

Megarry cleared his throat. The others fell silent. 'Are you in regular employment, Mr Delaney?'

'I want my solicitor. I know my rights.'

'You'll still have to answer my question. Are you in regular employment?'

'Yes. I work for McGurk's.'

'Who are they exactly?'

'They're pork butchers. In Amiens Street.'

'Do you live near the DART?'

'I live close enough. What's that got to do with anything?'

'Do you use it much?'

Delaney looked puzzled. 'Of course I do. Everybody uses it.'

'Do you have a car?'

'No.'

'So, for these trips you make out to Howth at the weekends, you would normally use the DART? Is that right?'

'Yes.'

'Tell me about the pubs you use. Where do you like to go?'

'The Lighthouse. The Cock. The Capstan. Anywhere there's a bit of craic.'

Megarry paused. 'Did you use the DART when you went to Howth on the weekend of April 20th last?

Delaney's eyes flickered for a moment. 'No,' he said. 'Definitely not.'

'How can you be so sure?'

He brought his face close to Megarry's and stared. 'Because I wasn't in Howth that weekend. I was in Galway. And I'll tell you something else. I've got witnesses.'

By 10.20 p.m. the last session was drawing to a close. They had interviewed three men in Bray, Delaney, Quinn and a forty-year-old builder called Harper with sunburnt arms and calloused hands, who had spent fifteen years in the sex offenders' wing of Arbour Hill prison for a string of attacks against women.

They had grabbed a sandwich in a pub in Dalkey before driving back across the city to Kilbarrack, where another eight men waited in the holding cells to talk to them. They'd been the usual bunch, devious and deviant, evasive, sullen and resentful. The man they were questioning now was small and middle-aged with a bald patch like a worn carpet on the crown of his head. He had tiny pink eyes that darted round the room, afraid to rest on anybody's face. Like an animal, Megarry thought, a rabbit or a rat.

He glanced once more at the man's file. His particular speciality was hanging around girls' schools with his fly zip undone, waiting for an opportunity to expose himself. His last conviction had been eighteen months earlier. He was plainly terrified at finding himself back inside a police station. He sat on the edge of his chair and spoke in a high-pitched voice that shook with fear. Once or twice, Megarry thought he was going to break down. But he had answered all their questions without pause or hesitation. He was telling the truth.

'You're free to go,' Kelly said at last.

The man looked uncertain.

'I said you're free.'

'That's it?' the man asked in surprise. 'Will you need me again? If you do, I'd prefer if you rang me at work. I don't want you calling at the house. My wife doesn't like it. The neighbours talk. You know how it is.'

'Just stay out of trouble and you'll hear no more from us.'

The man grabbed Kelly's hand and pumped it in gratitude. 'I'm straight now,' he said. 'All that stuff is behind me.'

He took Megarry's hand and shook it too, but hesitated when he came to Lawlor. Instead, he took his jacket from the back of the chair and hurried from the room.

'Jesus Christ,' Kelly said when he was gone. 'What a shower of degenerates.'

Megarry stood up and stretched his arms, stifling a yawn. 'At least none of those men murdered anyone,' he said wearily.

'How can you be sure?'

'I know it.' He took out his cigarettes, got up and opened a window. The rain had stopped but the air felt cold and damp.

'Most of those guys have convictions for indecent assault,' Lawlor protested. 'Several of them are rapists.'

'But we're investigating murder,' Megarry said.

'I don't see how you can be so certain.'

'Oh, for God's sake,' Megarry exploded. 'What do you want to do? Bring them in again and put them through the mangle until one of them breaks down and confesses to something he didn't do? I'm telling you. The man we're looking for wasn't there.'

He realised that he was tired. They all were. They were beginning to snap at each other. He had been on the go since 7 a.m., subsisting on cups of tea and station biscuits. Now he needed a stiff drink.

He spoke again to Lawlor, this time in a gentler voice. 'For what it's worth, Annie, I'd be far more interested in one of the people we interviewed in Bray.'

'Delaney?'

'Yes. We know he fancied the Lacy girl. We know he's now living here. In Kilbarrack. And we know he had the skill required to cut them up.'

'But he's got an alibi.'

Megarry smiled. 'Has he? If I asked *you* where you were on the weekend of April 20th, would you be able to tell me? You'd have to think hard about it. But Delaney came right out like a shot.' He tapped ash from his cigarette. 'He might have got some people lined up to say he was in Galway that weekend just in case.'

'I'll tell you what,' Kelly said. 'Why don't I talk to the Galway cops? Get them to check. They could call at this guesthouse he says he stayed in.' He consulted his notebook. 'The Macushla. And I'll put a tail on him. Follow him around for a bit.'

'How long is all this going to take?' Lawlor asked.

Megarry shrugged. 'As long as required.'

'What about all those women out there?'

'What women?' Kelly said.

'The God-damned women who are terrified to go outside their front doors because of this bastard.' Lawlor's voice was rising. There was colour in her cheeks. 'The women who look over their shoulders when they go out to the shops. Or when they use the train. The women who are worried sick when their daughters don't come home on time. There's near-hysteria out there on the streets and it isn't just a creation of the media. There's genuine fear. We've got to catch this guy. And we've got to do it soon.'

Kelly stared at her, his mouth half-open.

'These attacks in Kilbarrack might not be linked to the murder. But until we catch the man responsible, we won't know for certain.'

'And how do you propose we do that?'
'We could use a decoy.'

8

The following morning, Megarry went reluctantly with Kelly to see the superintendent. He'd had dealings with him before and they'd left a sour taste in his mouth.

They left Lawlor at Howth station to track down Mary Grogan's boyfriends and locate her parents, then drove into town. It was a bright morning, the sun high in the sky out over the bay. There was a breeze bending the palm trees on the sea front at Dollymount strand, a couple of sails bobbing in the water near Dalkey Island.

The superintendent's office was in a large white building near Trinity College, an imperial relic left behind by the British. Some workmen on scaffolding were sandblasting the stone-work as they parked the car in the compound.

As they were getting into the lift, Kelly said: 'Just take it easy, Cecil. This is nothing to get excited about. He just wants to talk to you.'

'I'll count to ten before I open my mouth,' Megarry said.

The superintendent was waiting. He was a tall man, round baby face, hair going prematurely bald, uniform carefully pressed and the buttons polished till they shone. He came from behind the desk and extended his hand, the flesh warm and sticky.

'Take a seat,' he said. He picked a pencil off the desk and rolled it in the palms of his hands.

'I'm glad you could come. I thought we should talk. Peter's told me about your arrangement. It's not the sort of thing we normally go in for.'

'But this isn't a normal case.'

'I know that.'

Megarry felt his temper rise. It was what he had feared. He pushed the chair back and stood up.

'I don't need this. If you've got a problem with my involvement, there's a simple solution. I can get out.'

The superintendent's face had gone pink. 'Please,' he said. 'You Northerners are so impulsive.'

'Don't patronise me. I didn't ask to get involved in this case. In fact, I resisted it. I have a garden at home that's going to rack and ruin and my wife is pleading with me to get it tidied up. I got involved because Peter asked me. I thought I was doing him a favour.'

The superintendent took a deep breath, then slowly released it. 'I didn't say I had a problem with you. Actually, I approve. While you're assisting Peter, you'll have my full support.'

'Good,' Megarry said. He glanced at Kelly and slowly sat down again.

On the desk, there was a photo of a younger version of the superintendent holding up a cup, a trophy from his days as a county footballer. He's a vain man, Megarry thought. Vain and ambitious. And like all bureaucrats, he's scared shitless about protocol. But he also wants this case solved, so he's caught between a rock and a hard place.

The superintendent turned to Kelly. 'I had the Commissioner on to me this morning. He's not a happy camper. These news bulletins. The newspaper reports. And now this other young woman in Bray. It makes us look foolish, Peter. To put it in a nutshell, the Commissioner wants a scalp.'

He tapped the pencil vigorously against the desk.

'It's going to take time.'

'What's the problem? You need more resources? I can give you more men.'

'It's not resources,' Kelly said wearily. 'Resources won't solve this one.'

'So what am I supposed to tell the Commissioner? How're you going to crack it?'

'Perseverance,' Kelly said lamely.

'Perseverance? Jesus. You try telling that to the Minister. You know what she'll say? She'll tell you to go whistle Dixie. She wants results. She wants to look good, get the media off her back.' The superintendent sighed. 'Peter, I'm not sure you know how this works. The Minister was on to the Commissioner this morning. Chewed his ass off. And you know what he did?'

'He got on to you and did the same,' Megarry said.

The superintendent swung round to observe him. 'Yes. That's exactly what he did.'

'I know how it works,' Megarry said. 'But it doesn't solve anything. There's no point harassing Peter so that he delivers a case that falls apart the minute he gets it into court. It might take the heat off for the time being, but it just stores up more trouble. We have to take our time and get it right.'

Kelly cleared his throat. 'We're thinking of using a decoy.'

'A what?'

'These sex attacks at Kilbarrack. It's not far from Howth. Just four or five stops on the DART line. It could be the same man. We're hoping to draw him out.'

The superintendent laughed. 'You're going to put a young woman on the street in the hope of catching this guy? What if it backfires? What if she gets injured?'

'She volunteered. It was her idea.'

'Who are you talking about?'

'A colleague. Annie Lawlor.'

The superintendent looked first at Kelly and then at Megarry. He began to shake his head.

'I don't like the sound of this. What if it goes wrong? Can't you see the meal the press will make out of that? And just say you do manage to catch this guy. How do you know his defence team won't plead entrapment?'

'We don't,' Megarry said. 'But I think it's worth a try. Lawlor's well able to look after herself. And we'll have people in the immediate vicinity at all times.'

The superintendent sat back, stared for a moment at the ceiling. Then he turned once more to Kelly, waving his hands in a shooing motion.

'Just go and solve this damned thing, will you? And for Christ's sake make sure she doesn't get hurt. I'll tell the Commissioner you're making progress. But you'd better deliver on this or, so help me God, you're going to be hitting the bricks again out in some God-forsaken beat in the inner city.'

Lawlor spent the next day preparing for the decoy assignment. She went back to her notes of the previous assaults and trawled through them again, looking for some further pattern. Was there some type that attracted this man? Petite women perhaps? Plump women? Busty women? Blondes? Brunettes? She could find no common thread. Since the assaults had first been reported to the police eighteen months earlier, a total of twenty-two women had been attacked. They had come in all shapes and sizes. And all ages. The oldest had been fifty-five, the youngest only fourteen.

She remembered something that Megarry had said. How can you be sure it's the same man? For the first time, she began to have doubts, began to consider the possibility that they might be dealing with several attackers. There were a lot of strange men out there; she had seen some of them in the last few days in the interview rooms in Bray and Kilbarrack.

She went back to the notes and started once more, paying close attention to the statements of the women, the circumstances, the descriptions they gave.

And then she stumbled on the pattern she was looking for. Not just one, but two. In almost all the cases, the attacker had forced the women to speak obscenities while he carried out the assault, to talk dirty, to encourage the abuse that he inflicted on them. And each time, he had used a knife. She felt a tingle of fear, a little worm of doubt about what she was getting herself into.

What should she wear? She rummaged through her wardrobe, taking out dresses and suits. Should she dress seductively like the hookers she had seen on night patrol around Fitzwilliam Square, short skirts, high heels, low-cut blouses revealing cleavage as they haggled with their Johns through the open windows of cars?

The notes gave her no clue. The women who had been attacked had worn an assortment of clothes. In the end, she settled for what she would normally wear for a night out.

Megarry met her at the station in Howth. As she settled into the passenger seat, he reached out and squeezed her hand.

'You're determined? You can still call it off. No one will think any less of you.'

She turned to face him. 'But I want to do it, Cecil. There's panic out there. The media won't let up. Even if this guy isn't the killer, we have to catch him. It's got to stop.'

It was getting dark, the street lights coming on. She had put on a little scent. The smell filled the car.

Megarry took a small radio from the dashboard. It was the size of a cigarette packet. He slipped it into the breast pocket of her coat. 'You don't have to touch it,' he said. 'It's on a VHF frequency. Just speak at voice level and we can pick you up. And remember, if you're frightened or worried at any stage, just say so and we'll take you off.'

They left the coast road near Black Banks. A big yellow moon was hanging over the sea. Megarry stopped close to Kilbarrack DART station and she saw another car swing across and flash its lights. She recognised Kelly and three cops from Howth station.

Megarry turned the engine off and they sat for a moment in silence. 'Now's the time to stop,' he said. 'If you're not sure.'

She felt her knees tremble. 'There's something I didn't tell you, Cecil. He uses a knife.'

'But you want to go on?'

'Yes.'

He pressed her hand.

'Okay. Remember we'll be in constant contact. Keep walking towards the station as if you're going to catch a train. Don't look around. Try to relax.'

She opened the car door. The night air felt cool against her face. Fear overwhelmed her in a rush. On impulse, she threw her arms around Megarry and kissed his cheek.

The entrance to the DART station was bathed in yellow light. It was approached by a narrow path surrounded by bushes. Down below in the darkness, she could make out the tracks of the railway line gleaming silver in the night. She heard a train draw near, the wheels clattering on the rails, and then it seemed to burst into the station in an avalanche of sound. She heard people getting off and then a horn blasted and the train started up again, rattling away towards Dublin. An eerie silence settled over the scene.

She stood in the shadows and waited. There was a stillness in the air, a handful of stars in the cold sky. She could feel her heart begin to thump in her breast. She started walking again towards the station entrance.

The place was deserted, the only sign of life the little office where the clerk dispensed the tickets. She could see him now, a small man with glasses. He was reading a book. She looked at the clock on the station wall; it was 10.15 p.m.

She started back the way she had come. She suddenly felt cold. She thought of what she had read earlier in the notes. The gloved hand, the mask, the hard steel of the knife. Her mind filled with terrible possibilities.

Perhaps, right now, the man was watching her, somewhere in the shadows, waiting for an opportunity to strike. Perhaps he had taken out the knife and was testing its sharp blade, preparing to press it against her neck. What if the radio didn't work? What if Megarry didn't see or hear? What if she was attacked and he didn't get to her in time?

She was walking now into the most abandoned part of the path. Beyond the bushes there was a ditch running down towards the railway line. The light from the station fell further away. Everything was silent. She listened to the sound of her own breath, the crunching of her shoes on the gravel path.

The thought came to her that she should call it off. Run back to Megarry and the waiting cops and tell them she couldn't go through with it. That it was just a stupid idea. A waste of time.

Just then, she heard a sound break the silence. She froze. She heard it again, closer this time, a muffled sound as if someone had stepped on a twig. She turned to go and heard a man's voice beside her.

84

'Excuse me,' he said.

A panic seized her. She started to run but it was too late. She felt a hand across her mouth, an arm dragging her towards the bushes. She tried to fight. Her shoes slipped on the grass and her legs gave way. Then a dark figure was on top of her and they were rolling into the ditch. She felt fingers tearing at the buttons of her shirt, searching for her breasts, the cold knife against her throat.

'Talk dirty,' the voice said. 'Say you like it.'

Megarry had watched her go with a sinking heart. Privately he had shared the doubts expressed by the superintendent. But he also recognised Lawlor's determination and the passion she felt about this man. And he knew that she was right to believe that men could not fully understand.

He switched off the car lights and took out his cigarettes. He saw her walk slowly towards the path leading to the station. Then she was gone from sight, obscured by the bushes and trees, swallowed up by the darkness. He heard the train come in, saw the handful of passengers leave the station to make their way home. A few minutes later he saw her emerge from the shadows and enter the bright pool around the entrance.

She stopped for a moment. He saw her glance around as if uncertain. It struck him how desolate she looked, a lonely figure suspended in the light. He was tempted to speak to her on the radio, but then she was off once more, moving back into the shadows, lost again. He looked across the road to where Kelly was parked. He had told him to come armed and had watched in the station as he strapped on his service automatic, first snapping it open to make sure it was loaded.

He had bent to tap ash from his cigarette when he heard the voice. It was a gruff Dublin accent. Male. 'Excuse me,' it said.

He flung open the car door and started to run.

Kelly had heard it too. He came sprinting across the street. He had three men with him, torches blazing in the darkness.

Megarry felt his heart race. He entered the path. He felt the branches slap against his face as he ran.

'Annie!' he cried. 'Annie!'

There was a bank tumbling down to the railway line. He could make out a shape in the darkness. As he got closer, he saw what it was.

He paused and held his arms out straight, hands clasped together as if in prayer.

'Police!' he yelled. 'We're armed.'

'I've got a knife,' the voice said. 'I'll cut her.'

Behind him on the path, Megarry could see the torchlights. Without thinking, he hurled himself into the ditch, fingers groping wildly for the man's face.

He felt a sharp pain across his arm and warm blood. Kelly and the others came sliding down the bank. He heard the click of the automatic.

'Drop the knife,' Kelly said. 'Or I'll blow your fucking head off.'

The man was panting. Slowly, he released Lawlor and she fell into Megarry's arms. He saw Kelly reach out and rip off the mask.

He recognised the man at once.

It was Sean Boylan.

Book Two

9

Swimming upwards in a dark pool towards the light. That's how she would explain it afterwards, whenever people asked. The first thing she became aware of was the scent of flowers, a huge bowl of roses on a table beside the bed. It mingled with a fainter smell of disinfectant. The room looked strange. White everywhere, even the curtains.

She realised there were people in the room. She could see them, like grey shadows flitting near the bed. One of them bent forward. She caught a whiff of cigarette smoke from his clothes. Then the voice, the flat Northern accent, the reassurance that came at her in a rush.

'Take it easy,' Megarry said.

Annie Lawlor struggled to sit up and felt a searing pain across her neck.

'You're in St Margaret's,' Megarry said soothingly. 'But there's nothing to worry about. You're only here for observation. They say you were concussed. How is your neck?'

She reached her hand up and felt the rough cloth of the bandage.

'It feels like I've been kicked by a horse.'

She recognised Kathleen and Rory, her boyfriend. He leaned over and kissed her softly on the cheek. 'You're going to be all right,' he said.

'What happened?'

'You don't remember?' Megarry said.

'Bits of it. I remember his hand, his voice, the knife.'

'Kelly disarmed him. You fainted. You were hurt. It was the way he was holding you. They gave you a sedative.'

Kathleen moved her chair closer to the bed.

'I think what you did was very brave. I'm proud of you. You were a star.'

'Please,' Lawlor said.

'No. It's true. Now that he's been caught, all those women can go out again.'

Megarry held up his arm, and she saw that it was bandaged. 'He got me with the knife before Kelly overpowered him. I had to have twelve stitches.'

'Have you identified him?'

'Yes,' Megarry said. 'Sean Boylan.'

Lawlor blinked.

'The *fisherman*?'

Lawlor sank back on the pillows, her face incredulous. 'Jesus,' she said. 'Who would have thought it? Sean Boylan of all people?'

'You'll have to give us a statement,' Megarry said. 'Whenever you're ready. There's no rush. What he said, what he did. We're going to nail this bastard through the breastbone.'

She paused and then she said: 'Don't you think it's some coincidence that Boylan should also be the person to find the head?'

Megarry smiled. 'You're thinking like a detective.'

She stretched her hand and linked it in his.

'I want out of here. I want to be back on the case.'

When he got back to the station, he found Kelly in great good humour. He was drinking coffee from a plastic cup and eating a chicken roll. He put it down on the desk and wiped his mouth with a paper napkin.

'We've got him, Cecil,' he said. 'We've got the fucker at last. I'm only sorry we didn't kick the shit out of him while we were at it. Resisting arrest. There's nothing he could have done.'

'You did enough,' Megarry said. 'You arrested him.'

'The super's having apoplexy, he's so excited. Now he's got something to keep the Commissioner happy. He wants to put out a press statement, start claiming some credit for a change.'

Megarry sat down. His arm was hurting. It was much more painful than he had admitted either to Kathleen or to the doctor.

'Don't you think that's a wee bit premature?'

'Premature? What are you talking about? I've had it up to here with the media. Now we've got something to shout about, why shouldn't we tell the bastards?'

Megarry shrugged.

Kelly leaned across the desk. 'Cecil, I swear to God. We've got something to celebrate and you sit there looking like somebody's just hit you in the face with a bag of shit.'

He grinned, sat back in his chair. 'The super was edgy as hell about getting you involved. You saw him, Cecil. You'd think somebody'd stuck a poker up his arse. This arrest is my justification.'

'But it was Lawlor who drew my attention to the Kilbarrack attacks. It was her idea for the decoy.'

'Of course. Nobody's arguing. It all confirms my judgement, Cecil. It proves I got it right when I picked you two. How is she, by the way?'

'She can't wait to get back on the case.'

'I can't wait to have her. She's going to file charges against Boylan. I'll see to it. He's going to be one sorry sonofabitch he ever laid a finger on her. And when we nail him for the murder . . .'

Megarry held his hand up. 'You're going too fast, Peter. Let's take this thing one step at a time. Have you talked to Boylan yet?'

'Yes.'

'Did he ask to see a solicitor?'

'Not yet.'

'Well, that's a start,' Megarry said.

Sean Boylan was sitting on a bed in the holding cell, his broad shoulders hunched like someone sheltering from a storm. It was a small room with a tiny window. He looked up when they came in. He had a bruise on his cheek and a deep scratch on his forehead. He was smoking a cigarette.

Megarry paused. He could feel Boylan's eyes on him. There was a dankness in the air, a stale smell of sweat and tobacco. On the ground near the bed there was a metal ashtray brim-full with cigarette stubs.

'Inspector,' Megarry said and turned to Kelly. 'Who gave the prisoner permission to smoke?'

'I don't know, superintendent.'

'Remove his cigarettes.'

'What the fuck . . .?' Boylan said and crouched into a corner of the bed like an animal about to strike. Kelly walked quickly to the door and opened it. He called out to the corridor and two guards came running into the cell.

'Remove the prisoner's cigarettes.'

The men approached the bed. 'All right,' one of the guards said. 'Give them over.'

Boylan hesitated and then his hand went slowly to his pocket and withdrew a crumpled packet of Rothmans.

'Now,' Megarry said. 'Someone open that window and let some fresh air in here. This place smells like a zoo.'

He sat down at the table and waited till the guards had left the room. He spoke to Kelly. 'The rules say clearly, no smoking.'

Boylan was staring at him, a confused look in his eyes.

'You smoke,' he said. 'You were smoking in our house, the day you talked to me and my da.'

Megarry turned once more to Kelly. 'Who is he addressing, Inspector?'

'I think it's you, sir.'

'Did anyone give him permission to speak?'

'No.'

'You're a bleedin' hypocrite. Taking my ciggies away. You smoke yourself.'

Megarry faced him. 'You trying to provoke me?'

'What?'

'Your insulting language. Are you trying to make me angry?'

'I was only making a remark.'

'When I need your remarks, I'll ask for them. In the meantime, if I was you, I'd get used to not smoking. Where you'll be going, you won't be smoking for a very long time.'

'What do you mean?'

'You'll be going down. Arbour Hill. Ten years minimum. Do you understand? Ten years in jail. In a cell like this. With two other prisoners. One wash-basin. One privy. No remission.'

'But I . . .'

'But nothing. It's an open-and-shut case. We've got witnesses. Solid reliable police officers, including a woman officer who's now injured as a result of your attack.'

'She asked for it,' Boylan said. There was an excited look in his eyes.

Megarry remembered that day he had visited his house in St Patrick's Lane. The suicidal drinking.

'She *what*?'

'She asked for it. All these bitches ask for it. She asked me to do it to her. They love it. They love a bit of rough. Only they won't admit it. Why do you think she was walking down there in the first place?'

Megarry caught his breath. 'She was going for a train.'

'No, she wasn't. I watched her. She walked to the station and then she walked back again. She was looking for a bit of rough. She told me. She said she enjoyed it.'

'You made her say that.'

'No, I didn't.'

'You think these women enjoy being assaulted by you?'

'Sure they do.'

'Jesus Christ.'

Boylan was grinning at him. 'They love it. They're sluts. You should hear them when they get going. The language they use. You wouldn't believe it. Just because they dress pretty. That means nothing. They're bitches. Dirty bitches. They love it.'

Kelly moved quickly and caught Boylan by the throat. 'You mad bastard. You injured my colleague. Do you realise the pain you've caused?'

He raised his fist, and for a moment Megarry feared he was going to strike.

He spoke sharply. 'Peter.'

Kelly turned and saw Megarry shake his head. He lowered his arm.

'You're just a piece of shit,' Kelly said. 'Take a good look at yourself. What woman in her right mind would let you near her?'

Boylan sat on the bed and laughed. 'They love it, I tell you. They beg for it. I've seen them. I've heard them.'

Megarry spoke again. 'Do you have a regular girlfriend?'

Boylan looked away.

'I asked you a question.'

'No.'

'Did you ever have a regular girlfriend?'

'Years ago.'

'What happened?'

'I got tired of her. Threw her over.'

'Tell me why you attack women.'

'I don't attack them,' Boylan protested. 'I just told you. They ask for it.'

'Why do you carry a knife, if you don't attack them?'

'That's all part of the excitement. They like that.'

'They like having a knife put against their throats?'

'Sure. It turns them on.'

Boylan was grinning again and Megarry suddenly realised that he must be enjoying this interrogation. In some perverse way, he was reliving the attacks. He found a piece of chewing gum in his pocket and stuck it in his mouth.

'How many women are we talking about here?'

'God knows. Dozens. There's loads of them out there. Randy as hell. They love that old knife against their throats.'

Megarry swallowed hard. 'We've had complaints from twenty-two women. Are you responsible for all of them? Do you admit that?'

'Probably.'

There was a tape recorder on the table.

'Our first report was in November 1995. Were you responsible for that?'

'When?'

'November 1995. It was winter. The boat would have been laid up because of the weather. You probably got bored. Isn't that what happened? All these incidents occurred when the boat was tied up. Isn't that right?'

'Just a bit of sport,' Boylan said. 'A bit of fun. There's no harm in it.'

'But you did them all? All twenty-two?'

'I didn't keep count.'

'Well, unless there's someone else out there. Maybe there's a copy-cat. Maybe there's somebody who's copying you. That's been known to happen.'

'There's nobody else,' Boylan said quickly. 'No one but me. I'm the only one can do these jobs. Nobody else knows how to turn those bitches on.' His voice was rising.

'So you admit them? We have the tape recorder running. This is on the record.'

'Yes.'

Megarry took a deep breath. He looked at Kelly.

'Tell us what you know about Imelda Lacy.'

'Who?'

'Lacy. Imelda Lacy.'

Boylan glanced from one face to the other.

'Who is she?'

'She's a woman we're interested in. She lived in Bray. You ever hear of her?'

'No.'

'You're sure?'

'I never went to Bray,' Boylan said.

'It's on the DART line. It's only an hour from Howth.'

'So?'

'You used the DART to get to Kilbarrack.'

'Well?'

'Maybe you felt like a change?'

'No way. Why would I go over there? I got all the sport I wanted round Kilbarrack.'

'Look,' Megarry said. 'We have you for the assaults. Why don't you just get everything off your chest? Tell us everything you did. We'll start again. What do you know about Imelda Lacy?'

Boylan looked confused. 'I just told you. I don't know any Imelda Lacy.'

'What about Mary Grogan?'

Boylan's eyelids flickered. 'Never heard of her.'

Megarry took out the photograph he had found in Crow's Nest Cottage and pushed it in front of Boylan's face.

'That's her. Do you recognise her now?'

'Was I with her? Sometimes I don't see their faces.'

'You tell us.'

'I don't think so. I don't know this woman.'

'She lives in Howth,' Megarry said. 'West Heath. You know West Heath, don't you?'

'Sure I do. It's up near the Summit.'

Megarry took out his cigarettes and placed them on the table. He saw Boylan's nose twitch and his face break into a smile. He waved a finger at the policeman. 'You're a devil,' he said.

'Am I?'

'You're trying to tempt me. You're trying to get me to say something I might regret.'

'I only want the truth,' Megarry said. 'That's all. Do you know her?'

'No.'

Megarry selected a cigarette and slowly tapped it on the side of the box. He could see Boylan watching him. He took out his lighter and stroked it with his fingers.

'You know, life in prison is very hard for sex offenders. They have to be segregated for their own safety. The other prisoners hate them. They try to attack them. Sometimes they succeed. One case I know of personally, they took a razor to this guy . . .'

'Why are you telling me this?' Boylan asked.

'I just want you to be acquainted with the facts. You'll be going down. For a long time. However . . .' He tapped the cigarette once more. 'If Inspector Kelly were to go into the witness box and say that you co-operated fully with the police, the judge would probably take that into consideration when it came to sentencing. It would be in your favour. It could mean the difference between ten years and maybe . . . five years.' He flicked at the lighter and bent the cigarette into the flame. 'Tell us what you know about Mary Grogan? You do know her, don't you?'

'If I said yes, what would happen?'

'We could talk about her. How well you know her, the nature of your relationship. When you saw her last.'

Boylan sniffed the cigarette smoke.

'Go on,' Megarry coaxed. 'Tell me about Mary Grogan.'

'But there's nothing to tell. What's she got to do with anything?'

He looked from Megarry's face to the cigarette box and back again.

Megarry suddenly pushed the packet across the table. 'You want one?'

'Sure.'

'Go ahead.'

Boylan's hand moved forward. And then, just as quickly, he recoiled as if suspecting a trap.

'What about them rules you mentioned?'

'I can bend the rules any time I want.'

'You're sure? I won't get punished for this?'

'No. Go right ahead.'

Gingerly, Boylan reached for the cigarettes. Megarry flicked the lighter once more. Boylan filled his lungs with smoke.

'Now,' the policeman said. 'We'll start again. You know Mary Grogan, don't you?'

Boylan swallowed. 'It's . . .'

There was a knock on the door. Their heads turned. A young policeman looked into the room.

The wild look came back into Boylan's face. He stopped.

10

'*Jeeeesus!*' Megarry snapped. 'What is it?'

The young man reddened. 'There's someone to see Inspector Kelly.'

Kelly rose quickly and went out to the corridor. Megarry could hear them whispering and then the sound of footsteps retreating. He turned again to Boylan.

He was sitting with a mischievous gleam in his eye, slowly blowing smoke from the side of his mouth.

'That rule you mentioned. About not smoking. You made that up, didn't you?'

'Did I?' Megarry said coldly.

'Yes, you did. I was right about you. You're a rogue. You're trying to trap me.'

'Listen,' Megarry said. 'I don't make things up. If I say it's not allowed, it's not allowed.' He snatched the cigarette from Boylan's hand and crushed it out. 'That keep you happy?'

Boylan stared.

Megarry felt his arm throb with pain. The man who had cut him and attacked Lawlor and twenty-two other women was sitting opposite and he was playing games. His instinct was to reach out and beat him till the rage he felt inside had been purged. Instead, he tried to control his spiralling anger.

'Let's start again. Tell me about Mary Grogan.' He checked to see that Kelly had left the tape recorder running. 'What do you know about her?'

'Never heard of her.'

'I don't believe you.'

'You can believe what you want.'

Megarry sighed. 'A town the size of Howth where every-body knows everybody else. You're telling me you don't know her?'

'There's loads of people I don't know. Jesus, there's new people coming all the time. I don't know everybody.'

'But you do know her. I saw it in your face when I showed you the photograph.'

'No, I don't.'

'You're lying.'

'Why should I lie?'

'To cover up.'

Boylan started to laugh. 'I've got nothing to hide.'

Megarry brought his fist down hard on Boylan's hand. There was a squeal of pain.

'I warned you not to provoke me. I warned you not to mess.'

Boylan nursed his injured hand. 'I'm not messing.'

'I'm only starting,' Megarry said. 'I can do what I want with you. I can beat the shit out of you. The guards will say you fell down the stairs.'

Boylan glanced nervously towards the tape recorder. 'Is that thing running?'

'Yes.'

'Knock it off.'

Megarry stretched out a hand and turned the switch.

Boylan stared past him towards the wall. 'What do you want to know?'

'Everything about Mary Grogan. I want you to tell me how you met her. I want you to tell me what you talked about. I want you to tell me what you were doing the weekend of April 20th.'

'All right,' Boylan said. 'But first you tell me why you're so interested in her.'

'Because . . .'

'Because what?'

The strange look was back in Boylan's eye. Suddenly, he slapped his thigh.

'Because she's the one was dumped in the sea. That's it, isn't it? Jesus Christ.' His shoulders began to shake. 'It was her head was caught in the net. She's the one got whacked. Isn't that right? And you think I did it.' He threw back his head and howled with laughter till the tears ran down his cheeks.

There was a noise at the door. Megarry looked up and saw that Kelly was back. He felt a tiredness wash over him.

Kelly looked at the scene before him, came across and whispered in Megarry's ear.

'Her parents have arrived. They're downstairs.'

Megarry left the holding cell with a heavy heart and went slowly down the stairs in Kelly's wake. Mr and Mrs Grogan were waiting in his office.

They looked like a typical retired professional couple. He was small and thin with a pinched face and blue veins that throbbed in his pale forehead. His wife had grey hair and nervous hands that wandered now and then to pick at imaginary threads on her coat. Megarry noticed that they had both dressed soberly. Mr Grogan had put on a black tie.

'Would you like coffee?' Kelly asked tentatively, but Mr Grogan shook his head.

'Mrs Grogan?'

'No, thank you.'

'We would just like to get this over as soon as possible,' Mr Grogan said.

'It's been an awful shock for us.'

'I understand,' Kelly said.

'Begging your pardon, but I don't think you do.' Mr Grogan's hands trembled as he took out a handkerchief and blew his nose. 'You ever have a child die like this, Inspector Kelly?'

'No, sir. I haven't.'

'Well then. How can you understand what it feels like?'

'What Henry means,' his wife said, 'is that you never expect this to happen. Nothing can prepare you. We just can't believe it.'

'She was so full of life,' Mr Grogan said. 'Full of vigour. She had everything to live for, and then to be told . . .' He paused and blew his nose again. 'We'd just like to identify her if you don't mind, and take her away so that we can make the funeral arrangements.'

Kelly cleared his throat. 'Do you mind if we ah . . . ask you a few questions? We'll keep it brief.'

'Is that necessary?'

'Unfortunately, it is.'

Mr Grogan shifted in his chair. 'All right,' he said weakly. 'Get it over with.'

'When was the last time you had contact with Mary?'

'About four weeks ago. She phoned.'

'What sort of mood was she in?'

'She was in a good mood. Mary was always in a good mood. She brought us up to date on her news. Little bits of gossip about work and her social life. She had a very hectic social life.'

'She was going away for the weekend,' Mrs Grogan put in. 'She was looking forward to that.'

'Do you know where she was going?'

'She didn't say.'

'Was she going alone?'

'I don't know. She just said she planned to be back on Sunday evening. She had to report for work on Monday morning. She promised to ring.'

'And she never did?'

'No.' Mr Grogan clasped his hands to stop them from trembling.

'Can you tell us a little about her social life, her friends, that sort of thing?'

Mrs Grogan spoke. 'She had lots of friends. Mary was the type who made friends easily.'

'Any particular friend?'

'There was some woman she was friendly with in Howth. A painter, I think.'

'Do you know this woman's name?'

Mrs Grogan shook her head.

'Anyone else?'

'Joyce Denvir. They'd been at boarding-school together, and later at university.'

'What does Joyce do?'

'She's a teacher in Dublin.'

'Do you have her address?'

'No,' Mrs Grogan said.

'What about men friends?'

'She had plenty of those,' Mr Grogan said.

'Anything serious?'

'There was one young man. Brian Casey.' Mr Grogan glanced at his wife. 'We thought there might have been an engagement, but in the end it all came to nothing.'

'Why was that?'

'Who knows? She didn't say.'

'Do you know which of them broke off the relationship?'

'We think she did. Mary was quite headstrong. Very confident. She didn't talk about it much, but we got the impression that he was the one pushing for an engagement. Mary resisted. She felt that marriage would constrain her.'

'And when did this happen?'

'About six months ago.'

Mr Grogan took his wife's hand and squeezed it.

'If you're finished now, Inspector, we'd like to see Mary.'

Kelly glanced nervously towards Megarry. 'I don't think that will be necessary, Mr Grogan. You see, we've made a positive identification from your daughter's dental records.'

The Grogans looked at each other. 'Nevertheless, we'd like to see her,' Mrs Grogan said.

Kelly took a deep breath. 'You *have* been informed of *all* the circumstances?'

'That she was drowned? Yes. We know that.'

Kelly's mouth fell open. 'She wasn't drowned,' he said. 'She was shot.'

Mrs Grogan gave a little gasp and put her hand to her mouth. 'I'm sorry.'

She began to weep. 'Oh, my God.'

'Why weren't we told?' Mr Grogan demanded. 'Why didn't someone tell us?'

'I thought you were told. I gave instructions for the local

police to inform you personally. I didn't want you hearing on the telephone. There's obviously been a misunderstanding.'

'The sergeant said she'd been drowned.'

'He was wrong.'

Mr Grogan's voice shook. 'Can we see her please?

Megarry spoke.

'I don't think that would be a good idea.'

They turned to observe him. 'What do you mean?'

'We only have her head.'

There was a silence.

Megarry thought of the awful object he had seen in Finnegan's lab, the bloated face, the eye sockets empty, the nose and ear gone, the skin scraped from the side so that the bare flesh lay exposed. This was not the daughter they had known, the smiling girl in the photograph. This was not how she should be remembered.

'You have every right to see her,' he said in a quiet voice. 'However, I would strongly advise against it.'

Mrs Grogan was weeping silently, a handkerchief pressed tight against her face.

'She was shot and then her head was cut off. There has also been a certain amount of damage. The head was in the water for some time. I'm afraid it's not a pleasant sight. You wouldn't recognise her.'

The old man's mouth trembled.

'Please,' Megarry said. 'Take my advice. I think it would upset you. Remember her the way she was when you last saw her. Or as a child on her Communion Day. You must have photographs. Remember her like that.'

Mrs Grogan had started sobbing now. It was like a dam had burst. Her breast heaved and she blew her nose in an effort to stem the tears. Her husband put his arm around her shoulder and drew her close.

I think I know the pain you are feeling, Megarry thought. Your only child. I too have a daughter who almost died. He watched the old man as he comforted his wife.

Kelly took the Grogans out to their car. When he returned, his face was pale.

'That idiot of a sergeant. Imagine telling them she'd been drowned. Where in God's name did he get that idea?'

'He obviously misunderstood,' Megarry said. 'These things happen.'

'That time they asked to see her. I thought for a moment I was going to die. You know, I hate this business. It's the worst part. Dealing with relatives. It's not my thing.'

'It's nobody's thing,' Megarry snapped. 'It's a dirty business. But it has to be done. I thought you handled it well.'

'You did?'

'Yes. All you can do is give them the facts and offer them what comfort you can. They have to deal with their grief alone.'

He got up and put his arm around the younger man's shoulder. 'C'mon,' he said. 'I'll buy you a drink.'

They walked to the Cock Tavern and sat in an alcove by the window, watching the sunlight streaming through the stained glass. There was an afternoon lull in the bar, a quiet that seemed to permeate the place. Megarry remembered the last time he'd been here, the uillean pipes, the ebb and flow of the music, the voices raised in song.

He sat now and watched the way the light reflected through the glass, spangles of green and blue, little particles of dust suspended in the air. He thought of Jennifer and felt a sadness take hold of him.

'You know, my heart goes out to them,' he said at last. 'Their only child. To die in the fullness of her life. It must be hard, the hardest thing a parent has to bear.' He sipped his whiskey, felt it warm his throat.

'At least we've got someone for it,' Kelly said. 'We've got Boylan. It's only a matter of wearing him down, getting him to confess.'

Megarry swirled the whiskey in the glass. 'I said earlier, Peter. You're going too fast.'

'We have him with a knife assaulting women. He's admitted that. And then, hey presto, he turns out to be the guy who finds the head in his fishing net. You're going to tell me that's all a coincidence? He probably dumped that head there himself and waited till his old da was with him to pull it up again. Make it all look like it was found by accident.'

Megarry took out a cigarette and tapped it slowly on the table top.

'Let me tell you a story. When I was your age, an inspector in the Special Branch in Belfast, I had an IRA guy in my sights for murder. I had a string of touts ready to swear on a stack of bibles that this was the guy. I brought him in, questioned him for days but I couldn't get him to crack. He used to sit there, staring at a spot on the wall, refusing to talk. In the end, I prepared charges anyway. And then a funny thing happened. One by one my informers fell away. Got cold feet. Refused to give evidence. I had no case. I had to let the guy go. Later, I discovered that he couldn't possibly have done the hit. He was being set up. Two years later we got another guy. Got a confession, forensics, the whole shooting gallery. We sent him down. He was the first man's brother-in-law and he was screwing his wife.'

'What are you trying to say?'

'That you have to be sure, Peter. You have to have a wrapped-up case. No loose ends. No little bits of string hanging out that a defence lawyer can pull so that the whole damned package unravels.'

'And you're not sure about Boylan?'

'No. I'm not.'

Kelly shifted. 'But we have him cold for the assaults. He admitted them on the tape.'

'The assaults are one thing, Peter. Murder is another. There's something just not right. The way he stares. The way he boasts about these attacks. That's not the way a normal person would behave.'

'You're not taken in by that shit,' Kelly said. 'It's all an act. The guy should get a friggen Oscar.'

'No,' Megarry said. 'Listen to me. He admits attacking twenty-three women. Makes no bones about it. But he shows no remorse. It's as if he believes he has done nothing wrong. Did you notice his reaction when I suggested there might be a copy-cat? He got possessive.'

'Jesus, Cecil. You're making excuses for him. We have the bastard cold.'

'I think he's mad,' Megarry said.

'Cecil. This guy is an actor. This is what he wants. Can't you see what he's playing at?'

Megarry put his glass down on the table. 'You think he killed Mary Grogan?'

'Yes.'

'Imelda Lacy?'

Kelly shrugged. 'Possibly.'

'But we've no proof. We can't even prove that he knew these women.'

'We'll get a confession, Cecil. We just need time to work on him. We've hardly started.'

'His confession will be no God-damned use if the court throws it out.'

'What are you talking about?'

'I think you should get a psychiatrist to look at him.'

Kelly threw his head back and laughed.

'Yes. His legal people are bound to demand one anyway. You might as well get in first.'

'Cecil, I don't believe this. Boylan's our best suspect and you want to let him off the God-damned hook. You know what psychiatrists are like. They're sure to find something wrong with him. They'll see it as a challenge.'

'Do it,' Megarry said firmly. 'And now that we've spoken to her parents, put out an appeal for anyone who knew Mary Grogan to come and talk to us. Get that photograph printed up and distribute it. And check out these men friends she had. Annie's got their names.'

Kelly sat back in his seat as if deflated.

'I'm sorry,' Megarry said. 'You can't rush this, Peter. You've got to be patient. Sometimes it's hard.'

He finished his drink. 'What happened with Delaney?' he said.

Kelly sighed. 'We lost him too. His alibi checked out. I had the Galway cops call to the place where he stayed. The Macushla Guest House. They checked the register. They had a John Delaney on the nights in question.'

Megarry considered for a moment. 'Did anyone talk to Delaney? Did anyone actually see him there?'

'Sure. Several people. They confirmed what he said. He was definitely in Galway that weekend.'

'Did the guesthouse say whether he had a companion?'

'A companion?' Kelly looked confused. 'I don't know. I don't think we asked. Why?'

'Because even if he was in Galway, it doesn't mean he didn't murder her.'

'I don't understand.'

'Mary Grogan was going away that weekend. You heard what her parents said.' Megarry's face broke into a slow smile. 'Just say she went to Galway with John Delaney?'

11

There was a train leaving for Galway at 5.30 p.m. Megarry got to the station with six minutes to spare, after a hectic taxi journey through the snarled-up evening traffic. He had called Kathleen from the bar.

'You're *what*?' she said.

'It's just an overnight. I'll be back tomorrow.'

'But you'll need a change of clothes. And what about your razor and things?'

'I haven't time. It's the only train this evening. I can buy a disposable razor. I'll survive.'

'Can't you leave it till tomorrow?'

Out of the corner of his eye, he could see Kelly talking to the barman. He held up two fingers to indicate a double. 'I need to go tonight. Something's come up. It's urgent.'

'What about your arm? Have you got your medication?'

Megarry lifted the glass of Bushmills that Kelly had just bought and held it up to the light. 'Yes,' he said. 'I've got my medication.'

A train from Cork had just come in and the station was packed. He fought his way to the ticket office, then to the barrier. He was beginning to perspire, all the rushing around, the whiskey, the hot sun streaming through the fanlights on the roof, casting shadows on the floor. He could feel his shirt sticking to his back with a warm, prickly heat.

He found a seat in the last carriage, just as the whistle blew, sat back and watched as, bit by bit, the city fell away. Soon they were out in the countryside, speeding across the flat expanse of Kildare, fields and trees a blur of green and brown in the evening light.

He was feeling drowsy. The sun through the window felt warm against his face. He fell asleep, dreamt of Sean Boylan and John Delaney and the Grogans. They were all in hospital together, lying in beds, one, two, three, four, along the ward. He heard Delaney speak: 'Have you got your medication?' There was a sneer on his face. He reached into a bag and laughed as he took out a boning saw.

When he woke, it was growing dark. He could see the lights coming on in the farmhouses, twinkling like fireflies in the dark fields. There was a sour taste in his mouth and his arm was hurting again.

He made his way along the train till he came to the dining carriage. He got a table near the back, beside a blonde, middle-aged woman who looked at him with interest. He studied the menu. There was salmon, chicken, roast lamb, pork chops. He thought of Dr Henry. No meat, low cholesterol. To hell with it, he thought and ordered a T-bone steak and a half-bottle of wine. When the waiter had gone, he took out his cigarettes and held them up politely for his companion's inspection.

'Do you mind if I smoke?'

She smiled, a teasing coquette's smile. 'What would you do if I said yes?' she replied.

The train got into Galway just before 8 p.m. The Macushla Guest House was to the west of the city, out along the Salthill Road. He got a taxi outside the station and they drove past Eyre Square and the docks, the streets crowded with revellers. He could hear music, the notes of a fiddle, raised voices pouring from the open doorway of a pub.

> *In Scartaglen there lived a lass,*
> *And every Sunday after Mass,*

She would go and take a glass,
Before going home by Bearna.

'What's going on?' he said to the driver.

The man spoke over his shoulder. 'It's a festival. To commemorate a local poet. All the pubs have got late extensions.'

'Right,' Megarry said.

He sat back on the soft upholstery of the cab and watched the narrow streets pass by. He had fond memories of Galway, weekends spent here years ago with Kathleen and Jennifer when she was only a child. They had taken a cottage once out in Spiddal and Jennifer had wakened to find a donkey grazing on the front lawn. That small event had made the holiday for her. For years afterwards she talked about it.

The Macushla turned out to be a bungalow on the shores of the bay. It was a converted farmhouse and the builders had made an attempt to retain its original features. He could see the open-stone walls, the wooden window frames, the hanging baskets of geraniums and aubretia beside the door. At the back of the house, where it sloped down to the bay, there was a big orange moon hanging like a balloon above the water. He could hear the gentle sighing of the breeze, the soft lapping of the sea rising and falling against the shore.

There was a sign in the window: 'Vacancies'. He pressed the bell and waited. Eventually a light went on and a plump, baggy-breasted woman in an apron emerged to open the door. He could see her examining him, his tie undone, the sweat matted in his hair, his arm encased in the grubby sling.

'Yes?' she said.

'You have vacancies?' He pointed to the sign.

'Well, now,' the woman began.

'I'd like a single room. Just for tonight.'

The woman squinted into the darkness. 'You've no luggage?'

'No. I had to travel in a hurry.'

'People staying here usually have luggage.'

'I hadn't time,' Megarry explained. 'I was in a rush.' He shifted uneasily from one foot to the other.

'Wait a moment,' he said and fumbled for his wallet. He

peeled off a twenty-pound note. 'I've money. I can pay you in advance.'

The woman reached out and quickly took the note. 'You're a lucky man,' she said. 'I just had a cancellation.'

'He followed her into the hall and she closed the door. There was a big, old-fashioned grandfather clock, a table covered in bric-à-brac, the sweet smell of baking bread.

'I'm Mrs O'Malley.'

'Megarry.'

'Will you be needing an evening meal, Mr Megarry?'

'I don't think so. I had something to eat on the train.'

'Breakfast in the morning?'

'Yes.'

She produced a register for him to sign. 'I'll put you in Number Three. It's in the back so it's nice and quiet. Not that there's any noise anyway. All my visitors are quiet. We don't allow singing, drinking or uninvited guests.' She gave him a hard look. 'People have to get their sleep. Enjoy your stay, Mr Megarry. If there's anything you need, I'll be in the kitchen.'

She left him and he made his way along a corridor to Number Three. He ran the shower, got undressed and stood for a long while under the hot water, feeling it wash all the tiredness out of his body. Then he dried himself, lay down on the bed and listened to the sounds the sea made as it sucked against the shore.

He thought of Kathleen. He knew she'd worry about him, even though she hadn't complained. She didn't like this sort of thing, rushing off across the country on the spur of the moment. He decided to ring her later.

Eventually he got dressed and went back to the kitchen. Mrs O'Malley was drinking tea and watching television with a small man in a cardigan.

She looked up as he came in and put down her cup. 'Yes?' she said.

'Can I speak to you? Privately?' He struggled with his good arm to extract his old RUC identity card and lowered his voice. 'I'm a policeman.'

She glanced nervously at the man in the cardigan, got up and led Megarry out into the hall.

'It's to do with someone who might have stayed here. A man called John Delaney. He says he was here on the weekend of April 20th.'

Mrs O'Malley looked relieved. 'Oh him. He was here all right.'

'How can you be sure?'

Because some detectives came a couple of days ago, asking about him. We went through the register. He was here three nights. Friday, Saturday and Sunday. It's in the book. Do you want me to get it for you?'

'There's no need,' he said quickly. Could you describe him for me?'

'It's a few weeks ago. I see a lot of people.'

'It's important. Someone else might have stayed here and used his name to establish an alibi. To make it appear that he was here, when he was really somewhere else.'

'Right,' Mrs O'Malley said. 'Let me see now. I only have the two singles and Mr Clancy had the other one. Number Four. He's a commercial traveller and he stays once a month. He was here on the Friday so I had to put the other man into Number Three. That's the room you have now. He came about five o'clock. He must have got the early train from Dublin. He had a brown leather grip-bag.' Her face suddenly brightened. 'I've got him now. Medium height. Black hair. Untidy. A bit on the scruffy side, to tell you the truth.'

Megarry thought of the man he had interviewed in Bray station, the dirty blue anorak and jeans, the unkempt hair, the unshaven chin.

'What sort of accent did he have?'

'Dublin.'

'What did he do while he was here?'

'Slept mainly. He was out most of the time. Said he had come for a bit of a break. He'd got some friends in town. He used to get up in the morning and have his breakfast and then he'd be gone for the day. To tell you the truth, I hardly ever saw him.'

'One more thing,' Megarry said. 'Was he alone?'

'Yes.'

'No woman?'

112

'Definitely not. I told you I put him in one of my singles.'
'Did he bring a woman back with him at any stage?'
'Good Lord, no,' she said. 'That's against the rules.'

She stopped, slowly reached a hand to touch Megarry's sleeve. 'This Delaney man? Did he do something bad?'

He went back to his room, put on his tie and went into town. He checked the witnesses that Delaney had produced, a barman in the Scotch House down near the quays and a friend whose phone number he had given. Both confirmed that Delaney had been in town that weekend. Both confirmed that he had been on his own. No one remembered seeing a woman.

At last he found himself in a little pub near the Spanish Arch. The place was crowded with young people. There was a group of musicians playing jigs and reels, half a dozen couples dancing sets on the hard stone floor. Megarry ordered a pint and settled down to watch.

He felt disappointed. It had been a waste of time, a journey half-way across Ireland that had come to nothing. But behind the disappointment was an angrier feeling of frustration, as though Delaney had somehow outwitted him. He remembered the interview at Bray station, the cockiness, the self-assurance, the ease with which the alibi had spilled from Delaney's lips. He had seen that kind of confidence before. It was the mark of a man who felt himself on the high ground, untouchable, immune, secure. A man who felt invincible but was nevertheless lying.

He bought another drink and nursed it till the dancers gave way and the music fell silent and the people began to drift from the pub. He left shortly after 1 a.m. and walked back by the shore of the bay. The house was in darkness when he arrived. He remembered Mrs O'Malley's injunction not to make noise, so he took off his shoes in the hall and walked in his stocking feet to his room. As he opened the door, he saw that something had been propped up against the mirror of the dressing-table. It was a piece of paper, left there while he was out.

It was a note from the landlady. He saw her name scrawled along the bottom of the page. He screwed up his eyes and started to read. It was a simple message. One line.

'There was a woman,' the note said.

The following morning, the sun woke him just as the hands on his watch said 7 a.m. There was an early morning chill in the room. He had forgotten to close the window when he got back the night before.

He drew his bandaged arm from under the sheets and held it up, expecting the familiar drag of pain. But the pain had vanished in the night. He clenched his fist and turned his arm from left to right. It felt the way it always had. Thank God for small mercies, he thought, and got out of bed.

There was a smell of cooking bacon. It seemed to be all over the house. He dressed and went out to the dining-room and sat at a table near the window where he could see out across the bay. There was a radio crooning on the sideboard, two German tourists studying a map at another table just inside the door.

Megarry nodded a greeting, sat down and waited. A minute later, Mrs O'Malley came smiling in with a coffee urn.

'Beautiful morning, Mr Megarry. I take it you slept well?'

'Like a log.'

She looked pleased. 'You must have a clear conscience, so.'

'I wouldn't go that far.'

She poured a cup of coffee, pulled out a chair and sat down.

'I remembered as soon as you'd gone. There *was* a woman, but she didn't come in. It was the Saturday afternoon. Mr Delaney had gone out as usual after breakfast and then soon afterwards the rain started. I heard a car stop outside the door. It was Mr Delaney back again. He was the passenger. The driver was a woman. A young woman, well-dressed.'

Megarry slowly stirred a spoon in the coffee cup.

'Mr Delaney went to his room and came out with a briefcase. Then he got back into the car and they drove away.'

'Did you see her again?'

'No.'

'What sort of car was it?'

'A silver hatchback. Dublin registration. I remember that. It's one of the things you do without thinking in this business, is check the car registrations.'

114

Mrs O'Malley folded her arms beneath her heavy breast and looked satisfied.

'This woman. Did you get a good look at her?'

'Sure.'

He put down the coffee cup and took out his wallet. He flipped it open and took out the photograph of Mary Grogan.

'Is that her?'

Mrs O'Malley pushed her glasses hard against her nose and peered at the print. He held his breath and then he saw her slowly shake her head.

'Oh no,' she said. 'That's not her. That's not her at all. This one was blonde.'

12

He got home just before midday. As he opened the front door he could hear voices, people talking. He looked into the front room and found Kathleen and her sister and a group of women sitting round a table with notebooks and pens. They were drinking tea.

Kathleen came out to the hall and closed the door.

'Did you find what you were looking for?'

'Up to a point.'

'You didn't, Cecil. I can tell.'

'All right,' he conceded. 'It was a wild-goose chase.'

She looked at him, the crumpled suit, soiled shirt, unshaven chin.

'You look like you've been knocked down by a bus. You shouldn't do things like that, Cecil, dashing off without even a change of clothes.'

'I told you. I didn't have time.'

Kathleen took his hand. 'I wish you'd slow down, Cecil. You know I worry.'

He put his arms around her, kissed her full mouth. 'There's no need. I'm feeling great. Fit as a fiddle.' He held up his bandaged arm. 'This is getting better. The pain is gone.'

He made for the stairs. 'I missed you. Thought about you the whole time.'

'Like hell you did.'

'No. Honest. How's Annie?'

'She's up and about. I don't think she's going to stay there much longer. She's prowling the room like a caged tigress.'

Megarry smiled.

'Peter Kelly called. Wants you to give him a ring. Oh, and Trish Blake. She's in our group. Says you spoke to her before.'

'Ahhh . . . The woman in Paradise Regained?'

'That's her. She wants to talk to you.'

'What about?'

Kathleen shrugged. 'She didn't say.'

He went upstairs, shaved and put on fresh clothes. Then he rang Kelly.

'Any luck?' Kelly asked. Megarry caught the note of expectation in his voice.

'He was there all right.'

'Any lady friend?'

'Yes, there was a woman. But it wasn't Mary Grogan.'

'Ah, well,' Kelly said and sounded disappointed. 'We'll just have to persevere. I've got two guys tailing him, but they haven't come up with anything yet.'

'You think he's clean?'

'Well, he's behaving like a regular Joe. Leaves for work at the pork butcher's at 7.30 a.m. Goes to the local pub for lunch. Home by 6 p.m. Regular as clockwork.'

'What about the evenings?'

'Parties a lot. Hangs around with some trendy crowd. You know. Poets, piss artists. That sort of clientele.'

'Where is this pub?' Megarry asked, and checked his watch.

'The Dublin Belle. It's in Talbot Street. Do you know it?'

'I'll find it,' Megarry said.

He called at Paradise Regained on his way into town. It sat snug against the cliff, like a fort or a battlement built to repel invaders. There was a breeze coming up from the sea, cool against his face. As he approached the house, he saw the way it tossed the heads of the daffodils in the little front garden.

Trish Blake came to the door in an agitated state, her face pale, eyes staring. She looked like she'd been weeping.

'Thank God you could come,' she said. 'I only heard this morning. I can't believe this.'

'Heard what?' Megarry asked gently.

'About Mary.' She stopped and pointed to where the sea was rolling against the rocks. 'That it was Mary's head that was found down there. I can't get over this. It's like a nightmare.'

'You knew her?'

'Of course. She was my best friend.'

For a moment the sea seemed to sound louder, a tumult of noise crashing against the shore.

He followed her into the kitchen.

'I heard it on the radio,' Trish Blake said. 'There was a police alert. Jesus, to think we sat here just the other day and talked about it and I didn't even know.'

'None of us did,' Megarry said. 'How long did you know her?'

Her hand trembled as it went to her face. 'Since she came to live here. About four years ago. And now to hear this. Just smack on the radio. Like it was the weather forecast. I can't believe it.'

Megarry sat down and took out his cigarettes. 'Do you smoke?'

'Occasionally.'

'Here.' He offered the packet and flicked the lighter into flame.

Trish Blake inhaled smoke, sat back and pushed a lock of hair from her face. 'It *is* really her?' she said. 'There's no doubt?'

'I'm afraid not,' Megarry said. 'We've identified her.'

Trish Blake took out a handkerchief and dabbed her eyes. 'I'm sorry,' she said. 'But I can't take this in.'

Megarry waited.

'How did you get to know her?'

'Through the women's group. Mary was renting when she first came here, before she bought Crow's Nest and got it restored. I met her one Sunday afternoon in the Lighthouse bar and we hit it off right away. I was involved with the women's group and Mary joined too. She was very active at first. Threw herself into all sorts of work. She believed that women like her,

118

with a good education and a good job, had a duty to help less fortunate women.'

'You said she *was* very active?'

'Yes. She dropped out about a year ago.'

'Why?'

'Pressure on her time, I suppose. She was working very hard at her job. She had her painting circle. And her social life. She enjoyed that. She didn't want to give it up.'

'Painting circle?'

'Mary ran a painting circle. Mainly local people. She was a very good artist.'

'I've seen her work.' Megarry tapped ash from his cigarette. 'You know, we're treating this as murder. She'd been shot before being dismembered.'

'God.' Trish Blake shuddered. 'This just gets worse.' She dabbed her eyes again. 'Do you know why . . .?'

'Not yet. How much did you know about her social life?'

'It was mainly the yacht club and people she knew through work.'

'Men friends?'

Trish Blake nodded. 'Loads of them. She was very attractive to men. She had so much energy, you see. And she was very sure of herself. I think that appealed to a certain type of man. And she didn't care whether or not they were married. We used to argue about that.'

'You did?'

'Yes. I thought it was immoral and unfair. She was supposed to be a feminist. I used to think about these men's wives. Mary cheating with their husbands. I love my husband very much. If another woman came between us, it would break my heart. But Mary didn't care. She had double standards that way. And she was callous. Mary could be hard as old boots when she wanted to.'

'Did you know a man called Brian Casey?'

'Sure. They were a regular pair for a while.'

'There was talk of an engagement.'

'Was there? I didn't hear about that. I don't think Mary was the marrying type. She was enjoying herself too much.'

'Do you know why it broke up?'

'She took up with somebody else.'

'Was he married?'

'I think so.'

'Do you know his name?'

'No. She didn't say.'

'And was this affair going on at the time of her death?'

Trish Blake swallowed. 'I don't know. Once she took up with him, it ceased to be a subject of conversation. She knew how I felt. I just refused to talk about it.'

'How did Brian Casey react?'

'He took it very badly. He was devastated, in fact. I think he had some sort of breakdown. Mary used to laugh about it. Said he was too possessive. She said she was well rid of him.'

'When did you see her last?'

'About a month ago. We had lunch.'

'What sort of mood was she in? Anything bothering her?'

'No, quite the contrary. She was organising an exhibition. She was very excited.' Trish Blake stopped and wiped a tear from her eye. 'That's how I'll always remember her. Sitting at that little table in Luigi's. At least I have a good memory of her. Even though Mary could be a bitch, she had a loving side. A good nature. She could be very generous.'

'And you had no contact since then?'

'No.'

'Did you not find that odd?'

'Not at all. I'd often go for long periods without hearing from her.'

Megarry crushed out his cigarette. 'Did she have enemies?'

'Not serious enemies. She upset people from time to time. She was very assertive and some people don't like that, but we all do it.'

'Do you know any reason why someone should want to do this?'

Trish Blake shook her head. 'I've been trying to figure that out all morning. Ever since I heard that radio bulletin.'

'We found a severed doll's head in her cottage. It's a strange coincidence, given what happened to her. Maybe someone sent it as a warning. Maybe the killer. Did she ever mention that?'

Trish Blake turned pale. 'Jesus, no. That's the first I've heard of it.'

'Is there anything you know that might help us with our investigation? Even small things can sometimes be useful.'

'I don't think so. I've been racking my brains for a reason. The whole business is . . .' She stopped. 'Just unbelievable.'

She went with him to the door.

He started to walk to his car, shimmering in the afternoon heat. As he approached he saw a gate and, behind it, the beginnings of a path. He stopped.

'Where does that lead?'

'Down to the sea.'

He looked back to where the car was parked on the road. He opened the gate. It was rusty and had to be forced. He could see that the path was overgrown with weeds and grass.

'Is it used much?'

'By kids. In the summer. The mackerel fishing is good down there.'

Megarry let his eye travel down to the rocks, the channel in the sea where the head was found.

'It's very dangerous,' Trish Blake said. 'A young lad fell last year and broke his leg. We were thinking of fencing it off to prevent them going down. But it's not our property, you see. It's a right of way.'

'Right,' Megarry said and walked back to the car.

The Dublin Belle had once been an old working-men's pub, but a development company had bought it, ripped it apart and put it together again in the style of what they imagined was a Dublin pub of the Victorian era.

Now it boasted chandeliers, brass footrests, polished counters, bric-à-brac and political posters on the walls proclaiming 'Home Rule for Ireland'. There were lots of these pubs springing up now, dealing in fake nostalgia, and normally Megarry avoided them, preferring the gloomy discomfort of the real thing. But the service here turned out to be fast and friendly. He had barely seated himself near the door when a young waiter in a long white apron swooped to take his order. He bought a pint of Guinness and settled down to wait.

The pain in his arm was completely gone, replaced by an irritating itch, and he had dispensed with the sling. He looked quickly around the bar. It was filling up with lunch-time trade, young men and women from the nearby financial centre with smart business suits and mobile phones, jostling for space at the food counter. There was a buzz of electricity in the air. Someone had left a newspaper on the seat beside him and he opened it. All at once his heart sank.

'New Link in Howth Murder Inquiry' the headline ran, and below it was a smiling picture of Imelda Lacy. He studied it. She looked so young and innocent, barely more than a child, laughing at a party, her arm around someone's shoulder. The photograph had been cropped to exclude her partner.

The report covered half the front page. It detailed the arrest of Boylan without mentioning his name. There was another picture of Mary Grogan and an appeal for information. A sidebar story claimed the police now believed the same man was responsible for both murders. Megarry cursed, folded the paper and put it away in his pocket.

As he did so, the door swung open and a shaft of sunlight cut across the bar. Delaney stood in the doorway. He paused for a moment to take in his surroundings, then marched quickly to the counter. He had put on his anorak and underneath, Megarry could see the butcher's bloodstained vest. A barman called out his name and moved to get him a drink. Delaney picked up a toothpick from a jar, stuck it in his mouth and began to chew.

Megarry slid from his seat and went to the counter.

'Can I buy you a drink?' he said softly.

Delaney swung round. The colour drained from his face. 'You?' he said. 'What the hell . . .?'

Megarry smiled. 'I'm offering to buy you a drink.'

'You can stick your offer. This is harassment.'

'Harassment?' Megarry said innocently. 'C'mon now, John.'

'You're persecuting me. Following me around. That's police harassment in anybody's book. That's illegal.'

'Hold on a minute,' Megarry said. 'You're going a wee bit far. I just came in here for a quiet drink and I happen to see you, so

I'm being sociable. What's the matter with you? You got a bump on your brain or something?'

'I told you everything the last time,' Delaney protested. 'You can't keep doing this to me. I have my rights.' He looked around for a means to escape, but Megarry blocked his way.

'You're being foolish. I can interview you any time I want. I could call at your place of work if I wanted. But I'm being considerate. I don't want to cause problems for you. What would your employer, Mr McGurk, think if he found out you were featuring in a murder inquiry?' Megarry signalled to the barman for a whiskey. 'Well?' he said. 'What will it be? You mightn't get this offer again.'

'I'll have a pint of stout,' Delaney said reluctantly. 'But I'm paying for it myself.'

Megarry saw the door open and a youngish man in a blue serge suit come in and stare at them, then walk to the end of the bar. Kelly's tail had arrived.

'Why don't we sit down?' Megarry said. He gestured to the seat he had just vacated. 'It's quieter there. No one to hear us.'

Delaney took his drink and followed. He glanced at his watch. 'Make it snappy,' he sighed. 'I've only got half an hour.'

'This won't take long. Just a few small points I want to clarify.'

'Like what?'

'Mary Grogan.'

'Jesus,' Delaney said. 'Not that again.'

'Afraid so.'

'I told you before. I don't know the woman.'

'I brought a photograph,' Megarry said.

He opened his wallet. At the other end of the room, the man in the serge suit was pretending to watch the racing on television. Megarry passed the photograph over and Delaney glanced at it quickly before handing it back.

'No,' he said.

'You hardly looked at it,' Megarry said and pushed the photograph back.

Once more, Delaney took it and this time he made a pretence of studying it, turning it sideways and examining it, before putting it down again on the table. He shook his head.

'Never saw her before in my life.'

'Look at me.' Megarry caught the other man's eye and held it. Delaney stared back, defiant.

'If you're lying, I'll have your ass, so help me.'

'I don't know her, for Christ's sake. How many times have I got to tell you?'

'Let me show you something else,' Megarry said. He took the newspaper from his pocket and spread it on the table. 'You seen this?'

Delaney's face went pale. His hands trembled as he gulped his beer.

'That's all lies,' he said. 'They're making that up. I don't believe a word of it.'

'Neither do I,' Megarry said and folded the paper away. 'But it shows the way people's minds are working. Why don't you tell me the truth?'

Delaney squirmed in his seat. 'What is there to tell? This all started because I asked Imelda Lacy for a date. I wish to God I'd never set eyes on her. She's caused me nothing but grief. Her brothers beat me up, drove me out of my home. And now you guys are persecuting me.'

'I'm simply making inquiries,' Megarry said. 'No one's accused you of anything.'

'I told the Bray cops. I wasn't even around the night she was killed. I had nothing to do with it. I swear on my mother's grave.'

'Tell me about Galway,' Megarry said. 'This trip you took a few weeks back. What was that all about?'

Delaney shrugged. 'It was just a break. I know some people down there. I gave you their names, for God's sake.'

'I forgot,' Megarry said. 'Any women friends?'

'Jesus. What is this? Women, women, women. You got sex on the brain or something?'

'Have you any women friends in Galway?'

'One or two.'

'A blonde woman who drives a silver hatchback? Dublin registration. She brought you to the guesthouse on the Saturday afternoon.'

Delaney stared.

'Who is she?' Megarry insisted.

'You've been checking on me?'

'Of course. What did you expect?'

'Fuck it,' Delaney said. 'I want her kept out of this. You hear? She's got nothing to do with me.'

'Who is she?'

'She's a woman I met in a pub down there. That's all.'

'You picked her up?'

'What are you? Some kind of pervert? She was on her own. Just like me. She was down for the weekend. Looking for a bit of R and R. We got together.'

'Is she married? Is that why you're trying to protect her?'

'Yes,' Delaney said quickly.' Now you've got it.'

'Tell me.'

'She's got relatives in Galway, for God's sake. She told her husband she was going down to visit them. It's good cover.'

Megarry glanced along the bar. The plain-clothes man had shifted his position and was watching them intently.

'What's her name?'

'I just told you I don't want to get her involved.'

'It'll go no further.'

Delaney sighed. 'Deirdre O'Shea,' he said. He lifted his glass and regarded Megarry over the rim.

'Have you an address for her? Phone number?'

'Hell, no. Nothing like that.'

'Have you seen her since you came back to Dublin?'

'I just told you. It was only a weekend fling. It wasn't serious.' Delaney finished his drink and made to stand up. 'I have to get back to work now.'

As he put his glass down on the table, something caught Megarry's eye. He reached out and held Delaney's hand. In close, where the nails joined the tips of his fingers, there were little grains of something flaky.

'You've been doing some painting?'

'Yes.'

'As in painting and decorating?'

Delaney's face grew dark. 'No. As in Leonardo da fucking Vinci.'

'You won't have another drink?'

'Are you kidding?'

Megarry watched him get up and hurry out of the pub. As he turned he saw the plain-clothes man approach.

'You know that guy?' he asked.

Megarry looked at him. It would take too long to explain and it wouldn't help.

'Of course. He's a butcher. I'm planning a barbecue. I was ordering a couple of pounds of ribs.'

Back at the station, as Megarry turned into the parking bay he found a mêlée in progress. There was a camera crew, a jostling mob of reporters and, in the middle of it all, Kelly struggling to escape.

'Please,' he was saying. 'There's no more I can tell you. It's all in the press release.'

'Is there a link between the two murders?' an energetic young man with a microphone shouted.

'I'm sorry. I can tell you nothing more.'

'For God's sake,' a voice groaned. 'Women are getting murdered. Is that the best you can bloody well do?'

Megarry turned to see a portly man with a bow tie and a red face. He had a notebook in his hand. He began to push forward.

'Excuse me,' the man said. 'Out of my way.'

Megarry blocked his path.

'Out of my way,' the man repeated. 'I'm the *Echo*.'

'I don't give a damn who you are. You're going no further.'

The man stared in amazement, streams of sweat pouring down his face. 'I beg your pardon?'

'You heard me.'

From the corner of his eye, Megarry could see Kelly retreating towards the station entrance, reporters and cameramen following in a scrum. The portly man began to follow.

'Out of my way.' He put his hand on Megarry's shoulder and tried to push him aside. Megarry leaned forward, grabbed the man by the lapels.

'You want your ass in a bucket?'

'What?'

'You want me to arrest you for obstruction?'

The man gasped. 'You can't do that.'

'Why don't you try me? There's a murder inquiry under way. You're obstructing it. Now if you don't want to eat your supper off an aluminium dish, I suggest you be a good man and take yourself off. Right?'

Megarry released him and pushed his way through the crowd. With the help of the desk sergeant, he slammed the front door shut. Kelly was in his office, tie undone, face pale.

'Jesus,' Megarry said. 'How did that happen?'

'I got ambushed. Guy from RTE rang looking for an interview. He's been pestering me for days. I told him okay, I'd see him at two o'clock. Next thing, the sergeant tells me there's a crowd of reporters outside. I went out to see what was going on and bang, I'm in the middle of a riot.' He took out a handkerchief and wiped his face.

'I told you not to deal with them,' Megarry said. 'They're treacherous bastards. All they're interested in is getting a good story. I told you to let the Press Office handle it. Were those TV cameras running? Did anybody get pictures?'

'I don't think so.'

'Let's hope not. You saw this, I suppose?' He took the newspaper out of his pocket.

Kelly sighed. 'That's what started it.'

Megarry went to the percolator, poured two cups and gave one to Kelly. He sat down.

'Right. Here's the drill. No more interviews. Any reporter turns up here at the station, you give him two minutes to get off the premises or you bust his ass. Has the superintendent been on to you yet?'

Kelly shook his head.

'Give him time. This sort of thing just serves to rattle their cages higher up the line. You'll just have to keep your nerve. Has the radio appeal brought any response?'

Kelly sipped his coffee. 'Quite a bit. She seemed to know a lot of people. I've got a team working on it.'

'All right. I talked to Delaney again. He says the woman he was with in Galway was a casual he picked up. He says her name is Deirdre O'Shea. I think he's lying. See if someone can check her out.'

'Do we know where she lives?'

'He wouldn't say.'

'Jesus, Cecil. That's like looking for a needle in a haystack.'

'I know that. Delaney knows it too. Just see what you can do. And keep the surveillance on him.'

'Anything else?'

'These men friends of Mary Grogan's? Any luck?'

'We've talked to them. They're all clean. I've told Brian Casey we want to see him. And we've located Joyce Denvir. She teaches in a school on the southside. Blackrock College for Girls.'

'Good. We'll talk to her too.'

Megarry finished his coffee. As he put the cup down, he heard a cough. Both men turned to look. Annie Lawlor was standing in the doorway.

Megarry's mouth opened in surprise.

'What the hell are you doing here? You're supposed to be in bed.'

Lawlor grinned. She strode into the room and stood in front of Kelly's desk. She moved her neck from side to side. The bandage was gone.

'Look,' she said. 'I've been cured. It's a miracle.' She put her arm around Kelly and kissed him. 'Thank you for saving my life.'

'Saving your life?'

'You disarmed that bastard, didn't you?'

Kelly blushed.

She sat down beside Megarry and peered closely into his face. 'Glad to see me?'

'Of course. But are you okay?'

'What do you think, Cecil? There was nothing wrong with me in the first place. A few bruises is all. You'd get more injuries fighting your way to the bar in the Garda Club of a Saturday night.'

'What did the doctor say?'

'Doctors! What do they know about anything? They just make it up most of the time. What do you want me to do? A dozen press-ups? There's nothing wrong with me, I'm telling you.'

Kelly puffed out his cheeks. 'You discharged yourself, didn't you?'

Lawlor lowered her eyes.

'Did you, Annie?' Megarry said.

'Hell,' Lawlor said. 'I was bored out of my tree. Doctors, nurses fussing from morning to night, taking my blood pressure, sticking bed-pans under my ass. How would you like it?'

'I don't suppose I'd like it at all,' Megarry said. 'But you have to remember . . .'

'Shit, Cecil. I'm reporting for duty. How's the case going? Have you nailed that bastard Boylan yet?'

'I'll tell you everything in the car. C'mon.'

She glanced at Kelly. 'Where are we going?'

'Crow's Nest Cottage. I want to give that place a proper going-over.'

'There's a few things we need to get straight,' Megarry said as they settled into the car. 'First of all, you should *not* have discharged yourself from hospital. Just say something happens to you? Kelly could find his ass in a sling. Technically, he's responsible for you.'

Lawlor shrugged. 'I'm a grown woman. I'm responsible for myself.'

'Secondly, we've referred Boylan for a psychiatric report. I've doubts about his sanity.'

'You what?'

'You heard me.'

She turned in her seat. 'But that's just a cop-out.'

'It's not. It's a precaution. If Boylan's sane, he'll stand trial. We have him bang to rights. We've got witnesses. We've got a confession. There'll be no contest. But I don't want Kelly to prepare a case against him and then have it collapse because Boylan's defence team can prove he's only fit for the funny farm.'

'Hell, Cecil. That bastard tried to cut me up. You're saying I put myself through all that hassle just so some shrink can tell us there's air getting in?'

'What I'm saying, Annie, is that we're going to do this thing right.'

'And what about all those women he assaulted? You mean he's going to get away with that?'

'He'll get away with nothing. One way or another he's going down.'

'What about the murder?'

'I don't think he did it.'

Lawlor stared. 'I don't believe this,' she said.

West Heath was bathed in sunlight when they arrived. It stretched before them all the way across to Shielmartin Hill, brooding tall and majestic at the edge of the sea. They left the car at the quarry and started across the bridle-path to Crow's Nest Cottage.

On their right, they could see the grim outline of the Dudgeon house. It stood like some bleak outpost, the vast moor trembling behind it. There was a curl of smoke from the chimney, but no other sign of life. Megarry wondered if the old woman was there, seated where he had seen her last by the window, the blind eyes staring now as they went past.

When they came to Crow's Nest Cottage, Megarry stopped, his hand on the gate. Behind the cottage, he could see the washing still hanging forlornly from the clothesline. With Mary Grogan dead, it could remain there forever. He strode across and gathered it into a bundle in his arms and brought it towards the house.

As he approached, he saw that the ground was carpeted with tiny fragments of glass, scattered like confetti. There was more on the sill and a gaping hole in the kitchen window.

'Kids,' Lawlor muttered. 'It's amazing. They can spot a deserted place a mile off. You'd think they'd got some kind of radar system.'

Megarry bent to examine the damage. There was no sign of a stone or other missile. 'This wasn't kids,' he said. 'This was done with a hammer or some tool like that.'

130

Something else drew his attention. The snib holding the entire window had been prised open and now hung loose. It was obvious that the pane had been broken to gain entry.

'Someone's been in here,' he said. 'Don't touch anything. We'll have to get the fingerprint people out.' He took the key they had found on the previous visit and moved quickly to the front door.

There was the familiar silence in the empty house. The odour of dust and trapped air. But there was something new. Megarry sniffed. There was the smell of tobacco smoke. He looked down and saw a cigarette end crushed out on the hallway floor. He picked it up.

'Whoever was in here isn't too fussy about where they stub out their dog-ends.'

He examined the butt. There was about half an inch of cigarette remaining and the faint lettering of the brand name was still visible. He put down the washing and Lawlor went past him into the house.

The place appeared as they had left it. They opened a door and entered the spare bedroom. The bed was neatly made, a coating of dust visible across the top of the dressing-table, the flowers in a little vase by the window now dead and wilting. He thought of the happy moments Mary Grogan must have spent in this cottage, the laughter, the mornings she had wakened to see the sun spilling in from the heath. He closed the door and went back into the hall.

They tried each room in turn. Everything seemed to be in order. In the bathroom, Megarry noticed that the spider had returned, squatting near the plughole of the tub. It scurried away as he approached. It was only when they opened the door to Mary Grogan's office that the full extent of the damage became apparent.

The filing cabinets had been flung open, and files and papers scattered all over the floor. Drawers hung crookedly from the desk, their contents spilled out. It was as if someone had gone through the room systematically taking it apart.

'Jesus,' Lawlor said.

Megarry bent to lift a photocopied paper from the floor. It

was an article from a learned journal. 'Supply and Demand Factors in Small Business Enterprise.' He put the paper on the desk and tried to straighten some of the drawers.

Lawlor exchanged a glance with him. 'What do you think? Someone looking for something? Or someone with a grudge?'

'Maybe both,' Megarry said. He stared once more at the damage. It suggested a certain mind-set, someone in a hurry, who placed no value on the objects in the room.

He left and went back again to examine the other rooms. He paused in the bedroom, looking carefully at the paintings of local landmarks: Howth Castle, Ireland's Eye, the Bailey Lighthouse.

He went into the lounge. There was a painting on the wall but it was a pastoral scene, horses grazing in a broad meadow. He went quickly to the studio. Again it was as he remembered it: the easel, the pots and brushes, the smock hanging limp behind the door. Nothing here had been disturbed. He looked at the painting in execution and saw the heath, Shielmartin Hill in the background.

He returned to the bedroom, slipped on a pair of surgical gloves and began to search. The house was still, the only sound the muffled movements of Lawlor in the other room. He started with the drawers, pulling them out one after another, lifting the contents carefully and then replacing them.

He wasn't sure what he was looking for; some clue perhaps, some indicator of Mary Grogan's life-style, some pointer to why she had met a violent death. He opened the wardrobe, rifled among the dresses and coats, catching their fragrant scent. He felt the pockets. On a shelf above the wardrobe was a collection of hats. He took them down, examined them one by one, put them back again. He was about to close the wardrobe door when something caught his eye.

On the shelf, tucked well into a corner, almost out of sight, was a white plastic bag. He took it down, opened it and withdrew a pair of handcuffs.

He stared for a moment in disbelief. Then he quickly tipped the contents onto the bed. There was a black leather mask, lengths of rope, a leather jump suit and a brown envelope. He opened it.

132

He called out to Lawlor.

'Take a look at these.'

They were photographs of a woman. She was dressed from head to toe in leather. She wore a black balaclava so that only her face was visible. She had been grotesquely made up, lips bright scarlet, eyes dark. In her hand she held a whip and she was in various stages of striking a naked man. He had been tied to a frame and was blindfolded.

Lawlor leafed quickly through the photographs. They showed the woman in different poses, all provocative, mouth and eyes leering seductively. She looked at Megarry. He had taken out the picture of Mary Grogan.

'Tell me if it's just my imagination.'

Lawlor studied the photographs again. There was no doubt. Despite the heavy make-up and the leather clothes, it was clearly the same woman.

13

'Blackmail?' Lawlor said and gave the prints back to Megarry. 'It could be the motive we're looking for.'

Megarry shuffled the photographs, selected one, studied it, took another. 'I'm not sure. It might be nothing. Something they took for their own amusement. It's not illegal, you know. Consenting adults. And if you go down that road, you're ruling out Delaney and you're sure as hell ruling out Boylan.'

'Why?'

'Because this guy has a mark on his left wrist and neither of them has. Here, look again.'

He held out a photograph. 'See it? It's a birthmark or something. And this guy is taller, broader built. His hair is different.'

Lawlor squinted at the picture. Despite the blindfold, there was no denying that the man looked nothing like Delaney or Boylan.

'Want to start again?' Megarry said. 'God knows who this guy is. Mary Grogan was promiscuous. I have that from her best friend. He could be anybody. Like I said, this could mean nothing. Just something they did for kicks.'

'All right,' Lawlor said. 'Let's try to be rational. Let's say this guy is a respectable member of the community. Married. Regular church-goer. Pillar of the establishment sort of thing.

Gets up to a little bit of hanky-panky with Ms Grogan, thinking it's all private and between themselves. Foolishly allows himself to be photographed. Let's say . . .'

'Let's say my aunt had balls. She'd be my uncle.'

'Cecil, listen. At some stage, she presents him with the photographs and makes some demand on him. In desperation, he decides that the only way out is to kill her.'

Megarry was shaking his head. 'Why should she want to do that?'

'The usual reason. Money.'

'She didn't need money. She was very well off. Is it likely she would risk her career for some crazy blackmail stunt?'

'Unrequited love?' Lawlor ventured. 'Let's say the guy in the photographs had agreed to leave his wife for Mary Grogan and then backed out of the deal. Revealing the pictures could have been her way of reminding him.'

'But would it be enough to drive him to murder?'

'Depends who he is. Depends how desperate.'

'And what about the break-in?'

'The murderer trying to recover the photographs?'

'No,' Megarry said. 'Whoever broke into the house was after something else. These weren't particularly well concealed. Anybody looking for them could have found them easily.'

'So you tell me. What *was* the burglar looking for?'

Megarry sighed. 'I wish I knew.'

However, when they got back to the station he went in at once to see Kelly.

'Who do you know in Vice?' he asked wearily.

Kelly looked confused. 'Vice, Cecil?'

'We found this lot in Crow's Nest Cottage.' Megarry put the bag on the desk, took out the mask, the leather suit, the handcuffs, the rope and finally the packet of photographs.

Kelly examined them, sat back and a grin broke on his face. 'Well, I'll be damned. S and M on Howth Summit. You know, Cecil, people said when they brought in divorce, it wouldn't stop there. I take it this is Mary Grogan?'

'That's right.'

Kelly chortled. 'And who's the lucky man?'

'I don't know. Lawlor thinks it might be blackmail.'

'Sounds reasonable.'

'I'm not convinced. The man in the photographs doesn't fit either of our two main suspects. I still see Delaney as our principal guy. I think he's lying about Mary Grogan and this woman he says he met in Galway.'

'Right,' Kelly said. He opened a drawer and leafed through a notebook. 'The man you're looking for is Charlie Strong. You want me to ring him for you?'

'No. I'll do it myself.' Megarry searched in his pockets for his cigarettes. Kelly watched from behind the desk.

'Can I make an observation, Cecil? Purely an observation and made with the best possible motive?'

'Sure.'

'For a man who's just had a heart attack, I think you're smoking too much.'

Megarry hesitated, a cigarette half-way to his mouth. 'You ever smoke?'

'No. Thank God. I never got started.'

'So you don't know what you're talking about. In fact, you're full of shit.' He paused. 'One other thing you should know. Somebody broke into Crow's Nest Cottage. Turned the place upside-down. Looks like the Parachute Regiment's just been through it.'

He put the cigarettes back in his pocket and left the room.

He rang Inspector Strong from the main office.

'My name's Megarry. Peter Kelly said you might be able to help.'

'Shoot,' Strong said. He had a broad Dublin accent which, Megarry had discovered, was rare in the force. Most of the cops he'd encountered were from the sticks.

'You know anything about leather clubs?'

'Sure,' Strong said. 'We've got everything in this town. It's not illegal, you know.'

'I'm investigating a murder.'

'An S and M murder?'

'I'm not sure.'

'Most of this stuff is innocent,' Strong said. 'Most of these people are harmless. They just like dressing up. Beats me what they see in it, but there you are. Whatever rings your gong, I suppose. There's a place in Richmond Close. You know it?'

'No.'

'It's over in the Liberties. A place called the Strangled Dwarf. Strange name for a club, what?'

'I find the whole thing strange.'

'It's a private club. You'll need a warrant.'

'I'll look after that,' Megarry said.

He went home. Kathleen was cooking; a sweet smell of onions and peppers filled the house. He went upstairs, showered and changed into jeans and a black leather jacket which he'd kept from his days in RUC Special Branch.

He poured a glass of wine, went out to the garden and sat on the wooden bench. The evening was coming down, the sun sinking behind Shielmartin Hill. There was a sound of birdsong, a dying echo from the trees at the bottom of the lawn.

Kathleen came and sat beside him. 'You're going out again?'

'Yes.'

'How much longer is it going to take?'

Megarry sighed. 'I don't know. The further I get into it, the more complicated it becomes.'

He waved a hand across the overgrown garden. In the gathering darkness, they could see the weeds sprouting through the grass, the brambles encroaching into the hedge. 'I'm sorry about this, Kathleen. I know I promised. I'll clean it up first chance I get.'

'Don't worry about it,' she said. 'The garden can wait.'

He took her in his arms, smelt her scent. There was a little line of freckles across her forehead. He bent his lips and kissed them.

'You're beautiful,' he said. 'From the first day I ever saw you.'

She laid her head across his chest. He took her hand. 'C'mon,' he said. 'Let's go upstairs.'

'What about dinner?'

'Turn the oven down. We'll eat later.'

Richmond Close was a narrow lane that ran off Thomas Street in the shadow of Christchurch Cathedral. It was one of the oldest parts of the city, the site of an early Viking settlement and later the home of the trade guilds that sprang up in the fourteenth century. Recently, the City fathers had decided on a restoration plan with a view to making the area a tourist attraction.

As he started down the cobbled street, Megarry could see the lights dancing off the river, the broad sweep of the once magnificent Dublin quays, fallen now into decay. He smelt the sweet cloying odour of malted hops carried on the breeze from the Guinness brewery.

Richmond Close seemed to consist mainly of solicitors' offices, antique shops and coffee-houses. There was a solitary pub with light spilling out onto the street and people drinking noisily on the pavement. He stepped into the roadway to avoid them, then continued, carefully checking the numbers on the doors.

He found it after about five minutes, just as he was about to retrace his steps. There was an intercom and a brass plaque recently screwed into the wall. It bore the grotesque figure of a dwarf, his fat tongue extended, his eyes staring wildly, his face like a gargoyle, contorted in pain. Two hands pressed hard against his neck. 'The Strangled Dwarf', it said. And beneath, 'Private Club'. Megarry pressed the buzzer and waited.

After a few moments, he heard a bolt being withdrawn and a swarthy man in cut-away denim jacket and jeans stared menacingly out at him.

'You a member?' he said. Megarry smelt his breath, a stale confection of tobacco and alcohol.

'No. But I'd like to join.'

Megarry could see the man appraise him.

'It's a private club. You need to be proposed and seconded.'

'I'm a visitor,' Megarry said.

'Where from?'

'Belfast.'

138

'Right', the man said and pulled the door wider. 'In that case, I can give you a temporary membership. It'll cost you twenty pounds.'

Megarry rustled in his pocket for the money and handed it over. The man gave him a form to sign. John Smith, he wrote.

'Right, John,' the man said. 'You're into leather?'

'I like denim more.'

'Ever been in a place like this before?'

'In Amsterdam once.'

'Okay.'

He pointed along a narrow corridor.

'Turn right for the bar. We've a full liquor licence. You're a little bit early. It doesn't normally hot up till after the pubs close. Then it gets *really* lively.' He grinned. 'There's also a lounge. You can watch the video if you like. Enjoy,' he said and clapped Megarry on the back.

There was a door at the end of the corridor. Megarry pushed it open and entered a small room. His immediate impression was of some clapped-out bordello. The lights were dim, the walls painted scarlet and there was a faded oriental carpet on the floor. There were settees and potted plants and in a corner he could see a magnificent parrot in a cage, its plumage a rush of yellow and blue. He went to the bar, pulled up a stool and sat down.

The barman was chatting to a small man in motor-cycle gear who sat at the end of the counter. He looked Megarry over and then casually made his way across. He was heavy-built, in jeans and leather jacket. His chest was bare, his head shaved, and in his lower lip a large silver ring shone in the dim light.

'What will it be?'

'Large Bushmills, please.'

'Ice and water?'

'Yes.'

Megarry pushed a ten-pound note across the counter. 'Keep the change.'

The barman scooped up the money without saying thanks. He leaned his elbows on the bar and considered Megarry. 'You're new,' he said.

'That's right. I just joined.'

'What's your name?'

'John.'

Megarry was aware that the other people in the room were watching him. There was an outrageous transvestite in fishnet stockings and black wig sitting further along the bar and two punk girls with orange hair on a settee behind him.

'Where you from, John?'

'Belfast.'

'Right,' the barman said. 'A tourist. We don't get many tourists. How'd you hear about us?'

Megarry took a sip of the whiskey. It tasted weak, as if someone had already tampered with the bottle.

'A friend. She's a member here. Mary Grogan. You know her?'

The barman ran a plump hand across his unshaven chin. 'Don't think so,' he said.

Megarry took out the photograph and put it down on the bar.

The barman studied it for a moment, then shook his head. 'No,' he said. 'Definitely not.'

'You're sure?'

'Absolutely.'

'That's funny,' Megarry said. 'She told me she was a regular.'

'Sorry,' the barman said. His tone seemed to have changed.

'But this is the only leather club in town, isn't it?'

'How would I know?'

'Well, for one thing, you work here.'

'Listen,' the barman said. 'I tell you I don't know the broad, it means I don't know the broad. Okay?' He turned away and began polishing glasses.

Megarry sipped his drink. Out of the corner of his eye, he saw the transvestite slip down from her stool and come over to join him. She put an arm around his neck.

'You'll buy a girl a drink, won't you, honey?'

'Mind your own business, Lorraine,' the barman interrupted.

Megarry drained his glass and put it down on the counter. 'Same again,' he said. 'What are you having, Lorraine?'

'Large pink gin, please.'

'She's had enough,' the barman said.

'Blow it out your asshole,' Lorraine screamed. 'Your mother's sucking cocks in hell.'

'Give the lady a drink,' Megarry said calmly and put another ten-pound note on the counter.

The barman hesitated, then turned reluctantly and poured the drinks. He put the money in the till and went back to the man in motor-cycle gear at the end of the bar. Megarry watched their heads bend in conversation. Every now and then they stared along the bar, and he knew they were discussing him.

'I couldn't help hearing what you said.' Lorraine began to stroke Megarry's thigh. 'You're looking for someone, right?'

Megarry took her hand and gently replaced it. 'You come here much, Lorraine?'

'Nearly every night, honey.'

'You know most of the people that come here?'

'Sure I do.' Her hand was back on his knee.

'Lorraine, I have to tell you something. I'm straight. Straighter than the Mormon Choir.'

'Don't make no difference. Lots of straight guys like me. And you're nice.' She ran her fingers along his cheek. 'I like blue eyes.'

Megarry sipped his whiskey. It was definitely watered. The barman was skimming the customers.

Lorraine tossed her dark mane and studied her painted fingernails. 'Who's this person you're looking for, honey?'

'Mary Grogan.'

'Don't know no Mary Grogan. What's she look like? Where's that picture you had?'

Megarry slid the photograph along the bar and Lorraine examined it. Then she gave it back.

'That's not Mary Grogan,' she said. 'That's Shirley.'

'Shirley?'

'Yeah. That's what she calls herself.'

'You know her?'

'Sure. She started coming in here a few months ago. Mainly weekends. She's a dom.'

'A dom?'

'A dominatrix, honey. She's into whips and chains. All that old bag of tricks.'

Megarry rattled the ice in his glass. 'Does she come alone?'

'No. She has a boyfriend. Big tall guy with silver hair. Bit like you, honey, only taller. And not so nice. Know what I mean? No personality.'

'Do you know his name?'

'Sure. Calls himself Clive.'

She emptied her glass. 'My, my. Finished already. I'm going to need a refill.'

Megarry looked along the counter but the barman was gone.

'Can you tell me anything about him?'

'Not really, honey. People here don't talk about themselves very much. They like to keep their business private.' She had taken out a cigarette and dangled it from her fingers while she waited for Megarry to light it for her.

'In fact, nearly everybody in here tells lies. You can't believe a word you hear.'

'Is that a fact?'

'Sure. Even you, honey.' She fluttered her eyelids at Megarry. 'You're telling me you're looking for your little friend Mary. But you and I both know she's dead. I saw her picture in the paper.'

Megarry puffed his cheeks and let out a slow jet of air. Just then, he saw Lorraine glance past his shoulder. There was a warning look in her eyes.

He turned quickly but it was too late. He felt a baton jab into his ribs, felt a spasm of pain. The barman and the doorman were standing behind him. He saw the muscles in the doorman's arm ripple like rope as he withdrew the baton and beat it slowly into the palm of his hand.

'It's drinking-up time, John.'

Megarry stared straight ahead. 'But I've only just arrived.'

'We're closing in five minutes.'

The barman took Megarry's whiskey and poured it down the sink. There was an ugly sneer on his face.

'That's against the rules of the club,' Megarry said.

'Rules don't apply to you any more. We're revoking your membership.'

142

'I don't think you can do that.'

'We can do what we damn well like, John.'

The doorman drew the baton back. 'Time to boogie,' he said.

Megarry tensed, put his palms flat on the counter and kicked. He caught the doorman hard on the knee. He heard a crack. The man groaned and limped towards him, baton raised above his head. There was spittle dripping from his mouth. Megarry kicked again and this time his boot crunched into the man's groin. He began to go down.

He felt a searing pain in the side of his face. He turned to see the barman take a glass, smash it against the sink and lunge. He heard Lorraine scream. Megarry quickly stepped aside and as the man went past he saw blood pump from his temple.

Lorraine stood with one high-heeled shoe in her hand. She raised it again and sunk it into the barman's face.

'You bitch!' she screamed. 'You fucking bitch! Why'd you go and do that?'

She kept thumping the shoe into the man's face. It was rapidly turning into a mass of crimson gore. The other people in the club were on their feet now. Everyone was shouting. Megarry grabbed Lorraine's arm and pushed her towards the door.

'You heard the man. Time to boogie.' He propelled her along the corridor and out into the street.

14

The following morning, he was up at 7 a.m., went for a brisk walk, came home, showered and had breakfast. By 8 a.m., Megarry was driving along the coast road towards Lawlor's flat, *en route* to their interview with Brian Casey.

It was a beautiful morning, the sun like a bright orange in the sky, a soft breeze rippling the water where it swept past the shore of Bull Island. In the distance, across the bay, the Dublin mountains shimmered in the morning haze.

Lawlor's flat was on the top floor of a terrace house near Clontarf boat club. As he climbed the stairs, he could smell the coffee brewing. He found her sitting in the kitchen, dressed in jeans and T-shirt. She was eating a croissant smeared with jam.

'Too much sugar rots your teeth,' he said as he sat down across from her.

'That's my problem. You want coffee?'

As she got up to fetch a cup, she noticed the ugly bruise on the side of his cheek and the plaster that he had put on over the cut. She stopped and stared.

'What in the name of God happened to you?'

'I had an altercation with a leather enthusiast. But I met a charming transvestite.'

'Cecil. Be serious.'

'You ever hear of the Strangled Dwarf?'

'Are you making this up?'

'It's a leather club over in the Liberties. Shirley used to go there.'

'Who's Shirley?'

'Mary Grogan's alter ego. She was accompanied by a man called Clive.'

'You must be joking. Nobody's called Clive these days. And you got beaten up?'

Megarry winked over the rim of his coffee cup. 'Let's just say there was a difference of opinion. Mind you, Lorraine held her end up well. For a man in high heels and tights, it wasn't easy.'

He told her what had happened. When he had finished, she ran a finger along his cheek.

'Poor Cecil. You're really taking a lot of knocks.'

'Yes,' Megarry said and finished his coffee. 'I'm thinking of suing the superintendent.'

The television station was on the south side. They drove over the toll bridge, past the docks, ships unloading, cranes, cobbled roads along the quays. They left the car in the car park and walked towards the reception area. As they approached, Megarry touched Lawlor's sleeve.

'This guy was Mary Grogan's boyfriend so he'll know a different side to her. Things that her parents didn't know or her employer. If you want to ask questions, feel free, but let me lead. We want to be singing off the same hymn-sheet at all times. Is that clear?'

She pulled a face. 'Yes, sir.'

'And don't mention the photographs.'

Brian Casey was waiting for them. He was tall and thin with untidy red hair. He had a narrow, nervous face and hollow cheeks. 'We can talk in my office,' Casey volunteered and led them along a corridor to a tiny room with two filing cabinets, a picture hanging crooked on the wall and a desk littered with books and papers.

'Sorry about the mess,' Casey said as he produced two chairs and made a space for them. 'It's just that things are a bit hectic right now. We're in the middle of casting.'

'What's your job?' Megarry inquired.

'I'm a drama producer.'

Megarry waited till Casey had settled himself, then looked across into his eyes. They were eggshell blue, with a way of avoiding Megarry's gaze, staring past him, darting around the room.

Casey tapped a pencil on the desk, tried to steady the quiver in his voice. 'I only heard the other day,' he began. 'It's awful. I just can't believe it.' He lowered his head and they heard him sob.

Megarry gently touched his shoulder, feeling uncomfortable.

'I'm all right,' Casey said. 'It's just . . . To tell you the truth, this breaks my heart. I loved her. I'd no idea it was Mary till I heard the radio appeal. I'm shattered.'

Megarry waited.

'How long did you know her?'

'A couple of years. We went out together. Mary liked to socialise. Dinner parties, receptions, opening nights at the theatre. She liked a good time. She liked to have a man on her arm. And she had the money to indulge herself.'

'What do you mean?'

'Mary was using me. She didn't really care for me.'

'You're sure of that?'

'I'm a romantic, Mr Megarry. I fall in love easily. Unfortunately, some people are more calculating. They don't mind hurting others. They just take it in their stride.'

Megarry glanced at Lawlor. 'You're saying that Mary was calculating?'

'Sure. She was hard as nails. She let nothing stand in her way. If Mary wanted something, she went for it with a single-mindedness that would have terrified you.' He looked away, fiddled with the pencil. 'I should have realised that she wouldn't really want to settle down with someone like me. If Mary was going to marry, she would have set her sights much higher. But I filled a gap for a while. Then, when she'd no further need for me, she dropped me like a hot brick and took off again.'

'Why did the relationship end?'

146

'She was very nice about the whole business. Said we both needed time to think about where the relationship was taking us. By saying that, you see, she roped me into it as well. Made it appear that this was some sort of joint decision. But really it was Mary saying that she wanted to pack me in. What could I do?'

Megarry remembered an earlier conversation with Trish Blake. 'Was there someone else?'

Casey took a deep breath and let the air escape through his teeth.

'I thought so at the time, but now I just don't know. Maybe it *was* just a question of space. Mary had loads of admirers.'

'Did she have enemies?' asked Lawlor.

'A woman like Mary was bound to make enemies. She just had no consideration for other people. It was all me, me, me. That sort of attitude is bound to get up people's noses.'

'Do you know any people she upset?'

Casey looked away. 'Not personally. But I'm sure if you root around among her colleagues you'll come up with something.'

'How close were you?' It was Megarry again.

'We were very close.'

'This is rather embarrassing, Mr Casey. But I have to ask you. Did you have sex with her?'

Casey glanced at Lawlor. 'What's that got to do with her murder?'

'Just answer,' Megarry said.

'Yes.'

'Normal sex?'

'Jesus, what's normal these days? Are you referring to deviations from the missionary position?'

'Did you indulge in any. . . .'

'Kinky stuff?' Casey said and shook his head. 'The answer is no. Mary was a healthy, red-blooded young woman. But that was it. She didn't go in for anything perverse. Not with me, anyway. If that's what you regard as normal sex, Mr Megarry, then Mary was normal in the extreme.'

'Something else,' Megarry asked. 'Do you think she was always faithful to you?'

'Certainly.'

'You never doubted her?'

Casey looked away again, past Megarry's shoulder to the crooked picture on the wall. 'Well, there were one or two times when doubts crossed my mind. Times when she would cancel an engagement at the last minute. Once I found a pair of men's socks in the cottage, but she was able to explain it away.'

'What did she say?'

'She said she'd had a builder in to do some jobs and he must have left them behind.'

'And you believed her?'

'Yes.'

'How would you describe your relationship with Mary? Would you say it was stormy?'

'No. Not at all. It was friendly. Anybody'll tell you that.'

'You never argued?'

'Of course we did. Once or twice. But that's to be expected. Every couple argues.'

'Mr Casey, you knew Mary better than most. Apart from her parents.'

Casey tossed his head back. 'Her parents? Don't make me laugh. They hadn't a clue about her. They were so proud of her, with her grand job in financial services. They thought their little daughter could do no wrong.'

'Do you know of any reason at all why anyone would want to murder her?'

Casey began to tap the pencil against the edge of the desk. Megarry's nerves snapped. He reached out and took the pencil away. 'Please,' he said. 'This is serious.'

'I'm sorry,' Casey said. 'Don't think this hasn't hurt me. I loved her. When I think of all the things we did together, the walks we took across Howth. We walked every part of the peninsula together. Mary loved that place.'

'Do you know of any reason?'

Casey hesitated. He squeezed his eyes shut. Megarry thought he was going to weep again.

'No,' he said. 'She was a bitch, but she didn't deserve to die.'

They got to Blackrock College for Girls shortly after 11 a.m. It

148

was on a shaded avenue above the town, with a view down to the sea. It had once been a grand house, home to some local dignitary, but now it had a beaten-up look, ivy crawling the walls towards the roof, a gutter hanging loose, paint peeling from the window frames.

As Megarry got out of the car he saw a tennis court, the net torn and sagging, a puddle of water gathered in the middle after some recent rain. Someone was watching from a window. He was just in time to see a curtain quickly pulled, catch a glimpse of a woman, middle-aged and bespectacled. As they approached the door, she came out to meet them. She had a plaid shawl slung across her narrow shoulders.

'Can I help you?' she asked.

The voice was upper-class, Anglo-Irish.

'We'd like to speak to Ms Denvir.'

'Might I inquire who's calling for her?'

'My name's Megarry. I'm a policeman. This is my colleague, Detective Lawlor.'

Annie smiled. The woman frowned. 'She's in class right now,' she said in a cold voice. They could hear a piano playing somewhere, children singing.

'Could you get a message to her? I think she might be expecting us.'

'Is this a personal visit?'

'Eh. Yes. You could say that.'

The woman studied Megarry, took a quick glance at Lawlor, pulled the shawl tighter around her shoulders and retreated into the cool hall. The sound of singing was louder. The woman closed the heavy front door.

'I'm Miss Moriarty. I'm the principal here. I'll ask Ms Denvir to see you when she's finished class.'

She pushed open another door and showed them into a large parlour. 'If you'd like to wait in here.'

There were a couple of old-fashioned armchairs, a table with a bowl of cut flowers and a cabinet with school trophies. There was a smell of mothballs. A series of photographs lined the walls.

Miss Moriarty turned and left without any more formality.

Lawlor made a face at her departing back. 'Brings back memories. French irregular verbs and netball. Only here, I'd say they play hockey.'

She went to inspect the photographs. They were school debating-teams, school drama presentations, pale-faced young women in white blouses, staring miserably into the camera. Megarry walked to the window and gazed out over the lawns at yachts scudding past Dun Laoghaire harbour in the distance, smoke curling from the orange chimney-pots of the town.

After a while, a bell rang somewhere. There was a sound of doors opening and a babble of voices. He went back to an armchair and sat down. The door opened and a young woman in skirt and pullover came bustling into the room.

'I'm sorry about the delay. It's just that things are very strict here. Rules, you know. Discipline.' She put a heap of exercise books on the table, then turned and frowned. She ran a finger distractedly through her hair. 'Anyway, you're here. You've come about Mary, I suppose?'

'Yes,' Megarry said.

Joyce Denvir sat down in an adjacent chair. 'I thought you would. It might have been better if you had contacted me at home. Miss Moriarty doesn't like visitors. Particularly men visitors. She's very peculiar that way.'

'This won't take long,' Megarry said. 'I realise it might be painful.'

'No.'

Megarry looked at her. She had dark hair cut in a sensible fringe across her forehead which gave her a solemn air, but underneath Megarry thought he could detect a playfulness.

'Oh, I'm sorry Mary's dead and all that. But I'm not shocked. In a strange way, I'm not even surprised.'

'You're not?'

'No. Mary had it coming to her. Don't misunderstand me. But she was living in the fast lane. That's the very phrase she used herself. She lived for the moment. Took risks. I always had a feeling she'd burn herself out.'

'But she didn't burn herself out. She was murdered.'

'It's the same thing.'

150

Megarry took a deep breath. 'You were very friendly with her.'

'At school and later at college. We were sort of . . . best pals. But we drifted apart.'

'Why?'

'Life-style mainly. Mary was earning very good money. Much more than me, I'm sorry to say. She liked a good time, parties, holidays. I couldn't keep up with her. I think she got bored with me. Anyway, I didn't care for the kind of company she kept.'

'What kind of company was that?'

'People like herself. Hedonists. Quite a mixture – writers, artists, dress designers, musicians. Money was no object to them. The sort of people who would think nothing of paying sixty pounds for a bottle of champagne. Or a line of coke.'

'Cocaine?'

'A lot of them were into drugs. They talked about pushing out the boundaries of experience. It sounds philosophical, but really it was just an excuse to indulge themselves.'

'And Mary?'

'I don't think Mary used. But she wasn't entirely disapproving. She used to say it was people's own choice. I didn't agree.'

'What about boyfriends?' Lawlor asked.

'She had loads of men. At one stage it was a different one every week. But she never seemed happy. It was as if she couldn't find what she was looking for.'

'There was Clive,' Megarry said.

Joyce Denvir looked up. 'You know about him?'

'A little.'

'Did you know that he was married?'

'No.'

'Well, he was. It was par for the course with that crowd she hung around with. Anything went.' She smiled. 'But that was Mary for you. It didn't matter whose man she got her hands on. You see, at heart she was very selfish. Oh, she could be generous all right. She gave a lot of time and money to some women's group she was involved in out in Howth. And she was very good company. But at bottom, Mary did what Mary wanted.'

'This Clive person,' Lawlor said. 'What do you know about him?'

Joyce Denvir shrugged. 'Nothing, really. I'm not even sure he was really called Clive, to tell you the truth.'

'Clive supplanted Brian Casey,' Megarry said. 'Would that be right?'

'More or less. But the Casey affair was on its last legs anyway. I'm surprised it lasted as long as it did. I never knew what she saw in him in the first place. Mary could have got the pick of the crop. And then he was so damned possessive. She couldn't go to the bathroom but he'd be following her. He wanted to marry her, but that was just a joke. Mary no more wanted to get married than the man in the moon. I thought Casey was a bit of a creep. He was always criticising her friends, but a lot of it was just envy.'

'So what brought it to a head?'

'It had been breaking up for a while. It was obvious to everyone but Brian. He couldn't see the writing on the wall. It was pathetic, the way he wouldn't let go. Then he tried to bully her.'

'Bully her?' Lawlor asked.

'He had a very quick temper. He would fly off the handle at the tiniest little thing. They used to have quite vicious fights. I even saw him strike her one time. Called her a selfish, two-timing bitch and said he wished she was dead.'

Megarry and Lawlor exchanged a glance. Joyce Denvir suddenly realised what she had said. She put a hand to her mouth.

'It was only words, of course. I'm sure he didn't mean it.'

She led them to the front door. The driveway and the lawns were thronged now with blue-smocked girls enjoying their lunch-break.

Megarry thanked her and as they turned to go, Joyce Denvir reached a hand to detain him. 'How are her parents taking it?'

'Not well.'

She nodded. 'I'll have to write to them. Send my condolences.'

152

15

They had lunch at a little bistro in Temple Bar. It was filling up and they were lucky to get a seat beside the window where Lawlor could watch the strollers in the afternoon sun.

'You know, in a way I envy Mary Grogan,' she said. 'Her life-style. It must be nice to be able to eat at good restaurants, drink champagne, spend three hundred pounds on a dress. Not have to worry about money. Rory and I are saving every penny we can. He wants to buy a house, get out of that bloody flat.'

'But was she happy?' Megarry asked.

'Who knows? Sounds happy enough to me. Nice cottage in Howth. Little bit isolated maybe, but nice all the same. Good job. Parties. Hectic social life. What's wrong with that?' She dipped a fork into her chicken salad. 'Sure as hell beats pounding the beat out in Ballymun.'

'I don't know,' Megarry said. 'I get a picture of someone driven. Never at peace with herself, always searching for something. I think she was a little sad.'

He thought briefly of his own career. How it started. That awful nightmare. A little house on the Falls Road in Belfast. Policemen rushing the front door. An IRA man sitting on the stairs with a gun held out in front of him. A flash like blue lightning. The smell of cordite. The blood splashing the walls like ink.

'I don't know, Annie. I think sometimes you've just got to settle for what you've got. Try and find some peace.'

A waiter came and took away their plates and another came with new ones. They chatted and watched the street. It was after three o'clock when they left to meet Kelly at the psychiatrist's rooms in Fitzwilliam Square.

Megarry had expected someone older. Dr Bristow wore a neat suit and tie and had his hair closely cropped. He had a sheaf of papers on his lap from which he glanced from time to time, to smile at Megarry and the other two detectives.

The consulting rooms were in an old Georgian house, painstakingly restored. Megarry had admired the high, moulded ceilings, the fine plaster, the elegant fireplace. He thought of A.E. and Yeats and literary soirées held in similar houses in Dublin at the turn of the century.

Dr Bristow leaned his elbows on the desk. 'In a nutshell, Sean Boylan is mentally ill.'

Megarry watched for Kelly's reaction. There was surprise at first and then disappointment.

'I examined him yesterday. We spent four hours together. He was very willing to talk. He feels no guilt at all about what he has done. In fact, he boasted about it.'

'Excuse me,' Lawlor interjected. 'This man has attacked over twenty women, myself included. And he isn't even sorry?'

'That's not how he sees it. He believes that the women were seeking sexual gratification from him. He's convinced they were willing.'

Lawlor shook her head. 'I don't believe I'm hearing this.'

'What about the knife?' Megarry put in quickly.

'That's all part of it. He says the knife and mask were to heighten the excitement.'

'But he tried to rape me,' Lawlor said. 'For all I know, he might have killed me. Now you're saying he thought I was enjoying it?'

'Unfortunately, yes.'

'And you believe him?'

Dr Bristow put the papers down on the desk and managed a weak smile.

'It's not a question of believing or not. I have to examine the medical evidence. Sean Boylan is a dangerous man. But if his counsel pleads mental instability and I am called as a witness, I can only give my medical opinion.'

He looked down at his notes. 'The regular use of words like bitch and slut. These are clearly derogatory terms. But in fact, Boylan really feels inadequate towards women. He would be unable to have a normal sexual relationship with a woman. To compensate for his feelings of inferiority, he projects this idea of women as base sexual creatures seeking satisfaction from him. In that way he is able both to convince himself about his own sexual prowess, and to bolster his self-image.'

'But he carried out a reign of terror in Kilbarrack for nearly two years,' said Lawlor. 'Women were afraid to go outside their front doors at night – they still are. Now you're trying to explain it away as if it was just some disorder that came over him. Don't you believe in right and wrong? Don't you believe in people taking responsibility for their actions?'

Dr Bristow's face coloured. 'This behaviour has its roots in an experience he had when he was a teenager. This is not uncommon. I asked him about girlfriends. He only ever had one. He was fifteen; she was older, sixteen or seventeen and much more sexually experienced. It was an adolescent infatuation but she treated him very badly. She used to belittle him, make fun of him. In the end she rejected him for an older boy. This was devastating for him, but eventually he rationalised it. Now he has convinced himself that it was the other way round and that he rejected her.'

'And that's what started it?' Megarry asked.

'Not immediately. The feeling of anger and humiliation festered. He became afraid of women, uneasy in their company. The fear of rejection and the memory of that original experience made it increasingly difficult to form relationships. At the same time, he has a strong sexual libido seeking an outlet. In the end, he hit on this method of attack as a means of achieving sexual gratification. But he couldn't admit that what he was doing was wrong. So he forced his victims to speak obscenities to him and in that way he convinced himself that

155

they were asking for it.' Dr Bristow shuffled the papers on his desk.

'Is there any possibility that he's malingering?' Kelly asked. 'Now that we've caught him, how do you know he's not making all this up? A stay in a psychiatric unit would be much more comfortable than a sentence in prison. And there's always the possibility of a review of his condition in a few years' time. He could suddenly claim to be cured. That's happened before.'

'I'm aware of that,' Dr Bristow said. 'I can only give you the result of my examination. I'm convinced he's not making it up.'

'Is he the type of man who gets pleasure from using violence? Might this be a way of exacting revenge on women for the humiliation he suffered?'

Dr Bristow smiled. 'He's not a sadist, if that's what you're trying to say. In Boylan's mind he is not using violence. You've got to understand how he views this. As far as he is concerned, these women were willing.' In fact, I'd go as far as to say that at bottom Sean Boylan is not a violent man.'

When he got home, Megarry found Kathleen with her coat on.

'I've left you something in the fridge,' she said. 'You can heat it up later.'

He took up a newspaper, sat down and switched on the television. 'What meeting is it this time?' he asked.

'The bazaar. Last-minute preparations. It's tomorrow. I hope you're ready.'

'Ready? What are you talking about?'

'You promised to lend a hand.'

He put the paper down. 'I what?'

'You said you'd man a stall for us.'

'I don't remember that.'

'You see, you never listen, Cecil. You're down for the bottle stall.'

'But I wouldn't know what to do. I've never ran a bottle stall in my life.'

Kathleen smiled. 'There's nothing to it. You just take the money and people pick a number. Then you simply match up the number with the bottle and give it to them. A child could do it.'

'Then find a child,' Megarry said.

16

The bazaar was in the church hall in Main Street. There was a crowd outside when Megarry and Kathleen arrived. Trish Blake met them at the door. There was a man with her, and she clung protectively to his arm. Megarry thought he looked somewhat out of place, although he seemed relaxed enough.

'Kathleen. Good to see you. Everybody's at their post. Or soon will be. We're aiming for a big increase over last year, and I think we'll get it.'

She saw Megarry. 'Cecil, it's great that you could come. I know you're very busy. But we'll get you out of here by one o'clock.' She lowered her voice. 'Are you making any progress? With the case, I mean?'

'Some,' Megarry said.

She shook her head. 'I still can't believe it. It's just so awful. Let's hope you get someone for it soon.'

She turned to the man beside her. 'Oh,' she said. 'This is Jim.'

'Ah,' Megarry said and extended his hand. 'So you got roped in too?'

''Fraid so. I get roped in every year.'

'There's nothing to this,' Trish Blake said. 'Did Kathleen explain?'

'Sort of. Do I have to shout or anything?'

'Well, you have to rustle up business, Cecil. You have to

158

encourage them. The whole idea is to part them from their cash.'

Megarry stared out over the hall. The doors were opening and people were starting to pour in, women rummaging over the second-hand clothes, children sucking ice-creams, babies screaming.

He groaned inwardly and turned to Jim Blake.

'What have they got you down for?'

'The book stall.' He pointed to a table heaped with children's comics and cheap paperbacks.

Megarry sighed. 'Well, I suppose we'd better get started.'

By ten to one, most of the crowd had melted away. Megarry collected the bottles which remained unclaimed, and counted the takings. Twelve pounds and sixty pence. It would have been simpler to have made a donation. He wandered over to where Jim Blake was talking to his wife.

'How did you do?'

'Just under thirty quid.'

'It all adds up,' Trish Blake said quickly. 'What about you, Cecil?'

Megarry told her.

'Don't worry. The bottle stall is never our best draw. But when we add up the door receipts and the tombola, plus the bric-à-brac and all the other bits and pieces, I'd say we'll make our target.'

Megarry looked around the deserted hall.

'Kathleen was on the cake stall,' Trish Blake said. 'At the end of the hall.'

Megarry turned to go.

'I'm really grateful for your help,' Trish Blake said. 'You must come and have dinner some time. You and Kathleen. When all this is over.'

'We'll do that,' Megarry said.

He went down the hill, past the church shimmering in the afternoon sun and into the town. It was that time of day when there were few people about, a handful of drinkers at the tables outside the Royal Hotel, an occasional car phut-phutting towards the Summit, a couple of cyclists resting on their handlebars. He kept walking and came at last to the harbour.

There was a calmness on the sea, the light shifting on the water like crinkled silver foil. He looked north, past Ireland's Eye and Lambay Island, along the shores of Portmarnock and Malahide. Up there on a clear day, you could see the dark humps of the Mourne mountains.

Suddenly he thought of the RUC collegues he had left behind in Belfast: Harvey with his carnaptious ways, loyal Nelson who never argued, Drysdale who he didn't trust but who had tried to persuade him to stay. They were similar in so many ways to Kelly and Lawlor and the superintendent. The same gripes and grievances, the same pressure, the everyday struggle to make a life. Cops were the same everywhere.

He realised, with a start, how quickly he had left that life behind, how rarely he thought of them now. He remembered the years they had spent together, the trials, the arguments, the petty betrayals. He felt a twinge of regret at the memory of times past, like ancient fingers straining to pull him back.

He started walking once more. And then, almost before he knew, he was outside the Capstan Bar.

He hadn't been here since the morning they had found Mary Grogan's head in the fishing net, the Boylans sitting like walking wounded on the scuffed banquette.

He entered the cool interior, pushed open the door to the lounge and immediately saw Tom Reddin's plump face smiling at him from behind the bar.

'Mr Megarry,' he said. 'It's good to see you. The North began, the North held on, God Bless our Northern men.'

Megarry blinked in the dim light. 'What are you talking about?'

'1798. The Presbyterians. Your forebears, Mr Megarry. Henry Joy. The unity of Catholic, Protestant and Dissenter. Surely you remember the United Irishmen?'

'Vaguely,' Megarry said and fumbled for his cigarettes.

'There's something about Northern people,' Reddin said and gave the counter a wipe with a wet cloth. 'When they say a thing, they mean it. They're straight talkers. You can trust them.'

Can you? Megarry thought as he took out his lighter. Sometimes I wonder about that.

'Isn't it a pity we can't all get together?' Reddin said. 'Forget past differences. Look to the future?'

'Maybe.'

'This little island is too small for people to be always fighting. We've got to learn to live together, share this common piece of earth. Mind you, we get no bloody leadership from the politicians.'

Jesus, Megarry thought, am I going to get a drink or do I have to listen all day to a lecture on Irish history?

'I'll have sparkling water,' he said sharply.

'Not drinking today?'

'What do you think I'm going to do with it, Tom? Eat it?'

'Certainly,' Reddin said and rushed away to pour.

Megarry looked around for somewhere to sit. The place was almost deserted, a couple of old sea-dogs smoking and drinking at the end of the bar, a man and a woman with the contented look of day-trippers sitting together at a table beside the door.

He lit his cigarette and when he looked up Reddin was back. He put down a drip mat and then the glass.

'No camera crews here today, Tom?'

'What?' Reddin said and then his face spread in a smile. 'You're pulling my leg, Mr Megarry.'

'No, I'm not. I understand you're well in with the media. You keep them informed of local developments. How does it work? Do they pay you a tip-off fee or something?'

Reddin's face went a bright red. 'I know one or two people,' he said defensively. 'Reporters. You know what it's like. They're always looking for stories. Sure, if people didn't tell them things, there'd be no news at all and then where would we be? Isn't information the lifeblood of democracy?'

'Sometimes,' Megarry said. 'Did you tip them off about the head?'

'Sure I did. It's what they call a good human-interest story.'

'But you see what they've made of it, don't you? They've got mass murderers on the loose. They've got half the old ladies in north Dublin afraid to go outside their front doors. And now, just for balance, they've spread the panic over to Bray.'

'That's not my fault. All I did was alert them.'

'We also had a mob of them besieging the station the other day. You might let them know, Tom, that if they ever do that again, I'll have them arrested.'

'Sure, sure.'

'They get in the way, clog up the investigation. And Tom . . .' Megarry softened his voice and Reddin drew closer. 'Sometimes we know things that it's best the public shouldn't know. Little details about the crime. Little things that only the perpetrator could know. Do you get my drift?'

Reddin smiled once more and dipped his hand into a bowl of peanuts on the counter.

'Sure,' he said. 'But isn't it gas all the same, that the man who found the head should end up getting jugged for raping women down at Kilbarrack? Sean Boylan, I mean. His poor parents are frantic with shame. It's the talk of the town.'

Megarry stiffened. 'How did that get out?'

'How does anything get out? People aren't stupid. The papers are saying that a man is in for questioning. Sean's been away for days. They put two and two together and nobody denies it. His poor ould father, now, is mortified. He was in here the other night and he sat over there in the corner and hardly said the time of day to anyone, he was so ashamed. Just sat and drank his couple of pints and went home.'

He drew closer to Megarry, his mouth smeared with peanut salt. 'Is that what you were hinting at just now, when you said there were things the police knew that the public didn't know. Do you think Sean Boylan is the murderer?'

'I can't talk about that.'

'You know, I'm not surprised. Now that I think about it. Sean was a real oddball. You should have seen him in here when he'd got a few drinks on him, lepping and roaring like a madman. There was times, you know, when I had to bar him out of the place. And here's another funny thing, too. For a man

162

that's in for rape, he'd hardly say "Boo" to a woman. He was terrified of them. In fact, to tell you the truth, it crossed my mind once or twice that he might have been the other way. You know,' Reddin said and dangled his wrist. 'Ginger.'

'What?'

'Ginger beer. Three-speed gear.'

Megarry lifted the glass of water, the bubbles beaded along the rim. He felt like a real drink, a pint of Guinness for instance, but he was trying hard to follow Dr Henry's instructions. He took a long sip.

Reddin dipped his fingers once more into the peanut bowl.

'And to think that the head belonged to poor ould Mary Grogan.'

The remark had almost slipped past before it registered. Megarry tried not to show his surprise. He put the glass down firmly and wiped his mouth with the back of his hand. He looked at Reddin with renewed interest.

'You knew her?'

'Of course.'

'Really? I didn't think she bothered much with the people in the town? I thought she was too . . . posh.'

Reddin shook his head. 'Not at all. She had her friends in the yacht club, right enough, and wealthy people from up the hill, but Mary liked to mix. She'd come in here regularly and have her glass of wine or a couple of gin and tonics and listen to the music.' Reddin pointed to an alcove where Megarry became aware for the first time of a framed picture of a piper.

'She was interested in traditional music?'

'Sure she was. We have a session here every Saturday night. Local musicians and singers. Mary would drop down most Saturday nights.'

'Did she come on her own, or with others?'

'It depended. Sometimes she'd be with a man.'

'The same man?'

'Yes.'

Megarry thought immediately of Brian Casey.

'Red hair?'

'No. His hair was black.'

'You're sure of that?'

At that moment, one of the old men at the top of the bar called out for more drink. Reddin hurried away. Megarry stubbed out his cigarette and looked at his empty glass. When Reddin returned, he ordered another.

'This man, Tom. What did he look like?'

'Medium height, medium build. Insignificant-looking creature, to tell you the truth.'

'What age?'

'Late twenties. Early thirties.'

'Local?'

'I don't think so.'

'Any name?'

'No surname that I can remember. But I heard her call him Jack a few times. You know, when she'd be sending him up to the bar for drinks. She'd call out after him. "Packet of crisps, Jack" or "Don't forget the tonic, Jack".'

'Jack?'

'Is that important?'

'It depends. It might be. Were they . . . lovers, do you think?'

Reddin chewed for a moment on the peanuts. 'I wouldn't know anything about that. I think he was a painter like her. I used to overhear them talking about galleries and that sort of stuff. But I know one thing.'

He paused and took out the cloth again and wiped the counter, even though there was nothing left to clean.

'I know he helped her out the time she had the row with Mick Dudgeon.'

Megarry leant towards him.

'She told me one time that Dudgeon's place was only a liability to her for all the rent she got out of it and the way he was always abusing her. He'd do nothing for himself, wouldn't even put a washer on a dripping tap. Always demanding that she repair every little thing because she was the landlord and the contract said she was responsible.'

Reddin glanced around. 'There was bad blood there, you see, from the very beginning. Poor ould Mary didn't know what she was walking into when she bought Crow's Nest. Dudgeon's

164

ould da, that would be George, he pissed the whole bloody lot away. He was an awful ould drooth. Nearly had the family out on the side of the road with the drinking.

'The land ended up with a property company, not that it's worth very much. But the houses are. With those views, you could easily get a couple of hundred grand for each.'

'That much?' Megarry said with surprise.

'Sure. Howth Summit. Views looking down over Dublin Bay and the whole city. People would be queuing up. That's what annoyed Mary, you see. She knew if she could get Dudgeon out she could make a killing on the place. Instead of which she was getting a pittance in rent and all this hassle about repairs.'

'And what was the row about?'

'What do you think? He came looking to get some damned thing fixed and Mary refused. He said he'd get the law on her, force her to fulfill the contract. And she told him that if he wasn't careful, she'd put him out altogether. I'm not sure legally she could do that, to tell you the truth. But it was enough to drive Dudgeon into a frenzy. He quoted his forefathers on the land right back to Oliver Cromwell's time. It almost came to blows. For a while, she was afraid to sleep alone in the place. I think she got this fella Jack to go up and have a word with Dudgeon and warn him off.'

Megarry toyed with his glass. 'This Jack? Has he been back to the music sessions since they . . .'

'Found her head?' Reddin finished the sentence. 'No,' he said. 'I haven't seen hilt nor hair of him since. In fact, it's months now since I saw him.'

Megarry finished his drink. 'Old Mrs Dudgeon. What happened to her eyes?'

Reddin shrugged. 'I don't know the whole story. She's mad. There's some people think she's a witch.'

Megarry laughed. 'In this day and age?'

'You may laugh, Mr Megarry. But there's people in this town are afraid of her. They think she can put a curse on things. Ask Gameball Geraghty.'

'The fisherman?'

'You know him. Drinks in the pubs around the town. He'll tell you all about her.'

Megarry considered. 'There's one more thing. Would Sean Boylan have known Mary Grogan, do you think?'

Reddin looked at him with a sly grin. 'You do think he did it, don't you?'

'Well? Did he know her or not?'

'It would be a good story,' Reddin said. 'The media would love it. But I have to tell you the truth. I don't think he knew her at all.'

As Megarry left the pub and walked along the seafront in the bright sunlight, he asked himself why he hadn't talked to Reddin sooner.

He started along the west pier, past the fish shops, the ice plant, the mariners' hall, the smoke house with its curl of grey smoke and the rich smell of kippered fish. Near the end of the pier, a couple of trawlers were tethered against the harbour wall. An old man in a sailor's cap sat on an upturned box, mending a fishing net. Megarry pulled over another box and sat down beside him.

'Gameball? You know me?'

The old man barely acknowledged his presence. He had a pinched face, small, button-like eyes, skin as brown and cracked as a dried tobacco leaf. His fingers worked deftly at the net, weaving the cord in and out in an intricate web.

'You're a cop,' he said. 'Or at least, you was. I see you drinking in the Lighthouse sometimes.'

'That's right,' Megarry said. 'I'm looking for some information. Old Mrs Dudgeon. You know her?'

The old man spat onto the cobblestones. 'Course I know her. She's bad. Bad, bad woman. You stay out of her way.'

'What's bad about her?'

'Just about everything. You tell me what's good about her?'

'She seems harmless,' Megarry said.

Gameball Geraghty snorted. 'Shows what you know. She can bring bad on people. She used to kill babbies.'

'Kill babies?'

'Years ago. Girl got herself into trouble, she went to see Ma Dudgeon. She got rid of it for her. Buried the bodies in that field they've got up there on West Heath. You dig up that field, you'll find their skilitons. They're still there.'

'What else did she do?'

'Killed cattle. You get on the wrong side of her, she'd put a curse on your livestock. People are afraid of her. I don't blame them.'

Megarry picked up a piece of cord, smoothed it with his hand. 'You ever hear that she killed people?'

Gameball shook his head. 'Never heard of that. But she could make things happen to you. Fella once had a row with them Dudgeons over money. Next day he crashed his car. Legs have been crippled ever since.'

'And Mrs Dudgeon did that?'

'Sure she did. Perfectly good car. Police checked it over. Brakes were working, everything.' He snapped his fingers. 'You tell me why that car crashed.'

'What about the land?' Megarry said.

'Land's too stony. Nothing will grow. Only good for grazing.'

'But they used to own it all?'

'That's right; owned it as far as Shielmartin Hill. But old George drank it away. He was another bad piece. Mean, violent. He used to beat them kids till they were black and blue. Beat her too. And he mortgaged the land to some company in Dublin. Took the money and drank it. Kids and all were nearly put out on the road. Parish priest had to intervene. Father Rickard. He's dead too. He went and pleaded with the development people to let them stay. Otherwise they wouldn't have had a roof over their heads.'

'They had that land for years?'

'Right back to the Vikings, some people say. They had it a long, long time. Sad to see something like that happen just because a man can't control his thirst.'

'What happened to George?'

'Died. Alcoholic poisoning. Some people say she did it.'

'His wife?'

'Some people say she just got so mad at him that she put something in his whiskey one night when he was fluthered. Rat

167

poison. Man would have been so drunk he'd never know the difference.'

Megarry paused. 'But that was never proved?'

'No. They just took him out and buried him. I think they were so glad to see the end of him, nobody cared.'

'And how did she come to lose her eyesight?'

Gameball Geraghty's fingers slowed on the net.

'George did that.'

'How?'

'They had an argument one night. George was drunker than a skunk as usual. Just took a poker and hit her right across the face. Blinded her. He was an evil ould bastard. Bad piece of work.'

Megarry stood up. There was cloud coming in from the sea and a cool breeze rippling the water at the harbour's edge.

'Thanks, Gameball,' he said. 'I owe you a pint.'

He started along the cobbled stones of the pier towards the town. He heard the old man shouting after him.

'You take my advice. Stay away from her. She's a bad woman.'

17

Megarry started back up the hill. As he climbed, the sky grew dark, clouds heavy with rain coming in from the sea. He reached the quarry and started along the bridle-path. The heath was charged with menace, Shielmartin Hill black with shadow. He stopped at Dudgeon's house. The dog stirred at the doorstep, baring its teeth. When he put his hand on the gate, it came barking to meet him. He saw the curtains flutter and Dudgeon's face at the window.

'It's me,' he shouted. 'Cecil Megarry.'

The curtains fell away and the front door opened. Dudgeon called the dog to heel. He looked angry and afraid.

'What do you want this time?' he asked. 'I brought that damned gun licence to the station. Just like you said.'

'This is about something else.'

'What?'

'Can I come in?' Megarry said. He placed his hand on the gate once more and started along the path to the front door. Dudgeon retreated inside the house and the policeman followed.

The place had the same defeated look. The peeling wallpaper, the cracked window, the scuffed furniture, the rifle resting just inside the door. There was a fire burning in the grate that combined with the heat rising from the moor to make the air in the house close and uncomfortable. The old lady was sitting as he remembered her by the window, sightless eyes gazing out over the vastness of the heath.

'It's Mr Megarry, ma,' Dudgeon said. 'You remember him? He called here before.' She stirred as he came into the room, but didn't speak.

'Do you want tea?' Dudgeon said and drew the policeman into the kitchen and closed the door. 'I don't want her to hear,' he said. 'What's this all about?'

Megarry took out his cigarettes and held the packet open for Dudgeon.

'Did you know that Mary Grogan is dead?'

The other man bent his head into the flame from the lighter. Megarry waited till he drew back again, puffing smoke. He reached a finger to pull a strand of tobacco from his lip.

'Dead?' Dudgeon said.

The policeman studied his face. There was no reaction. 'It was on the radio. We put out an alert.'

'We never listen to the radio.'

'She was murdered. Someone shot her and then cut her up. You must have heard about it. The head that was found in a fishing net off the Bailey?'

Dudgeon sniffed. 'She was a bad bitch. She gave me and ma nothing but grief. I'm not sorry for her.'

Megarry had expected some expression of horror or shock, but there was no response from the other man. It was as if he had already come to terms with the murder.

'I believe you had a row with her recently over repairs to the cottage?'

Dudgeon's eyes circled the policeman warily.

'I had loads of rows with her. Ever since she bought the land there's been nothing but trouble. She wanted us out so that she'd be able to sell this place. She didn't want tenants. She didn't give a toss about us. Tenants bring problems. It's much better if you've just got an empty house that you can sell.'

'What did you threaten her with?'

He saw Dudgeon's face grow dark.

'I never threatened her.'

'Oh, come on,' Megarry said. 'I know you did. You scared her so much that she had to get a man to speak to you. Guy called Jack.'

Dudgeon pulled nervously on his cigarette. 'Who've you been talking to?'

'It doesn't matter. It's true, isn't it? You threatened her.'

'She threatened me. Told me she'd put me out of my own place. Just because I asked her to get the damned roof fixed. It's in the contract. I showed it to her. But she just laughed at me. Told me if I didn't stop bothering her, she'd have me put out.'

'And you told her if she tried that, you'd harm her?'

'What am I supposed to do? Stand by like a little mouse and let her put us out on the side of the road?'

'Who is this Jack guy?'

'Some fella she was friendly with. He came here to see me. Trying to act the hard man. Telling me what he'd do and what he wouldn't do. But I soon ran him off the place.'

Dudgeon rolled his shoulders and for the first time he allowed himself a smile.

'What did he look like?'

'Greasy-looking bastard. He didn't scare me. I've dealt with tougher men than him in my day.'

There was a scraping noise at the window and Megarry saw the rain beginning to beat in tiny drops against the pane. He glanced around the cramped little room, the dirty, food-encrusted cooker, the damp patch on the ceiling above the door. Was this place worth killing for?

'Had you ever seen him before?'

'Once or twice. She used to bring him down to Crow's Nest. Sometimes when I'd be working around the yard, I'd see them go past on the bridle-path. But they just ignored me. She considered me beneath her notice.'

'Do you know where he lives?'

'Like I told you, I ran him out of the place. I didn't get his life story.'

'What did you do exactly?'

'I went for my gun.'

Megarry kept a grim face. 'You know that's an offence? We could take the gun off you. Revoke your licence.'

'He was threatening me. I'm entitled to defend myself.'

'Threatening, threatening. Everybody threatening someone. He remembered what Gameball had said. The beatings when Dudgeon was a child. It suddenly occurred to Megarry that Dudgeon's life had been totally circumscribed by intimidation and fear.

'Did you know that someone broke into Crow's Nest?'

Dudgeon looked up sharply.

'Someone smashed a window. Looks like it might have been done with a hammer.' He looked meaningfully at a tool that lay on a counter near the sink. It was a claw hammer. For a moment nothing was said, then Dudgeon spoke.

'I was just fixing the pelmet there.'

He pointed above the window and, sure enough, the policeman could see the evidence of recent work.

'It came loose,' Dudgeon said. 'I banged a few nails into it.'

'Whoever broke into Crow's Nest was after something. You didn't see or hear anything, did you?'

'No,' Dudgeon said, and kept his head down.

Megarry paused. The heat in the room had become intolerable, the windows misting over with the rain.

'Can you tell me where you were on the weekend of April 20th?'

'I'd have been here. Where else would I be?'

'Did you see Mary Grogan that weekend?'

'No.'

Megarry caught Dudgeon's glance and held it.

'I have to warn you that you are a suspect for Mary Grogan's murder. We may have to bring you in for further questioning. We may have to take your fingerprints.'

Dudgeon snorted. 'Are you finished now?'

'For the time being.'

He went to the door and walked into the other room. The hunched figure of the old lady still sat by the window. He could see that the rain was blanketing the heath now. He was going to get soaked.

Dudgeon followed him to the front door. As he was about to open it, he heard the old woman cough and then the cracked voice was speaking.

172

'She's dead, isn't she?'

Megarry felt his neck stiffen. He stopped and looked back towards her. She hadn't shifted. Her face was still staring out over the moor.

'Yes,' Megarry said softly. He could see from the curl of her withered cheeks that the old lady was smiling.

'I knew it.'

The policeman felt his blood run cold.

'She was wicked. She did wicked things. She mixed with men she had no right to be with. I said she would die. I knew God would punish her in the end.'

He made his way back to the Summit, the rain seeping into his shoes and hair, his trousers damp from the brambles and gorse. By the time he got to the bus stop, he was soaked. He stood in the shelter and waited, turning events over in his mind. And then, with a start, he realised that Dudgeon's description fitted Delaney. And Jack was a derivative of John, Delaney's Christian name.

The bus came panting up the hill. Megarry paid his fare and sat at the back in the warm. He felt a kind of exhilaration. If Reddin could identify Delaney then he would have caught him in a lie. For Delaney had denied all knowledge of Mary Grogan at the interview. It would be enough to warrant bringing him in again. And this time, Megarry would have the advantage.

He got off near the station and walked the rest of the way in the rain. There were several vehicles parked in the compound, but Kelly's car was not among them. As he came through the entrance he saw the sergeant's broad head bent over a ledger. He looked up and grinned as Megarry tried to shake the damp from his clothes.

'Bloody weather. Always chopping and changing. Did you not bring an umbrella?'

'Where's Inspector Kelly?' Megarry said tersely.

'He's over in Bray. There's been a development. He was looking for you all morning.'

'I was tied up with something else.'

'Well, you missed all the excitement.'

'Tell me,' Megarry said. 'And make it quick.'

The sergeant sat back and rubbed his thick hands together. 'Man just walked in off the street this morning and confessed to murdering Imelda Lacy. What do you think of that?'

Megarry felt his heart skip.

'Inspector Kelly's over there now. He said for you to go across and join him.'

Megarry started for the door, then stopped. 'Do we have a name? What's he called?'

'Jack something . . .' The sergeant rifled through some papers on his desk.

'Delaney?'

'No,' the sergeant said and looked disappointed. 'Man called Jack Thunder.'

18

It was a grim-faced Inspector O'Connor who met him at Bray station.

'We're in my office,' he said. He looked at Megarry's bedraggled state, hair plastered across his forehead, suit crumpled with the rain. 'I'll get you a towel. And a hot cup of tea.'

Megarry dried himself and they went through to O'Connor's office. Kelly and Lawlor and two other men were already waiting.

'What happened?' Megarry asked.

O'Connor sat down, pointed to a plump, uniformed cop.

'Hard to credit it. This morning, shortly after nine o'clock, Joe there was manning the desk. Guy just walked in off the street, said he had a confession to make. Joe brought him into the interview room and, straight out, he says he murdered Imelda Lacy.'

'Did he give any explanation?'

'Yes. Said he wanted to get it off his chest. Said he couldn't forget it and the recent publicity about the Grogan murder was making it worse.'

'He's not a nutter?'

'Doesn't seem to be. He's rational. Cool and collected. Knows a lot of detail about the case.'

'He could have picked that up from the papers.'

'Not all of it.'

'Local?'

'He's from Dun Laoghaire. Barman. Married with three kids.'

'What reason did he give?'

'He says he doesn't know. Says it was just something came over him. He had been out in Bray for a drive. Had a few pints in some of the local pubs. Says he was feeling a bit drunk. He was going home when he saw her waiting for a bus on the outskirts of the town. Gave her a lift and then attempted to get amorous. She resisted and there was a struggle. She was shouting and kicking. He tried to restrain her and in the confusion he says he strangled her.'

'And raped her?'

'Yes.'

Megarry glanced at Lawlor. She looked away.

'What happened next?'

The cop called Joe took up the story.

'Says he panicked. He thought of taking her up the mountains, digging a grave and burying her somewhere. He had a hunting knife in the car which he used for fishing trips. He stopped at a garage and bought a can of petrol. Then he took her to a field outside the town.'

The man's voice shook for a moment.

'Says he cut her up and tried to set her on fire.'

There was silence. Joe swallowed hard.

'Sonofabitch says he had trouble trying to burn the body and in the end he just abandoned it. Got into the car and drove home. Threw the knife and the petrol can into the sea and destroyed his clothes.'

'Have you been able to confirm any of it?' Megarry asked O'Connor. 'Where did he buy the petrol can?'

'Donnelly's garage in Bray.'

'Does anyone remember selling it to him?'

'No. It's too long ago.'

'Has he any record for sexual assault?'

'No.'

'Any record at all?'

'Nothing.'

'What about his wife? Has anyone talked to her?'

'Not yet. I thought maybe we should assess this thing first. Make sure we're on solid ground. There's no point shocking the life out of the poor woman unless we're certain.'

'Someone should talk to her. She might have seen him when he came home. And if he set about destroying his clothes, she might have known.'

'I'll do it,' Lawlor said quickly.

'I'll get someone to go with you,' O'Connor said. 'It's dirty work.'

They had Jack Thunder in the interview room. Megarry glanced at him as they came through the door. He looked nothing like the description they had been given of the man last seen with Imelda Lacy. Thunder was small, with glasses and close-cropped hair like a scuffed tennis ball. He was neatly dressed in a blazer and dark trousers. Megarry calculated that he was about thirty-five.

He sat down across the table from him and stared into his face. Thunder's brown eyes met Megarry's and didn't flinch. He showed no sign of agitation or fear. It struck Megarry that he was almost at peace, like someone who has come to an important decision about his life and is determined to see it through.

Megarry opened the files. O'Connor walked to the corner of the room where a tape recorder rested. The others pulled out chairs and waited.

'You may smoke if you wish,' Megarry began.

'I don't use them.' Thunder's voice was firm and steady.

'Is there anything you need? Glass of water? Cup of tea?'

'No, thank you.'

'Do you wish to have a solicitor present?'

'No.'

Kelly had a notebook out. Megarry took a deep breath.

'This is an official interview.' He nodded to O'Connor, who started the tape.

'We are inquiring into the murder of Imelda Lacy, eighteen years of age, of McDevitt Villas, Bray, County Wicklow. You have the right to remain silent, but anything you say to us voluntarily may later be used in evidence if we bring charges against you. Do you understand?'

'Yes.'

'Your name is John Thunder, of Twenty-five Abercorn Street, Dun Laoghaire?'

'Yes.'

'You wish to make a statement regarding the murder of Imelda Lacy?'

'Yes.'

'Would you recount for us again the events of the evening of November 13th, 1995?'

Jack Thunder cleared his throat.

'It was a Saturday evening. I'd been working in the bar all day. That's Coogan's pub in Glasthule. I finished at 6 p.m. and instead of going home, I decided to go for a drive down to Bray. I felt like a couple of beers. I went into the White Horse and watched football on television. I had two pints there. I left the White Horse and went to McDermott's and had another couple of pints and a few whiskies. I was feeling a bit tipsy, but I was able to drive. As I was going through the town, I saw this girl waiting at a bus shelter. I stopped the car and asked her if she wanted a lift. She said she was going into Dalkey, so I offered to take her.

'She got into the car. She was wearing a short skirt and it was riding up above her knees. She kept pulling it down, but it only drew attention to it. She was wearing this perfume and it got me excited. I thought she was giving me the come-on, so when we left the town I drove off the road and along a dirt track. She started to protest, but I thought she was only playing hard-to-get. I put my arm around her and tried to kiss her. She started to kick up a row, screaming and shouting. I put my hand across her mouth to keep her quiet, but she bit my fingers.

'I don't know what happened next. It was like I had a black-out, but when I came to, she wasn't breathing. She had these red marks on her neck. I tried to revive her. Shook her and slapped

178

her face but she wouldn't come round. That's when I realised that I must have strangled her.' Thunder lowered his face.

'And then?'

'I undressed her and had sex with her.'

'What happened next?'

'I lost my head. Here I was with this dead woman in my car. I decided to get rid of her. I was going to dump the body and then I thought of burying it. In the end, I decided to burn it. I drove to Donnelly's garage and bought a gallon of petrol, then drove to a field at the back of the town and cut her up with the hunting knife. I burnt her clothes first. Then I poured the petrol on her and set her alight, but the flames kept going out. I was in a terrible panic. In the end, I just left her and drove away. I threw the knife and the petrol can into the sea at Sandycove. Then I went home and dumped my clothes and had a shower.'

He stopped, looked at the other policemen in the room staring at him with hard faces.

'Can you describe her for us?'

'Tall, slim, good-looking. Dark hair. She had a little mole about the size of a penny on the side of her neck.'

'What was she wearing?'

'Short skirt, like I said. White blouse. Black leather jacket, black high-heeled shoes.'

'Anything else?'

'She was full of chat. Bubbly girl. When she first got into the car, she was talking away twenty to the dozen. She said she was going into Dalkey to meet some of her pals in one of the pubs. She said she had a job in Neary's bakery in Bray. Saturday night was her big night out.'

He put his head in his hands.

'Why didn't you contact us before?' Megarry asked.

'I was afraid. I thought it would all blow over and eventually I'd come to terms with it and be able to live with myself. But that didn't happen. When I try to sleep at night, I keep thinking about her. I can see her face smiling at me. I can hear her laughing.

'Then this other case started up on the radio. It just made matters worse. I've been thinking about it night and day. It's driving me crazy. I want to pay the penalty for what I've done.'

For the first time, Thunder's calm began to crack. 'I don't know what came over me. Honest to God. I've never done anything like this in my life. When I think of that poor girl. Of the misery and pain I must have caused her parents. I want to apologise to them. I wish to God I'd never been born.'

'Who else knows about this? Did you talk to anyone? Your wife?'

'I told the priest in confession. He advised me to go to the police. But I hadn't the nerve. Until now.'

Megarry scrutinised the files. The tape recorder whirred gently in the background, and he could feel Kelly's eyes on him. He paused and closed the files.

'There's another matter we're inquiring into. Do you know Howth?'

'I've been out there a few times. But not very often. I rarely go over to the north side.'

'When was the last time you were there?'

Thunder put a hand to his brow and tried to think. 'It must be a year, eighteen months. It was a Sunday. I went over with the wife and kids for the day.'

'Do you know the Capstan Bar in Howth?'

'No.'

'Did you know a woman called Mary Grogan?'

'No.'

'Mary Grogan was murdered and cut up. Just like Imelda Lacy. Do you know anything about that?'

'She's the woman whose head was found?'

'That's right. Do you know anything about it?'

'No. Nothing at all.'

'If you do, it would be best for you to tell us. You have already confessed to one killing. If you are responsible for the murder of Mary Grogan, you have nothing to lose by telling us now.'

Thunder shook his head. 'No,' he said. 'Honest to God. I know the papers are saying the same man did both murders. But it's not true. I don't know this other woman. I'm telling you the truth. I never set eyes on her in my life.'

Megarry glanced across at Kelly. There was a look like despair on his face.

180

On his way home, Megarry stopped in Doyle's on College Street. There was a group of journalists drinking in the snug, but otherwise the place was quiet. He sat at the counter and waited for Peggy, the manageress.

'What's on the menu?' he said. 'I could eat a horse.'

'I've got roast chicken, roast potatoes, garden peas, stuffing, gravy. I've got pork chops, scampi, cod in batter. You want me to go on?'

'Is the chicken good?'

Peggy put her hands on her hips and tried to look offended.

'Okay. Okay. Tell the chef to go easy on the stuffing. And give me a glass of Chianti.'

He went to the end of the bar and rang Kathleen. 'I got delayed,' he said. 'Had to go over to Bray. Man just confessed to murdering Imelda Lacy.'

'What's wrong with that? You sound disappointed.'

'Well, it's not the man we thought had done it. It just throws the whole damned thing up in the air. We'll have to start all over again.'

'Sinead Kelly called. About an hour ago. She wants you to ring her.'

'Did she say what about?'

'I think there's something wrong. She sounded . . . well . . . she sounded upset.'

He found some more coins in his coat and rang Kelly's wife.

'It's me,' he said. 'Cecil.'

'Is Peter with you? I need to talk to you. Without him. Can you come out?'

'Tonight?'

'If it's not inconvenient.'

Megarry saw Peggy put a steaming plate down on the bar, pour a glass of wine. 'Sure.' he said. 'Give me half an hour.'

When Megarry got to Kelly's house, the evening was beginning to come down. There was a smell of damp earth, wet grass, rotting leaves. Someone had left a kid's bicycle on the lawn. He pressed the doorbell and waited.

Sinead Kelly had put on make-up but her face looked worn and pinched. She seemed to have aged since he saw her last.

She brought him into the kitchen. Jamie was sitting at the table with an exercise book spread before him. He jumped down when he saw Megarry and came running with his hand out.

'You owe me a pound,' he said. 'Celtic beat Rangers. Three one. You bet me the last time. Remember?'

'But I never bet. I'm not a gambling man.'

'Please, Jamie. Leave Cecil alone. He's tired. So am I.' She turned to Megarry. 'Tea? Or would you like coffee?'

'Tea'll be fine.'

He fumbled in his pocket and brought out two pound coins. 'Here,' he said. 'If I remember right, it was fifty pee. Put one of them in your money-box. Right? Then when it comes holiday time, you'll have loads of pocket money.'

The boy grabbed the coins. 'We're not going on any holidays,' he said.

His mother spun round from the cooker where she was making the tea.

'Go to bed, Jamie.'

'Can I not stay a while longer? I never see Cecil.'

'No,' she said and gathered the books together. 'I want you bright-eyed and bushy-tailed in the morning. C'mon.' She clapped her hands and Jamie got up reluctantly from the table. He kissed his mother and left the room.

'Night, Cecil. You want to bet some more?'

'Get out of it,' Megarry said. 'What is this? You trying to clean me out?'

The door closed and Jamie was gone.

Sinead sat down across from him and poured.

'Thanks for coming,' she said.

He looked into her eyes. They were filling with tears.

'I'm at my wits' end. I needed to talk to someone and you were the best person I could think of.'

'What is it?' Megarry asked gently.

'It's Peter. I'm worried sick about him. He's practically living in his office. He never sees the kids. He barely sees me. And he's changed, Cecil. You must have noticed that. He's got morose, bad-tempered. There's times he's like a devil. He snaps at the least little thing.'

182

'He's tense, Sinead. That's all. He's got a big case on his hands. It's important for him. He's giving it everything he's got.'

'But we seem to spend all our time arguing. It's beginning to affect our relationship.'

Megarry stirred a spoon in his cup. It was the old story. He remembered the rows he used to have with Kathleen when he was younger. Working on a case till the wee hours of the morning. Adjourning to the back room of the Montrose Hotel. Stumbling home at daybreak, half drunk. And later, when things became too much for her, moving out of the house altogether to that grotty flat on the Lisburn Road in Belfast.

'Look, Sinead. If it's any comfort, all police wives complain about the hours their husbands work. But he's doing it for you and the kids. He could take a soft number, sit in the office and doss, fill in traffic reports all day long. But he's made of better stuff than that. He wants to do well. And he will. I can see it in him.'

She lowered her eyes and the tears began to fall like rain down her face.

'I'm sorry,' she said. 'But what use is all of that, if we've no marriage left?'

'Don't talk like that,' Megarry said quickly. 'The case is going well. We may have someone for the Bray murder, and another for the Kilbarrack assaults.'

'But this woman who was found out in Howth, Cecil. That's the one the superintendent is squeezing Peter about.'

'He's squeezing Peter?'

'He called him in yesterday afternoon. Told him if the Howth murder wasn't wrapped up soon, he was pulling him off the case. He even hinted that he might transfer him down the country somewhere.'

Megarry took a deep breath. He felt a flash of cold white anger. 'The bastard,' he said.

He finished his tea, gently patted Sinead's hand. 'Don't worry about it,' he said. 'Peter's being transferred nowhere. Leave this with me.'

She walked with him to the front door. A big moon hung like a lantern above the roofs of the city. She gripped his arm.

'Cecil, don't tell him I told you that. Don't tell him we had this conversation.'

'Don't worry,' he said and walked off into the night.

19

The night was filled with wild dreams. Megarry woke about six o'clock, the sheets twisted, his face and chest bathed in sweat. The room was suffused with a pale light. He got up and went into the bathroom. The dawn was creeping across the cold morning sky, bright blues and pinks dappling the edges of the horizon where it sank into the sea. Out beyond the harbour wall, he could see the island rising like some giant sea beast out of the mist.

He went back to bed and dozed again and at last was wakened by the phone ringing in the hall. He put on his dressing-gown and padded downstairs in his bare feet, the floor cold to the touch. It was Lawlor.

'I talked to that woman.'

'Thunder's wife?'

'Yes. She confirms what he said. She remembers him coming home that night very agitated. He had a shower and then burnt his clothes in the backyard.'

'Did you get a statement?'

'Yes. The poor woman's in an awful state. Imagine someone coming to your door and telling you that your husband's a rapist and a murderer.'

'She may have known already,' Megarry said. 'Perhaps she just didn't want to believe it.'

'We've also checked with Tom Reddin. Brought him a photograph of Thunder. He says it's not the man who was with Mary Grogan those times in his bar.'

'Ah well,' Megarry said.

Lawlor waited on the line. 'You know what this means?' she said.

'Yes, I do. Thunder knew too much about the crime. He knew things that he could not have known unless he killed her.'

'Which rules out Delaney.'

'For the Lacy murder, yes.'

'And with Boylan out of the frame now, we have no suspect left for Mary Grogan.'

'No obvious suspect,' he corrected her. 'There are other people. There are other things we can do. You could see if you can find a recent photograph of Delaney for a start. Try the Bray cops.'

He ran his fingers through the stubble on his chin. 'We really need to find her body, Annie. We've hardly any forensic evidence. We're conducting this case with our hands tied behind our backs.'

'You sound depressed,' Lawlor said.

'No,' Megarry said quickly. 'Nothing like that. We haven't reached the end of the road yet.'

'You're sure?'

'Wellll,' he said, and he realised that his voice lacked conviction. 'Who can ever be sure of anything?'

He went back upstairs and got dressed. When he came down again, Kathleen had the coffee percolator going. The smell filled the kitchen.

'You had a bad night,' she said. 'Tossing and turning. You kept waking me up.'

'I know,' he said wearily.

'You kept muttering in your sleep. What's wrong with you?'

'It was probably indigestion.'

He finished the coffee and she walked with him to the front door. It was another bright day. He could feel the heat already.

He bent and kissed her.

'What's bothering you?' she said.
'It's nothing. Forget about it.'

He went the way he always did in the morning: up the road past the church and across the golf course. There was only a handful of golfers out. He could see the marks their feet had made on the dewy grass.

He skirted the edge of the course till he came to the wood. The town lay beneath him. Beyond the harbour, the sea was churning, lashing the rocks off Ireland's Eye. He entered the wood. It was cool, filled with bird-song. The sun filtered through the branches in shards of light.

As he walked, his mind returned to the case. He remembered the promise he had made to Kelly in the early days of the investigation. *We'll see this through to the end.* But sometimes promises couldn't be kept. Sometimes promises were better not made. He thought of Sinead and what he had said to her. *Don't worry about it. Leave this to me.*

What's the matter with me? he thought. Who do I think I am? Some kind of superman who can solve everybody's problems? What right have I to go about talking to people like that? Raising hopes I can't deliver.

He felt a depression settle over him, and a feeling of guilt he'd experienced before. He reminded himself that murder inquiries got stalled all the time. There were files in every police station in the world, marked 'ongoing', but effectively closed because the investigators had grown weary of chasing down false trails, coming up against dead ends. What made the Grogan case any different? And yet it was different. Something told him that all that was required was one happy shaft of insight, one more little push. Was it one of the people they had interviewed? Was it someone who had uttered regret? Someone who had looked into his eyes and expressed sympathy for the dead woman. He thought of the photographs they had found in Crow's Nest Cottage, the blindfolded man. Who was he? Where did he fit into the whole business? And one thought above all the others kept forcing itself into his consciousness. Why was Mary Grogan killed?

With a heavy heart, he left the wood and at last he saw the lake, the trees bending into the light, the ripple on the surface where the breeze caught the water. He sat down with a sigh and took out his cigarettes. He felt the heat of the sun. He closed his eyes and stretched out on the grass.

For a few moments, he dozed. When he woke, there was a stillness in the air. He looked out over the lake. A couple of waterbirds were diving near the shore. Something caught his attention. It looked like a piece of wood, sticking up out of the water, pale and white and smooth. He wondered why he hadn't noticed it before.

Out of curiosity, he got up and walked to the water's edge. At once, he felt the hair rise on the back of his neck. It was like something he remembered as a child, an illustration from a Bible text, God's avenging finger pointing.

What he was looking at, floating upwards from the dark recesses of the lake, was a human arm.

Book Three

20

Megarry stood on the shore and watched with mixed emotions as the divers raised Mary Grogan's body from the lake. It came yellow and bloated, like a life-sized doll, the water dripping off the skin in a thousand diamonds of light. There was something that looked like a rope tied around the belly and thighs. He could see the indentations it made in the enormous folds of flesh, like cord tied into a balloon. He became conscious of a smell carried off the lake, an overpowering odour of putrefaction. Beside him he heard Kelly gasp, raise a hand to his mouth, then turn and walk away.

Inspector Walshe's men had got a dinghy into the centre of the lake and the divers were awkwardly pushing the torso towards it. Megarry saw a man in a black wet-suit lie flat and kick, the splash of water rippling the surface of the lake as the body moved slowly forward. Another man leant over the side of the boat, hands outstretched to receive it.

For a moment there was a struggle. The body trembled as the man pulled it towards him. He put his arms around it and hugged it close as if in an act of embrace, the legs hanging limp, the light glinting off the nest of pubic hair. The man pulled hard and all at once the body slipped into the dinghy. Megarry stood transfixed as the man laid the sodden corpse on the floor of the boat and pulled on a cord to start the engine and turn back to shore.

He felt a strange sensation, the fields so calm and peaceful, the trees, the birds, the sun casting shadows on the water of the lake. And here coming towards him through the waves, the terrible fruits of murder. His first thought was an odd one: *At last they have something to bury. At last they can put her to rest.*

He turned to where Kelly was now standing under a clump of tall oaks. Inspector Walshe came to join them.

'Rope must have snapped or something,' Walshe said. 'She would have been tied down to keep her submerged. Probably tied to a stone. I'll bet that's what's happened. Rope has come loose.'

He seemed to be in good humour. There was a twinkle in his eye, a satisfied look on his face, as if he was pleased that they had found the body at last. It was as if the whole business of Mary Grogan's body had been a personal challenge and he had successfully mastered it.

Megarry said nothing.

'Didn't I say my men were professionals?' Walshe continued. 'I told you we wouldn't let you down.'

'But you meant the sea,' Kelly reminded him. 'You said if it was in the sea you would find her.'

'*Wellll*,' Walshe said. 'That was only logical. The head was in the sea. It was natural to assume that the rest of her would be in there too.'

He stroked his chin. 'Mind you, it is a bit of a conundrum. You'd think the murderer would have put the whole damned lot in the sea and be done with it. Why would he put the head in one place and the body in another?' He gave a little chuckle. 'Well, that'll give you guys something to think about, eh?'

The dinghy was almost at the shore, two men still in the water clinging to the stern. They had a stretcher and body bag ready and a van waiting on the road.

'You want her brought to the morgue or where?' Walshe asked.

'The forensic lab,' Kelly said. 'Finnegan is expecting her.'

Herbie Finnegan was waiting for them, his red face shining with excitement. He had put on his white coat and plastic surgical gloves and a linen mask across his face. He didn't shake hands, just nodded a brief acknowledgement, then stood aside while the stretcher was taken from the van and carried into the building by two young officers.

'Down here,' Finnegan said and went before them giving directions in a brisk, businesslike voice. They followed him silently along the grey corridors. No one spoke till they reached the dissecting room and the body was laid out on a table.

'Well now,' Finnegan said, and rolled back his sleeves. 'Are you sure you guys want to see this? It's not a pretty sight.'

He looked from one man to the other but neither spoke.

'You can wait outside if you want. There's a kitchen down the back. You could make tea. This shouldn't take long.'

'We'll stay,' Megarry said.

Finnegan switched on an overhead lamp and began his examination. 'Well now. Let the dog see the hare.'

He bent with his scalpel and began to scrape away portions of yellow skin. The smell that Megarry had noticed at the lakeside was stronger now, the odour of decay, like the smell of dead fish. Finnegan kept turning his face away to breathe. The windows were open and a breeze ruffled the thin, white curtains. Megarry glanced at Kelly. His face was pale and tired-looking. He had taken out a handkerchief and held it clasped against his nose.

Finnegan was working on the body, examining the finger-nails, the toes, the genitals, the ears, the hair. He stopped every now and then to cut away tiny pieces of flesh and place them in a tray. He worked busily, as if enjoying himself, shifting the lamp from time to time to present a new angle. He studied the neck, took out a magnifying glass and peered at the loose grey skin, took swabs and blood samples.

At last, he seemed satisfied. He stood back from the table and stripped off his gloves. Then he went to the sink and began to wash his hands and arms with carbolic soap.

'I'll have to open her stomach,' he said. 'Examine the contents. But I can do that later.'

'What did you find?' Megarry asked.

Finnegan dried his hands with a towel and took off his mask. There was a tight little grin on his face.

'What did I find? You Northerners always want to get straight to the bloody point. I found what I found the last time. The head was removed with a saw. An electrical saw, I would say. The cut is very clean. There's also some bruising on the upper arms and chest. That's consistent with a struggle. I'm assuming she tried to resist when she was shot.'

'An electrical saw?' Megarry said. 'Not a boning saw?'

'That's what I said.'

'The type of saw you would use for cutting trees?'

'Or metal. A boning saw would leave certain serrations. This is a clean cut. It's like I told you when I examined the head.'

'What about sexual assault?' Kelly asked.

Finnegan shook his head. 'The body has been in the water for some time, which complicates matters. However, I can see no bruisings on the genitals, nothing that you would expect to find if there had been violent sexual activity.'

'And the time of death?'

'I'd have to carry out more tests on the skin samples. By the look of it, I'd say that the body was in the water for maybe three weeks.'

'That's not what you told us the last time,' Megarry said.

Finnegan turned to stare. 'What did I say the last time?'

'You said ten days.'

'Well then. Ten days to three weeks.'

'Which is it, for Christ's sake?' Megarry said.

'I beg your pardon?' Finnegan's lip was trembling.

'It's important to be precise. What's the point of examining her, if you can't even tell us when she was killed?'

'Mr Megarry, I'd remind you that we're dealing with a corpse that's been dead for some time.'

'And I'd remind *you* that you're supposed to be able to tell us these things.'

Finnegan's red face glowed with anger. 'I won't be abused, Mr Megarry. Not by you nor by anyone.' He turned away from them, began to take off his laboratory coat.

'Look,' Megarry said. 'The head was in the sea.'

'I know that.'

'But the body was found in a lake. Would that not make a difference?'

194

'You didn't tell me it was found in a lake.'

'Jesus,' Megarry said. 'Didn't your examination show that?'

'I wasn't looking for it.'

'Would the rate of decay be the same?'

'*Wellll*,' Finnegan said. He squeezed his mouth like you would squeeze an orange. 'There would be some variations. A body in fresh water would probably decay faster.'

'But there would be damage in sea water too?'

Finnegan took a deep breath. 'Look, Mr Megarry. These things can't be exact. I can only give you estimates. If it was a fresh corpse, I could be more precise.'

'Nevertheless . . .'

'Neverthless what? What does it matter? What are you driving at?'

Megarry felt a surge of anger. 'What if the head wasn't in the sea for ten days? What if it was in the lake with the rest of the body? What if it was only put in the sea shortly before it was found?'

He could feel Kelly staring at him.

For a moment, none of them said anything, and then Finnegan reached once more for his gloves.

'All right,' he said wearily. 'I'll examine the head again.'

Megarry left the laboratory shortly after midday and drove back to Howth with Kelly. He went home and stood for a long time under a hot shower as if trying to wash away the contamination he had just witnessed.

In the kitchen was a note from Kathleen. '*I've taken the car. Gone to visit Nancy. Breakfast's in the oven.*' He found a shrivelled plaice, its eye pale and glazed. He poured some coffee and sat at the table for a long time, picking at the fish without appetite. At last, he scraped the remains of his breakfast into the wastebin and went out to the garden. It had a wild, desolate look, the grass so overgrown that it would take shears to cut it. He pulled a few weeds, took up a pair of secateurs and began mechanically lopping the dead heads off the roses. After a few minutes, he went back into the house, washed his hands and walked down to the station.

He found Kelly in his office. The tired look he had noticed earlier seemed more pronounced. There was a grotesque-looking drawing on the desk.

'What's this?'

'It's Finnegan's reconstruction of the head. Remember I asked him to do one for us?'

Megarry picked it up. It was a face like some hideous mask, hair tumbling down the cheeks, eyes staring. It was like something out of a horror comic.

'It looks nothing like her,' he said and tossed the drawing back on the desk. 'The man's an idiot.'

He leaned back in his chair and searched in his pockets for his cigarettes. 'I want to talk to you,' he said.

Kelly looked up.

'You know, Peter, often cases never get solved.'

'I know that.'

'In fact, it's worse than that. Sometimes cases *are* solved. Totally wrapped up to the investigators' satisfaction but no charges are ever brought. There are people walking the streets of this city who have literally got away with murder. The cops know it. They meet in the street and the villains smile. They know they're safe. Maybe there's not enough evidence. There's different reasons. It can be very hard for a cop to meet a killer and know there's nothing he can do.'

'What are you trying to tell me?' Kelly said irritably.

'I'm saying that no matter how this case pans out, no one can blame you. You've put your back into it. I've never seen an investigator work harder. I'm proud to have worked with you. Sinead is proud of you. Jamie is proud of you. If we don't bring this business to a satisfactory conclusion, you have nothing to reproach yourself about.'

He put the cigarettes back in his pocket and stood up.

'There's something else. It's hard on wives too. It's hard on families. Remember that.'

Kelly was staring at him. His eyes had grown moist.

'Thanks,' he said.

Lawlor was at her desk. He went and sat beside her.

'You're looking good,' he said.

'Am I? I got my hair cut.'

'It suits you.'

'Sometimes getting your hair cut can make you feel better. Don't you find that?'

'I suppose so.'

'Well, I needed to feel better, so I got my hair cut.' She lifted a pencil and doodled on a pad. 'Is the super hassling Peter?'

'I think so.'

'What can we do about it?'

Megarry took a deep breath. 'Sometimes there's nothing you can do. If the superintendent behaves like a shit, you just grin and bear it. Doing what's right is the important thing.'

He made a steeple with his fingers. 'Did you get a picture of Delaney?'

She opened her drawer and took out an envelope. 'Here.'

It was Delaney. A tidier version than they'd been used to. Clean-shaven, hair cut and actually smiling for the camera.

'Where'd you get it?' Megarry inquired. 'Bray cops?'

'No. It's from his driving licence. I've got contacts.'

Megarry put the photograph back in the envelope. 'Bring it with you,' he said.

'Where are we going?'

'To see Trish Blake.'

They went in Lawlor's car to the Bailey and down to the lighthouse. The sea was shining like polished steel. As they approached Paradise Regained they could hear it crashing on the rocks below.

Trish Blake came to the door at the first summons. She seemed surprised to see them. She opened her mouth as if to say something and then appeared to correct herself.

'I thought it was the postman,' she said. 'He's getting later and later. Some days he doesn't come till the afternoon.' She opened the door for them to enter. 'I was just doing the washing. Today's my washing day.'

'This is my colleague, Annie Lawlor. She's working with me on the investigation.'

Trish Blake's mouth parted in a broad smile. 'Well, I must say I approve, Cecil. Women can sense things that men can't. And women will tell women things that they might not tell a man.'

'Is that a fact?'

'Yes, it is. Incidentally, you know how much the bazaar netted? Over £600. Isn't that great? I didn't get a chance to thank you properly.'

'Bazaar?' Lawlor said.

'Yes. The local women's group. Cecil ran the bottle stall. It was for Children in Need,' Trish Blake said. 'I've a soft spot for them.'

She lowered her voice. 'It's partly a personal thing. You know I was orphaned?'

Megarry turned to look at her. 'I didn't know that.'

'How would you, Cecil? I hardly ever mention it. My parents both died when I was very young. I can barely remember them.' She tossed the information out as if it was of no great importance.

'But that must have been terribly sad for you,' Lawlor said.

'Not a bit. Didn't do me any harm. I had good foster homes.'

'You know, I used to work in that area,' Lawlor continued. 'I did a degree in Sociology at UCD.'

Megarry coughed to clear his throat.

'Look, Trish. I need to go over again the events of the day before the head was found.'

Mrs Blake turned an anguished face to him. 'Jesus, Cecil. Not all that again?'

'I'm afraid so. You see we've recovered the rest of the body. It was found this morning in Harpoon Lake.'

'My God.'

Trish Blake pushed back her hair, then twisted her wedding ring with her fingers.

'Hell, Cecil. If you're going to talk about that stuff again, I'm going to have a drink. The very thought of it gives me the creeps.'

She opened a cupboard and took out a bottle of sherry. 'Anybody else?'

'Too early,' Megarry said.

She poured herself a large sherry, then came back and sat down on a settee opposite them.

'Get this over fast,' she said and raised the glass to her lips. 'This business gives me nightmares.'

'You remember that day?' Megarry began.

'Fairly well.'

'Can you recall if anybody went down the path to the rocks?'

'No,' Mrs Blake said. 'No one.'

'You seem quite sure.'

'I'm positive.'

She took another drink of sherry, then puckered her brow for a moment.

'Actually, now that I think about it, there were some kids fishing.'

'Really?' Megarry said. 'You didn't mention that before.'

Mrs Blake looked confused. 'Hell, Cecil. I can't remember every damned thing.'

'And to get down there, they would have had to use the path?'

'Yes. I suppose so.'

'But you said yourself that people rarely use the path. Surely if you had seen someone down there, you would have remembered?'

'I didn't think it was important at the time. How was I to know that . . . Mary's head would be found down there? It just didn't register. I'm sorry, Cecil. I'm not being a very good witness, am I?'

'You're doing fine,' Lawlor said and patted her arm. 'People can't always remember every little thing. Particularly a woman like you, busy the way you are.'

'Can we get back to these children?' Megarry frowned. 'How many were there?'

'Two or three. Three, I think.'

'And how long were they down there?'

'I'm not sure about that. I saw them going down around lunchtime. I remember now because I had just put the radio on for the lunchtime news. They had fishing poles and bags and things.'

'What age were they?'

'About fourteen or fifteen. I remember thinking that they should have been at school.'

'And you didn't see them come up again?'

Trish Blake shook her head. 'I was organising the bazaar. I was busy on the phone for most of the afternoon, ringing round different people. I didn't stop till it was time to prepare Jim's dinner.'

'Apart from these kids, did you see anyone else use the path?'

'No,' Mrs Blake said firmly. 'I'm quite sure of that. But then, like I said, I was busy. I wasn't paying any particular notice.'

'So if someone else had used the path, you might not have seen them?'

'No.'

Megarry sighed. The interview was going nowhere.

'There's something else you mentioned before. You said your husband heard a noise late at night.'

'Did I?'

'Yes, you did, Trish. You said something woke him at 1 a.m. The dog was barking and he went out to investigate.'

'Oh yes. That's right. But it was nothing.'

'He was sure there was no one there?'

'Well, he didn't see anyone.'

'Did he go down the path?'

'I don't think so. He wasn't gone very long.'

'And the dog didn't bark any more?'

'No. Jim got into bed and we went back to sleep.'

Megarry sat back in his chair, closed his eyes and rubbed them with the heel of his hand.

'I think we'll have to talk to him,' he said. 'Where does he work?'

'You could see him here,' Mrs Blake said quickly. 'He'll be home around six.'

'Trish, this is urgent. Can I have the address?'

'Rossmount Machines,' she said. 'It's in Parkgate Street. Up near the Park.'

Megarry stood up. 'I'm sorry to keep bothering you. But we have to check everything.'

'I know, Cecil. But sometimes it gets wearying.'

She finished her sherry and put down the glass. As Megarry stood up, his eye was drawn to a painting on the wall. It was a seascape. Suddenly there was a flash of illumination. This was the painting he'd been looking for in Crow's Nest Cottage.

He bent to examine it.

'P.B.?' he said.

'A local artist,' Trish Blake said coyly.

'It's very good. I like it. Who's the artist?'

'Me,' she said and gave a little smile.

As they got to the car, Lawlor's mobile began to ring. He watched her speaking for a moment and then she passed it over. 'For you.'

It was Finnegan.

'I've just been talking to Inspector Kelly,' he began. 'I've examined that head again. I've revised my original opinion. I believe it was only in the water for a short time.'

'How short?'

'Less than twenty-four hours.'

'That's what I thought,' Megarry said. 'Thank you.'

'Excuse me,' Finnegan cut in. 'I'm not finished. I didn't like the way you spoke to me today.'

'I don't care what you like. If you did your damned job properly in the first place, there'd be no argument.'

'In fact, I'm taking it up with the superintendent.'

Megarry took a deep breath. 'Now you listen to me, you little runt. You make any trouble for Peter Kelly, I'll personally come down to your damned lab and kick you so hard in the Henry Halls, they'll look like boils on the back of your neck. You got that?'

He handed the mobile back to Lawlor. She was laughing.

21

The Rossmount Machine Plant was part of a sprawling industrial estate, a warren of small factories and offices making everything from car tyres to filing cabinets. They found a small man in an ill-fitting security uniform picking his teeth with a matchstick in a corrugated hut. He put down the newspaper he was reading when Megarry and Lawlor appeared.

'Where could we find Jim Blake?' Megarry inquired.

The man examined them with red, rheum-filled eyes. 'Who's looking for him?'

'We're friends of his.'

'That's all right then. You'll get him over there.'

He picked up the newspaper again and pointed to a red-bricked building.

Jim Blake was in the commercial section, in a neat office with potted geraniums and a desk littered with technical drawings and plans. He was wearing blue overalls and had a pair of industrial goggles pulled back on top of his head. He seemed to be expecting them.

He stood up from his chair. 'Trish rang to tell me you wanted to talk. It's about the murder, isn't it?'

'Only in a tangential way. I really wanted to find out about the night before the head was found at Piper's Gut.'

Blake seemed uneasy. A few people were passing along the

corridor outside. Megarry could see them glancing into the office as they went by.

'Look,' Blake said. 'Would you mind if we did this somewhere else? You know what it's like. People gossip.'

'Sure,' Megarry said. 'It's purely routine. It'll only take a few minutes.'

'There's a coffee shop up the street. We could go there.'

Blake locked the office and they all trooped down the stairs and into the bright sunshine. As they crossed the yard, they passed a long shed. They could hear the rattle of machines, a loud hum like a plane engine revving up. Megarry stopped.

'Do you mind if I take a look?'

'Why not?'

Blake strode over and pulled a door wide. The noise was louder. There was a smell of oil and grease. Men in overalls stood by clattering pistons, whirling lathes. A man with a blow torch welded a sheet of steel in a shower of sparks and blue smoke. Megarry and Lawlor watched the scene for a few minutes, then Megarry closed the door and spoke again to Blake.

'I haven't seen anything like that since I was a little boy. My father took me on a tour of the Belfast shipyards.'

'What do you make?' Lawlor asked.

'Car components, mainly. For export. I programme the machines.'

'You're an engineer?' Megarry said. 'Where did you study?'

'Trinity College.'

They were out on the main street now. Across the road was the entrance to the park. There was a procession of schoolkids being ushered into line by their teachers. A sign with a pointing finger said 'Zoo'.

'I've always regretted not going to university,' said Megarry. 'But in my time there was no free education and my parents could never have afforded it. So it was straight out of school and off to the police training depot for me.'

'The main thing is to enjoy what you're doing,' Blake said.

'And you enjoy your work?'

'It has its moments. But yes. I think on balance I probably do.'

They came to the coffee shop. A waitress gave them a table and took their order.

Megarry could see Blake checking his watch. It was expensive, with a silver strap.

'I have a meeting at 3 p.m.,' he said.

'This won't take long,' Megarry said. 'You know we've found the rest of the body?'

'No. I didn't.'

'We found it this morning. You see, we thought at first the head had been in the sea for some time. But now our examination suggests it was only put there shortly before it was found. Our tests suggest twenty-four hours at the most.'

Blake nodded.

'I think whoever dumped the head in the sea may have used the path beside your house. Some local fishermen had put a net down there. They only did that occasionally and as luck would have it, the head got washed into the net.'

'And what about the rest of the body? Was it in the sea?'

'No. It was in Harpoon Lake.'

Blake's face had gone pale. 'My God,' he said. 'That's awful.'

'You know it?'

'Of course. I take the dog up there for walks. I was up there only yesterday.'

The waitress came with their order. Megarry waited till she was gone.

'Trish was at home the day before the head was found. She says she saw some kids fishing off the rocks below your house but no one else using the path. She also says the dog woke you that night about 1 a.m.'

Blake looked confused. 'What night are we talking about exactly?'

'May 13th.'

Blake scratched his head. 'I honestly can't remember. If Trish said it happened, then I suppose it did.'

'Does the dog wake you often?'

'Sometimes.'

'And what would usually cause it?'

'Various things. He's very sensitive. We have him mainly as a guard dog. We're quite isolated and we were advised that a good barking dog was the best deterrent against burglars.'

'Can you remember the events of that night? Your wife says you went out to investigate.'

'May 13th?'

'It was a Tuesday.'

Blake suddenly slapped his thigh.

'Yes. I remember it now. I got up and took the torch and went out to see what the hell was causing the commotion. But there was nothing. The whole thing only took a few minutes.'

'Did you see anything at all? Think hard now. This could be important.'

Blake shook his head. 'You think maybe someone was down there, dumping the head in the sea?'

'That's exactly what I think.'

'I didn't see anything. But then, I didn't look down the path. I just didn't think about it, to tell you the truth. My main concern was the house and the car. When I saw that they were both safe, I came back indoors and locked up and went back to bed.'

Lawlor put down her coffee cup. 'So what *do* you think caused the dog to bark?' she asked.

Blake shrugged. 'God knows. I thought at the time it might have been the wind.'

'The wind?' Megarry said.

'Yes. You know, rattling something. We get a lot of wind where we are.'

'But there was no wind that night,' Megarry said.

Blake stared. 'How can you be sure?'

'Because I checked with the fishermen. There'd been no wind for days.'

Blake walked with them to where Lawlor had parked her car.

'I hope I was some help,' he said and extended his hand.

Megarry took it, held it for a moment, then slowly rolled back Blake's sleeve.

'That really is a beautiful watch,' he said. 'It must have been expensive.'

Blake glanced at the watch and then he smiled. 'I don't know,' he said. 'It was a birthday present.'

'An admirer?'

'Yes. Trish.'

Megarry laughed. 'She must be fond of you.'

'Yes,' Blake said. 'Extremely fond.'

Megarry bent to open the car door and then he turned back.

'Did you know her at all? Mary Grogan? Did you ever meet her?'

'Vaguely. Trish and her were very good friends. She brought her to the house once or twice. But I couldn't say I knew her well.'

He paused. 'I was shocked when I heard about it, of course. What a bloody awful way to die.'

They left the factory behind and drove out into the afternoon traffic along Parkgate Street. As they passed the railway station, Lawlor reached over and turned on the radio. A breezy announcer was reading the news.

'Police hunting the killer of thirty-two-year-old Mary Grogan in Howth are expected to charge a man with a series of sexual assaults in the Kilbarrack area. And there are developments in the case of Imelda Lacy who was murdered in Bray in November 1995.'

'Jesus,' Lawlor said. 'I'm sick of this.'

She went to knock off the radio, but Megarry restrained her.

'No, Annie. Let's hear it.'

'However, there is growing concern that so far no one has been charged with the Grogan murder. As public anger mounts, police chiefs are said to be increasingly worried at the delay in bringing charges. This report from our security correspondent.'

There followed an excited account about concern in the local area. Several people were interviewed, including the chairman of the chamber of commerce who said that traders had noticed a marked fall-off among shoppers, particularly the elderly. He put it down to panic and said that the police should redouble their efforts to find the man responsible. 'They owe it to the community,' he said in grave tones. 'The community is being held to ransom.'

Megarry listened, his face giving nothing away, as Lawlor battled the traffic along the quays.

At last she said, 'Heard enough?'

He nodded.

She switched the radio off.

They crossed O'Connell Bridge and passed the Custom House. There was a row of seagulls on the lawn, sitting like plastic ducks in the sun. For a while they drove in silence.

'So, Annie,' said Megarry, 'what do *you* think about all this?'

'Me?'

'Why not? You know all the facts.'

Lawlor turned her face away. 'I think it's looking grim,' she said. 'I think we're up shit creek without a paddle.'

'You believe it's that bad?'

'Yes.'

He smiled. 'I would have agreed with you until this morning. But now that we've found the body, things have changed. Remember what they used to impress on you at training college? Motive. Motive. Motive. Isolate the motive and you are half-way to solving the crime. What was the motive for murdering Mary Grogan?'

Lawlor took her eyes off the road. 'Is this some sort of game?'

'No. I'm perfectly serious.'

'Well,' she said. 'We could begin with revenge.'

'So who might it be?'

'Someone she crossed in her career? We know that she was ambitious and ruthless. Maybe she stood in the way of someone else's success. That might be enough to drive a person to murder.'

'But who?' Megarry pressed.

'I don't know.'

'Start again.'

'Thwarted love? Brian Casey was obviously upset that she broke off their relationship. He sounded very bitter. And we have the word of Joyce Denvir that he could be violent. He said he wished she was dead.'

'Anyone else?'

'I would have said Boylan or Delaney. But they seem to be ruled out.'

They were passing the Point Theatre. There was a queue of people milling about in the concourse. A billboard said: 'The Cranberries. Three Nights only.'

'When people talk about murder,' Megarry said, 'they always mention greed, revenge, sex, love, jealousy. They leave out one of the most common causes of all.'

'What's that?'

'It's what I call the Peace of Mind factor.'

Lawlor turned to look at him.

'It's very common, Annie. Its attraction lies in the removal of a threat or a perceived threat. The person who is murdered is holding some power over the murderer. The murderer eventually comes to believe that the only way he can achieve peace of mind is to kill the person who is threatening him.'

'Blackmail?' Lawlor said.

'Not necessarily. Keep thinking.'

'Jesus, I give up,' Lawlor said. She swung the car onto the Howth Road. 'But I'll tell you one thing. Whoever murdered her is local.'

Megarry looked up quickly.

'Why do you say that?'

'Because of the way the body was disposed of. Dumped in Harpoon Lake. The person who killed her knows the geography intimately. How many people know of that place? It's not particularly beautiful or interesting. Most people wouldn't even be aware of its existence.'

They came into Howth along the coast road and past the harbour. The sun was beginning to go down, yellow-gold rays slanting across the ocean. As the car approached the Capstan Bar, Megarry said to Lawlor, 'Have you met Tom Reddin?'

Lawlor shook her head.

'Let me introduce you. He's a very interesting man.'

The front garden of the pub was full, the wooden tables crammed with day-trippers drinking beer. Inside it was cool. It still smelt of beer and stale tobacco.

Reddin was washing glasses in the sink as they came in.

'Mr Megarry. You're back again. And a charming young lady with you. I am indeed honoured.'

'This is Annie Lawlor, Tom. She's working on the case.'

Reddin showed immediate interest. 'I'm delighted. And a difficult case it's proving to be, by all accounts. What are you having to drink?'

'Diet cola.'

'Make that two.'

Reddin poured the drinks and put them in frosted glasses on fresh drip-mats.

'Have this on me,' he said, and waved away Megarry's proffered cash. 'It's my pleasure. You know I always enjoy a conversation with you, Mr Megarry. I always gain . . . sustenance from it.'

'Is that a fact, Tom?'

'Yes, indeed, Mr Megarry.'

Reddin scooped up a handful of peanuts from a bowl and stuffed them in his mouth.

'What did you mean just now about the case proving difficult?'

'Well, I'm relying on our friends in the media for that information, but by all accounts the heat is on. Nobody charged yet with poor Mary's murder. People are concerned, Mr Megarry. They feel the police are not doing enough.'

'But how do they know what the police are doing? Don't you think the police want to solve this murder too, Tom?'

'Of course. Don't misunderstand me. I'm talking about perception.'

'You're talking about gossip, Tom.'

'Well now.' Reddin took a cloth and gave the counter a wipe. 'Gossip is really just what people are talking about.'

Megarry lifted his drink and felt the bubbles catch in his nose. He put the glass down and spoke to Lawlor.

'I don't know how you can drink this stuff.'

'Perhaps something a little stronger?' Reddin suggested.

'No, Tom. It's all right.' Megarry wiped his mouth with the back of his hand. 'Remember the last time I was here? You mentioned a young man who used to accompany Mary on occasions to listen to the music?'

'Yes indeed, Mr Megarry.'

Megarry motioned to Lawlor. She opened her bag and took out the photograph of John Delaney.

'Is that him, Tom?'

Reddin had taken out a pair of horn-rimmed glasses from his shirt pocket. He pressed them hard against his nose and raised his eyebrows to peer at the print.

'Yes,' he said at last. 'That's him.'

'You're sure?'

'I'm certain, Mr Megarry.'

22

'They're what?' Lawlor said in astonishment.

'They're taking me off the God-damned case.' Kelly tried to sound casual. He made an effort to smile but it came out lopsided. 'They're shafting me.'

'And who's taking over?'

'The superintendent. He's taking personal charge.'

'Jesus Christ. They can't do that. Not after all the work you've put in. You've been busting your ass since this thing began. It's not your fault if we haven't made an arrest.'

She appealed to Megarry. 'They can't do this, Cecil?'

Megarry sat down across from Kelly. 'Tell me what happened,' he said wearily.

'The superintendent said he wanted to see me. Said he'd been talking to the Commissioner and they were concerned about the lack of progress in the case.'

'What are they talking about?' Lawlor protested. 'We've got Boylan for the Kilbarrack assaults. And we've got Thunder for the Lacy killing. What more do they want?'

'Someone for the Grogan murder. That's what started all this media hullabaloo. The superintendent said that perhaps I was a bit inexperienced for a major murder inquiry like this.'

Megarry took a paper-clip from the desk, studied it and put it down again.

'You're wrong,' he said. 'This isn't about the Grogan murder. This is about politics.'

Kelly looked up.

'It's about giving the impression of activity. When the Minister starts asking questions, the Commissioner can point to the number of people he's had on the case. All the different things he's done. Even if he has nothing to show for it at the end of the day, no one can accuse him of inactivity. You're just a casualty of politics, Peter.'

Kelly looked totally deflated.

'However.' Megarry paused. 'He didn't actually tell you to stop working on the investigation, did he?'

'Not in so many words.'

'Then technically you're still in charge.'

Megarry walked to the desk and took all the phones off their cradles. He turned to Lawlor.

'Give me your mobile.'

Kelly watched in amazement. 'What are you doing?'

'I'm rendering you incommunicado. If the superintendent wants to take you off the case, then he'll have to come and tell you personally.'

They piled into Kelly's car outside the station.

'Where are we going?' Lawlor said.

'Dudgeon's place. I think Mick and his old ma know more about this whole business than they've told us.'

Dudgeon was working in the field behind the house when he saw them coming along the bridle-path through the gorse. He stopped and leaned on his spade for a moment and then he put it down and made his way to the gate to meet them.

He stuck out an unshaven chin. 'It's her, isn't it? Her in the Crow's Nest?'

'That's right,' Megarry said. 'We've got the rest of the body now. We found it in Harpoon Lake this morning. You know it, don't you?'

'Of course I do.'

'She'd been stripped naked and tied up and dumped in the water.'

212

A shadow flitted across Dudgeon's face. 'It wasn't me. I didn't do it. I told you that before.'

'How do I know that, Mick?'

'Because it's true. I didn't kill her. Honest.'

'But you know about it, Mick. You know who broke into her cottage. Don't you?'

The dog got up from the door and made its desultory way towards then, growling as it came. Lawlor stood back.

'Sit,' Dudgeon commanded and the dog slowly lay down at his feet.

'I don't know nothing about that.'

'Yes, you do.'

Megarry paused and looked out over the heath. It seemed to tremble with colour, yellow and green and purple all the way down to the sea.

'This is a beautiful place. Some people would pay a lot of money to live here. But you probably don't realise that. You're not all that interested in money, are you, Mick?'

'I have enough. I get by. I see that ma don't starve.'

'Your family has lived here all these years. And then this upstart comes and threatens to put you out. Just because you ask her to repair the roof, which is something she is meant to do under the terms of the lease.'

The gravel scraped as Dudgeon shifted his feet. 'She was a bitch,' he said.

'You almost lost the house once before, isn't that so? You were almost put out. Your father drank the lease away. You were only a child, but you never forgot the fear and shame that you saw every day on your mother's face. The threat that hung over you that you would end up like tinkers on the side of the road.'

Dudgeon looked away.

'You've had no peace of mind since she came to Crow's Nest. Isn't that so?

'Yes.'

'You threatened to kill her, Mick.'

There was no reply. Megarry became aware of the stillness of the place.

'You tried to frighten her, didn't you? You sent her a severed doll's head as a threat. Ma probably suggested that. It was meant to intimidate her, to get her to back off. And then when you heard that her own head had been found in the sea, you got worried. You realised that the doll could be damning for you. So you went back to Crow's Nest. You took a hammer and broke the window and let yourself in. You ransacked her study looking for that doll's head.'

Dudgeon said nothing.

'Have you got a cigarette?' Megarry asked and Dudgeon took out a packet.

Megarry took it from him and examined it.

'B & H? You smoke these all the time?'

'Sure I do.'

'You left a stub behind in Crow's Nest, Mick.' He opened his hand and a cigarette butt lay curled in his palm. The lettering was clearly visible along the edge.

Suddenly Dudgeon was appealing to Megarry and Lawlor and Kelly, staring from one face to the other.

'I did threaten her. I did send her the doll's head, just like you said. I did break into the cottage. All that is true. But I didn't kill her. Honest to God. I didn't do that. I'm not violent. Even though she gave me a terrible time, I would never have laid a finger on a woman.'

He was weeping now, the tears tripping along his cheeks. He lifted a sleeve and wiped first one eye and then the other.

'You've got to believe me. I didn't do it.'

Megarry felt a lump rise in his throat. He looked at the miserable farmhouse, the missing slates on the roof that had caused the enmity between neighbours, the grass sprouting from the gutters, the peeling paint.

He heard a rattle of glass. It shattered the silence of the heath. And then he realised it was coming from the house. The old woman was sitting by the window. She was banging on the pane with her stick.

'She wants you,' Megarry said.

But Dudgeon was shaking his head.

'No,' he said. 'It's you she wants.'

There was the same fetid smell Megarry remembered from the last visit, the odour of boiled vegetables, of human sweat, of trapped air. Dudgeon led them through the house to the room where the old woman sat by the window gazing out over the heath.

'Yes?' Megarry said.

'Sit down,' she commanded, and Megarry did as he was told. Kelly stood back.

'You have the girleen with you,' the old woman said. 'Where is she?'

Lawlor's mouth opened in amazement. She came forward and old Mrs Dudgeon grasped her hand in her own. She began to caress it, calloused fingers gently stroking the soft flesh.

'Mick didn't do it. You believe me.'

Lawlor looked into the milky eyes that didn't move but stared straight as an arrow across the heath. She smelt the old woman's smell and felt a slight unease. Mrs Dudgeon pulled her shawl closer around her chest.

'Why should I believe you?' Lawlor said.

'Because you're a woman. A mother knows her own son. I reared him. I know what he can do. I know he didn't kill her.' The old hands gripped tighter. 'I've had a hard life, daughter. I scraped and saved to rear six children. I had a husband who was no good. Never worked. Drank all day. Nearly got us put out of the house, only for the priest. Mick was protecting us. That's why he sent her that head. But he didn't kill her.'

'Who did it then?'

The old lady pulled at the shawl once more. 'That's your job to find out.'

'Mrs Dudgeon, if you know or suspect who killed her, you have a duty to tell us.'

The old woman sniffed but said nothing.

'We can bring Mick to the station. We can charge him with intimidation.'

Suddenly Mrs Dudgeon banged her stick on the floor. 'Talk, talk, talk. Why don't you listen for a change? He didn't do it, I tell you.'

'Who did it?'

'The wicked people she went with. She used to have parties down there in Crow's Nest. I would hear them at night when Mick was in bed, going past out there on the path. They'd be drunk. I'd hear them laughing and talking. All sorts of bad language. She had no respect for herself. She went with men who were already married. Did you know that?' She squeezed Lawlor's hand and pulled her closer.

'Who did it, Mrs Dudgeon?'

The old shoulders heaved and the lips began to tremble. A line of white spittle dribbled along her chin.

'A man called James. He did it.'

For a moment there was silence. Lawlor glanced at Megarry. 'James who?'

'I don't know his other name.'

'How do you know he killed her?'

'Because I used to hear them talking. They think because I'm blind I don't know what's going on. But I could tell you when the hare is on the mountain. I could tell you when the fox has left his lair. I may be blind but thank God I can hear. He did it.'

'Do you know where he lives?'

'He lives here. He lives in Howth. He killed her. I'll stake my life on it.'

Lawlor persisted. 'How do you know?'

'Oh, for God's sake. Questions, questions, questions. Yap, yap, yap.'

The old woman fumbled wildly till she grasped her son's hand.

'Mick, show them what you found in Crow's Nest,' she said.

Lawlor read the letter that Mick Dudgeon gave her in silence, then handed it to Megarry. It was a single sheet of paper, letters cut from a newspaper.

Why did you do it, Mary? Why did you betray me? I always trusted you. I opened my heart and in return you did this to me. I put my faith in you, but you threw it away. You laughed in my face. You took our friendship and crushed it in your hands. You betrayed me, Mary, and now you must die.

'You found this in the cottage?' Megarry asked.

Dudgeon nodded. 'In a drawer in her desk.'

Megarry put the note back in its envelope and slipped it in his pocket.

'Why didn't you bring it to us sooner?'

'I was afraid.'

'Did you tell anyone else?'

Dudgeon shook his head. 'Only me and ma knows.'

'Keep it that way,' Megarry said.

They left West Heath and went in along the coast road, past Sutton and Bayside.

'You believe him?' Lawlor said at last.

'Of course,' Megarry said. 'He's an uneducated man, limited intelligence. I doubt if he could think up something like this on his own.'

'But if Mary Grogan was getting threats like this, why didn't she report them?'

'Who knows? She didn't report the doll's head either. Maybe she just didn't take them seriously.'

'And you take this seriously?'

'Sure as hell. Whoever sent her that note delivered the goods.'

Delaney's address turned out to be a block of flats close to the railway line. There was a playground nearby and some kids kicking a ball in the fading light. As they got out of the car, Megarry said: 'I want someone to stay outside in case he tries to make a run for it.'

'I'll do it,' Kelly said quickly.

'Have you got your personal weapon?'

Kelly pulled back his jacket to reveal the shoulder holster nestling under his arm.

'Right,' Megarry said. 'Let's go.'

They started on foot for the mouth of the tower block. It was cool and dark. The lift wasn't working so they had to climb the stairs to the sixth floor. Megarry was out of breath by the time they arrived.

They could hear music from inside, guitars and drums

played by a heavy metal band. The door was opened by a young woman with dyed, cropped hair. She had a silver ear-ring in one ear.

'Yes?' she said and observed them defiantly from the hallway. The music was louder. It seemed to have no discernible rhythm.

'We're looking for John Delaney.'

The woman turned into the hall and shouted. 'Jack! Some people here to see you.'

There was a pause and then Delaney appeared from one of the rooms. He was wearing a smock and there were paint stains on his arms. When he saw Megarry, he immediately began to protest.

'I warned you the last time,' he shouted. 'This is pure harassment. I'm ringing my solicitor.'

Megarry took a piece of paper from his pocket and waved it in front of Delaney's face. 'This is a warrant to search the flat. Duly made out and authorised. It's all above board. And this is my colleague, Detective Lawlor.'

Lawlor gave a little bow.

'I don't think this is funny,' Delaney said.

'We never said it was.'

'This is fucking police intimidation. You could get away with this sort of thing when you were in the North, but you're in the Irish Republic now. We don't put up with this shit down here.'

Megarry fixed him with a stare. 'I'm well aware of where I am. I'm well aware of the law and my responsibilities. We're not doing anything illegal.'

'You're harassing me. You pulled me in a few days ago. You followed me into the boozer and now you're here in my gaff. How did you know I'd be here?'

'Because it's Monday. You told me you had Mondays off.'

'You're harassing me,' Delaney said again. 'You're persecuting me.'

'But if you're innocent, you have nothing to worry about.'

'That's not the point,' the young woman with the ear-ring put in. 'It's our civil liberties we're concerned with. We have a right to go about our business without having the oppression of the state brought down on top of us.' She glared at Megarry and then at Lawlor.

'Leave this to me, Noreen,' Delaney said and pushed her aside.

'I see you're still decorating, Jack,' Megarry said and pointed to the paint on Delaney's arms.'

'Ha, bloody, ha,' Delaney said.

'You know, I find it interesting that Mary Grogan should be a painter and you should also be a painter and yet your paths never crossed. What are you working on?'

He pushed further into the flat and entered the room where Delaney had been. An easel stood before a window, with a canvas stretched on it. Megarry turned to find Delaney in the doorway behind him.

'What is it?' he asked.

'It's an abstract. It's not finished. What do you know about art?'

'Perhaps I know more than you think.'

Lawlor had begun moving through the flat, quietly lifting cushions, poking into recesses, opening cupboards.

'Hey,' Delaney said. 'What are you up to?'

'Just executing the warrant,' Lawlor said and smiled.

The young woman with the ear-ring started up again. 'This is Fascism,' she said. 'This is state harassment of working people. I'm lodging a complaint. I'll get on to our local party man about this. What's his name, Jack?'

'For Christ's sake,' Delaney groaned.

'As I was saying earlier,' Megarry said. 'I find it odd that you never knew each other. And you lived only a few miles apart. How far is it to Howth on the DART?'

Delaney didn't reply. The music on the stereo system came to an end with a wailing guitar blast. Megarry raised his voice.

'Can't be more than fifteen minutes from your front door to the Capstan Bar. You know the Capstan, don't you, Jack? You did tell me that?'

Delaney's face flushed. 'What's that got to do with anything?'

'You'd be surprised. You know the proprietor, Tom Reddin, I suppose? Bit garrulous, but otherwise not a bad sort.'

'Do I?'

'Well, he knows you.'

'What?'

'And you also know Mick Dudgeon, don't you, Jack? I think you and he had an altercation?'

'For Christ's sake, my name's not Jack. Why do you keep calling me that? My name is John.'

Megarry saw the young woman glance at Delaney. She opened her mouth to speak and then thought better of it.

'Mary Grogan knew you as Jack. When you went with her to the Capstan Bar to listen to traditional music, she addressed you as Jack. She used to say things like "Packet of peanuts, Jack". Why did you lie to me?'

Out of the corner of his eye, he could see Lawlor move from the kitchen into a bedroom.

'You're trying to say I murdered her. Just like you tried to pin the Imelda Lacy job on me. I know the way you bastards work.'

'Who's Mary Grogan?' the woman with the ear-ring said.

'Oh, shut up, Noreen!' Delaney said.

'I'm going to bring you in,' Megarry said in a soft voice. 'You can get a solicitor if you like. We have a car downstairs.'

He saw Lawlor come out of the bedroom with an envelope in her hand. Delaney saw it too and tried to grab it.

'What the fuck . . .?' he said. 'That's personal stuff. You can't do this.'

Megarry opened the envelope. Inside was a strip of photographic negatives. He held one up to the light. A woman in an outfit posed with a whip.

'Good work, Annie,' Megarry said, and took Delaney by the arm.

By the time they had finished interviewing Delaney, it was almost nine o'clock. Megarry was ravenous. He left the interview room and went up to Kelly's office where the phones lay idle on the desk, as he had left them. He reconnected one and dialled home.

Kathleen came on the line. 'Where have you been all day? You didn't finish your breakfast. I saw it dumped in the wastebin.'

'I wasn't hungry,' Megarry said. 'I am now. I should be home in about an hour. Can you rustle up something?'

'Like what?'

'What about a nice steak?'

'Something's about to happen,' Kathleen said. 'I can tell.'

'Yes,' Megarry said. 'Open a bottle of wine.'

Next, he rang Joyce Denvir.

'Cecil Megarry here. We talked the other day at the school.'

'Yes.'

'I need to ask you something. When you were at Trinity, did you know a man called James Blake?'

'Sure I did. Everybody knew everybody else. He was studying engineering.'

'Did Mary know him?'

Denvir paused. Megarry held his breath.

'Yes,' Joyce Denvir said. 'Sure did. They were lovers.'

23

They were at Paradise Regained shortly after 9 p.m. There was a big orange moon like a ball of fire over the ocean. Out by Rockabill, they could see the lighthouse winking in the gloom.

'It's amazing the things you miss,' Megarry said as they parked beside a silver hatchback outside the house.

'Like what?' Kelly asked.

'Like that car. Do you remember if it was here the last time?'

'I don't think so.'

They rang the doorbell. The cries of the sea-birds rose like a lament on the night air.

Trish Blake opened the door. 'My God,' she said and gave a small laugh. 'Three of you now. This must be serious.'

'Is Jim at home?' Megarry said.

'Of course. But I thought you spoke to him at work?'

'We did. We have to speak to him again.'

'He's just finishing dinner. Come in.'

She held the door wide. They trooped through the hall and into the kitchen. Jim Blake was seated at a table near the window. It gave a view out over the night sky. He looked up as they came in, put down his knife and fork and wiped his mouth with a napkin.

'I'm sorry to burst in on you like this,' Megarry said.

'Sit down,' Blake said. He called out to his wife. 'Trish. Get Mr Megarry and his colleagues something to drink.'

'No,' Megarry said quickly. 'It's all right.'

They sat down.

'Would you care to join us?' Megarry said to Trish Blake. She hesitated, then smoothed her skirt and sat beside her husband.

Megarry pointed to the seascape on the wall. 'You know, it's amazing. I've never run into so many painters as I have in the last few days. Mary, Trish.'

'But there's so much here to paint,' Jim Blake said. 'The local scenery. It inspires people.'

'I ran into another one today. Jack Delaney.'

Trish Blake averted her eyes.

'Do you know him?'

'Sure. He was a member of Mary's painting group.'

'*Was?*'

'He had a row with Mary. I think he was jealous of her.' Megarry took out his cigarettes. 'Do you mind if I smoke?'

'No. Go right ahead.'

'It's a very bad habit. My wife and doctor want me to give it up. But I'm finding it very hard. I'm addicted, you see.'

'That's all right,' Blake said. 'I used to smoke myself. I know how difficult it can be.'

Megarry blew out a thin trail of smoke. It drifted grey and blue towards the ceiling.

'How well do you know Delaney?'

'Not very well. It was Trish who met him first.'

'We arrested him this afternoon.'

There was a sharp intake of breath.

'My God. Are you telling us *he* killed Mary?'

'No,' Megarry said. 'I've arrested him for something else. I've arrested him for blackmail. 'He had some compromising photographs of Mary. There was also a man in the photographs.'

Jim Blake pushed his plate into the centre of the table. 'And you want to talk to us about Delaney?'

'Partly. I also want to talk to you.'

'But I told you everything I know this morning.'

'Not everything,' Megarry said.

He reached out and took hold of Blake's left wrist. He pushed back the sleeve.

'You have a birthmark, I see.'

Blake smiled. 'It doesn't bother me. Lots of people have birthmarks.'

'The man in the photographs also has a birthmark. Just like yours. Here, see for yourself.'

Blake's hand shook as he lifted a photograph. 'But this man is blindfolded.'

Megarry tapped ash from his cigarette. 'This man is you.'

Blake began to laugh. He glanced towards his wife.

'This is preposterous.'

'No. Look. The hair, the build, the birthmark. It's you. Isn't it? You're the man in the photographs. You knew Mary Grogan from your college days. You were at Trinity together.'

Outside the window, they could hear the wind begin to howl.

'You had an affair with her when you were students. Then you drifted apart. You married Trish. You didn't see Mary again till she came to live in Howth. Did your wife introduce you through the painters' group?'

'This is nonsense,' Blake said.

'Mary was going out with Brian Casey at the time. You resumed your affair with Mary behind your wife's back. Your wife who was Mary's best friend. Who trusted her. Who had unwittingly brought her back into your life.'

'For God's sake,' Blake said.

'You used to go to the Strangled Dwarf with Mary. You called yourselves Shirley and Clive. How did you get into that scene? Was it Mary's idea? She was the dominant type. Did she like that kind of stuff? Leather, whips, handcuffs? Was it her idea to take the photographs?'

Trish Blake was staring at her husband. Her lip was trembling.

He ignored her.

'Tell me something,' Megarry said. 'The factory where you work? You have an electrical saw there?'

'What?'

'I saw it this morning.'

'Jesus,' Blake said.

'Have you got keys to the factory?'

'Of course. I'm senior management.'

'You used that saw to cut off Mary Grogan's head.'

There was a silence in the room.

'I don't believe I'm hearing this,' Blake said and tried to get up from his chair.

Megarry put a hand on his shoulder and pressed him down.

'I want a solicitor. You can't come barging into my house, tossing accusations about.'

'I think I can prove them,' Megarry said calmly.

'You're trying to say that *I* murdered Mary Grogan? Is that what this is all about? You're trying to say I killed her?'

'No,' Megarry said.

He turned to Trish Blake. She moved closer to her husband and gripped his arm.

'Your wife killed her.'

'I didn't do it,' Trish Blake said.

Her nails bit into the flesh of her husband's arm.

'You were in Galway on the weekend of April 20th. You were driving that car out there.' Megarry gestured with his hand. 'The hatchback. You met Jack Delaney.'

'No. It isn't true.'

'You met him there to buy back the photographs. He was blackmailing your husband.'

'No.'

'Yes,' Megarry said and thumped the table. 'Why don't you tell the truth? I've already interviewed Delaney. He's confessed.'

Trish Blake started to weep, silent tears that tripped along her cheeks.

'Delaney was friendly with Mary. They used to go drinking together in the Capstan Bar on Saturday nights to listen to the music. She got him to intervene in a row she was having with her neighbour, Mick Dudgeon.

'But Delaney has a chip on his shoulder. He resents his background, a poor boy from Bray. He resents his job as a butcher. He would have liked to move in arty circles, to become a full-time painter. But that would cost money he didn't have.

'For a time, he was a regular visitor to Crow's Nest Cottage. While he was there one day, poking around, he had a stroke of luck. He found the negatives in a drawer and realised they might have value. He first tried to blackmail Mary but she sent him packing. Then he started on your husband. Delaney says he was looking for £50,000 and when Jim couldn't raise that sort of money, he contacted you.'

'No!' Trish Blake screamed. 'It's not true. Jim loved only me. He never loved that bitch. This is all lies.'

'It's not lies. You wanted to avoid a scandal. You agreed to go to Galway to negotiate with him. I have Delaney's confession. I also have a witness who saw you together on the Saturday afternoon. You were driving that silver hatchback.'

Trish Blake shook her head violently from side to side.

'You were devastated when you discovered that your husband and Mary Grogan were having an affair. You couldn't come to terms with it.'

'No.'

'Yes,' Megarry said. 'She was threatening your marriage. Threatening to bring chaos and disorder into your life. You couldn't face that.'

Mrs Blake hung her head.

'You bought the pictures. How much did you pay him?'

She said nothing.

'It was a waste of money. Delaney had kept the negatives. You should have known that a blackmailer would do that. But of course you were desperate. You drove back to Dublin and waited till Mary came home. You rang her and invited her to this house. When she came, you begged her to give up the relationship. When she refused, you shot her.'

'No.'

'I also have this.'

Megarry reached into his pocket and took out the letter he had been given by Mick Dudgeon. He unfolded it and read.

'Why did you do it, Mary? Why did you betray me? I always trusted you. I opened my heart and in return you did this to me. I put my faith in you, but you threw it away. You laughed in my face. You took our friendship and crushed it in your hands. You betrayed me, Mary, and for that you must die.'

He held up the letter. 'You sent that, didn't you?'

'No.'

'It was found in her house. Crow's Nest Cottage. You sent it.'

Suddenly, Trish Blake's face crumpled like a paper mask. Her chest heaved and she was sobbing uncontrollably.

'I didn't mean to kill her. I wanted to scare her. I wanted her to give Jim up. She was destroying everything I'd built. My home, my marriage, my security. I pleaded with her, got down on my bended knees. She had everything she wanted, a good job, money, boyfriends. But it wasn't enough. She wanted to take Jim as well. You can't believe how selfish she was. She told me to grow up. Said I was being a stupid little housewife. I lost control. Pulled the trigger.'

She turned her tear-stained face towards Megarry.

'I didn't mean to kill her. Honest to God. It was the last thing I meant.'

Lawlor walked across the room and took her by the arm.

'We're arresting you for the murder of Mary Grogan,' Kelly said. He turned to Jim Blake. His face had gone a sickly grey colour. 'We're arresting you for being an accessory.'

24

Ten days later, Megarry and Kathleen had a barbecue. He'd finally licked the garden into shape, sawing down branches, cutting a swath through months of neglected undergrowth. He'd had to borrow a scythe for the lawn; the grass had grown so thick and tall. It had been hard work, hot and dirty. But now the garden looked trim, a semblance of order had been restored. He had dug the borders and Kathleen had put down rows of summer plants.

They had invited Peter Kelly, Sinead and Jamie, Annie Lawlor and Rory, and Kathleen's sister Nancy and her husband Andrew. The early morning haze had cleared and by one o'clock the sun had broken through. The air was filled with the smell of gorse and burning charcoal. There was a cool breeze drifting up from the sea. It was a perfect day.

Megarry poured a cold beer and looked with satisfaction across the lawn. The guests were chatting at a long wooden bench beside the rose bed. Kathleen had put out a barrel filled with ice and sunk bottles of beer and wine into it. Andrew had got Rory into conversation and was gesticulating vigorously with his arm. Jesus, Megarry thought, he's going to bore him witless about darts.

He tied on his apron and looked at Jamie. 'You ready?'

The boy nodded. He was wearing a green and white jersey, the Celtic FC strip.

'This is a very important job. You're my assistant. Right?'
'Right.'
'Your job is to keep turning the meat. You got your fork?'
Jamie produced a long, two-pronged meat fork.
'Okay. Let's start.'
Megarry dipped the meat into the marinade dish and began laying the pieces on the grill. The sweet scent of cooking meat began to fill the afternoon air.
'You ever done this before?' Megarry asked.
Jamie shook his head.
'My dad always does it. He never lets me help.'
'He will after this. By the time we're finished, you'll be an expert.'
Jamie smiled and cautiously stuck the fork into a chicken breast. The juice dripped down onto the coals.
'How's that ould team of yours doing?' Megarry asked.
'What do you mean? They're top of the league. Four points clear.'
'Jam,' Megarry said.
'It's not jam. Did you see them against the Hibbies?'
'I missed that,' Megarry said. 'I was busy.'
'They stuffed them. Four nil.'
'The Hibbies must have been asleep,' Megarry said. 'Wait till Rangers get them again. You'll be paying me that money back.'
'You'll have some wait,' Jamie said.
Eventually the meat was cooked. Megarry piled it on a large serving dish and Jamie carried it proudly back up the lawn to where the guests were waiting. Megarry pulled the top off another beer and went to join them.
'Everybody enjoying themselves?' he said.
'Cecil. We were just talking about that murder.' It was Nancy. She'd got her hair done and it sparkled in the sun.
'Please,' Megarry said. 'I thought we'd put that business to bed.'
'What I want to know is, why did that man cut her up? His wife had shot her, so she was already dead. Why didn't they just dump her in the sea and be done with it?'
Megarry looked around the table and caught Peter Kelly's eye.

'You've a morbid curiosity, Nancy. Did anybody tell you that?'

Nancy fluttered her shoulders like a little bird. 'I'm just interested, that's all. Everybody's interested. I was in the supermarket this morning and it was all they could talk about.'

'He cut her up because he thought it would be easier to dispose of the body,' Kelly said.

Nancy turned towards him. 'Really?'

'Yes. Here's what happened. Jim Blake came home that night to find Mary Grogan dead in their kitchen and his wife having hysterics. He was in a state of shock, as you can imagine. His first reaction was to get rid of the body. He thought of dumping it into the sea, but there was no guarantee that it wouldn't get washed up on some beach somewhere. So he hit on a different plan. He decided to take her into his factory and cut her up with the electrical saw and then dispose of her in Harpoon Lake.

'If he'd been thinking straight, he would have realised what an awful job it was going to be. A fresh corpse. He started with the head. There was blood everywhere. The place must have been drenched with it. The walls, the floor, the saw. He cleaned it up as best he could, but he couldn't remove it all. The forensic team had no difficulty finding traces when they went to the factory. It was Mary Grogan's blood.

'In the end, he couldn't go on. He was overcome with nausea. He was desperate. He was filled with remorse and guilt. And the sight of all that blood. He just gave up, bundled her back into the car and drove to the lake. He tied her down with stones and threw her in. And that might have been the end of the matter if the body had stayed submerged. But the head floated free. Blake saw it when he was out walking his dog, panicked and dumped the head in the sea below his house where it got caught in the Boylans' fishing net. Which is how we came to get involved.'

Nancy nodded. 'So he was only helping Trish?'

'You could say that.'

'You know,' Kathleen said, 'I never would have thought Trish Blake was capable of murder. She was so concerned about people, up to her neck in charity work. So disciplined.'

230

'She was driven to it,' Megarry said.

'But she didn't seem the type.'

'What *is* the type? What sort of people commit murder? Do you think they all go around wearing flashy suits and sunglasses, like something out of *Reservoir Dogs*? I've seen all sorts of murderers. From clergymen to little old ladies. People commit murder when it seems the only way out.'

He turned to Lawlor. 'Remember what I said about peace of mind? Trish Blake is obsessive. Remember that schedule she had, cleaning one day, baking the next, everything in order, everything spick and span? She was orphaned. She craved security. She thought she had found it when she married Jim Blake and then she discovered that he was being unfaithful. With a woman she considered her best friend.

'She appealed to Mary Grogan to end the relationship and she refused. Trish Blake could see everything she had built about to come crashing down, her marriage, her stability, her security. Removing Mary Grogan for good seemed like the only option left to her. That's why she committed murder.'

'What will happen to her?' Andrew said.

There was an embarrassed silence.

'She'll be convicted.'

'You know, I feel sorry for her,' Kathleen said. 'She *was* betrayed.'

'And what about Mary Grogan?' Rory asked.

'I have no feelings for her. She strikes me as a wilful, calculating woman. Arrogant and selfish. To steal her best friend's husband.'

'Maybe he was easy to steal,' Lawlor said. 'There were two of them in it. Why blame her?'

'Either way, she didn't deserve to die,' Megarry said.

He saw Jamie come out of the house. He had a hamburger in one hand and a football in the other.

'Fancy a game, Cecil?' the boy said. 'Shooty in?'

'What is this?' Megarry said. 'You trying to kill me?' He drained his beer, put the bottle down and started to get up.

'There is something I'd like sorted out,' Annie Lawlor said and leaned across the table to pour more wine. 'That warrant you produced the day we raided Delaney's flat. Where did that come from?'

Megarry felt in his pocket for a piece of paper and handed it across. Lawlor read out loud, 'Baked beans, cornflakes, sugar, bread, milk, kippers . . .'

That's my grocery list,' Kathleen said. 'What are you doing with that?'

The evening was starting to come down when the party finally broke up, the garden filling with night sounds, bird-song, crickets, a frog croaking somewhere in the gathering gloom.

The Kellys were the first to go. Megarry went with Sinead through the house while Peter went off to collect Jamie. She squeezed his hand.

'Thanks for everything you did, Cecil.'

Megarry shrugged. 'I didn't do anything.'

'We all know that's not true. You gave Peter back his confidence. The superintendent's delighted. And the Commissioner. He sent Peter a note to commend him for the way he handled the case.'

'Just shows you how volatile those buggers can be,' Megarry said.

Jamie came in from the garden with the ball. 'Did I tell you we're going to Scotland for our holidays?' the boy said.

'That sounds good.'

'It's brillo,' Jamie said. 'And dad's taking me to Parkhead. We're going to see Celtic play.'

Megarry looked at Kelly and saw him smile.

'Well, bully for you,' he said.